CHASERS

THE
DREAM
CHASERS

VIPUL MITTRA

RANDOM HOUSE INDIA

Published by Random House India in 2013
1

Copyright © Vipul Mittra 2013

Random House Publishers India Private Limited
Windsor IT Park, 7th Floor
Tower-B, A-1, Sector-125
Noida 201301, UP

Random House Group Limited
20 Vauxhall Bridge Road
London SW1V 2SA
United Kingdom

978 81 8400 429 8

Typeset in Melior by R. Ajith Kumar

Printed and bound in India by Replika Press Private Limited

For my wife Gitanjali, my daughter Megha, and my son Mehul—whose love, care, and affection keep me inspired.

1

IT WAS 3 AM. THE ONLY PLACE WE COULD FIND PARANTHAS was at Omi Dhaba near the PGI Hospital opposite University Gate. The three of us had gotten onto the dilapidated Vespa scooter semi-naked. It was not unusual for us to ride out like that, as a threesome; though it was indeed unusual to be virtually naked at this hour. All our smelly clothes lay soaked in a blue bucket beneath the waterless tap, in the froth and lather of cheap washing powder. So we had no other way of getting out but in our undies that had holes in all the wrong places.

Sandeep Galgotia or Sandy drove the scooter. It once belonged to his father who had given away his scooter and his son to each other. Sandy was the eldest among us, having done his two MAs in subjects as diverse as Music and Anthropology, before joining the present course, MBA. The only question that he had answered wrong in the interview for the B School was the full form of the acronym 'MBA', and the interviewers had laughed so much, so loud and for so long that in that moment of excitement, they awarded him 80 upon 100. They thought he was joking when he said MBA meant 'Management of Business Aims'; but had stopped laughing when he had stuck to his description saying that's what they should call the degree even if it had a different nomenclature. Because business without an aim is like a lost buffalo. They selected him.

Sandy remembered only love songs and a few romantic odes by Keats from his previous two degrees. He was short and as fair as bleaching powder sprinkled on a commode seat. He had no moustache, no beard, no chest hair, no hair on his arms and legs or any other parts that peeped through his underwear. Due to his utter fairness and hairlessness, girls considered him harmless. But he thought they loved him. He was also the richest of us all because he owned the Vespa.

Karan Kaushal sat in between Sandy and me. He compensated for Sandy's hairlessness in a way that made them appear as though they were made for each other. His forehead was always covered with a mop of hair that fell from from his head, while the rest of his face was hidden behind a generous beard. His eyebrows were Gorbachevian, and his arms and legs too were well-carpeted. When I met Karan for the first time, I resisted shaking his hand, afraid to be left clutching clumps of hair that he might shed. Later, I discovered that he used shampoo instead of soap while bathing. Karan spoke slowly and with emphasis, stressing each word, as though he was forever on the podium. He laughed without a smile. He wore thick glasses that hid the fact that he had once flunked his Math paper. He had an inbuilt defect that made him treat even unknown girls with excessive decency. His slow-motioned, emphatic speech made him the brunt of many girlie jokes. Girls felt safe pulling his leg and he too, like Sandy, thought they loved him because they always giggled in his presence, without reason, like passers-by bowing in front of roadside shrines.

The last chap was me, Viraat Nijhawan. I was the youngest of them, the tallest and the most reserved. I had whiskers and a tough jaw and my hair was always slicked backwards. I was focused on studies and had rarely spoken to a girl before I joined university. Sandy told me that at times my large eyes scared the girls, like police beacons scaring away innocent people. At times, I thought that was a good thing. I always tried to be meticulous in my ways and so my undies had fewer holes. I lived in town with my parents, but had come to stay at the boys' hostel for the past few weeks to help the others during exam time. Girls kept away from me, and at times, I too believed they loved me, but were only being shy. The three of us hung around together all the time—except for when we were chasing Mallika.

Mallika Mattoo was the most attractive girl in the entire university, and she was our classmate. She was part of our gang during the day. In her presence, the three of us boys were like three rivals—separate, distinct and competitive. We were like three blades of a fan jutting out of a common axis, connected yet rotating around an unattainable utopia. Following one another in a wild goose chase; going fast, but going nowhere. We were obsessed by the same dream while Mallika was generally indifferent to our approaches. Together we were a gang of dream chasers, infected by the new-age mantra that made a virtue of chasing one's dreams and following one's heart, irrespective of where that might lead one to.

'Sandy, stop the scooty man!' shouted Karan. 'There is a puncture in the tube.'

Sandy made the scooter wobble and shake as if to prove Karan right, and brought it to a screeching halt. I swung my leg over the stepney to get off the scooter, feeling the breeze enter the side of my underwear to tickle my crotch. Karan got off in the same fashion and must have felt no breeze brush him as he was too hairy. Sandy got down from the front like a lady. He never risked revealing his hairlessness and so he always got off his scooter from the front, coyly.

Often, I had wondered why girls' bicycles had no rod connecting the seat to the handle; and why girls alighted their bikes, mopeds, and scooters from the front, not lifting and swinging their legs all the way back and over, the way the boys do. But as we alighted the Vespa, it suddenly struck me and I shouted, 'Hey dudes! You remember, I keep

4

wondering why girls get off bikes from the front? Now I know the answer. I think it's a hymen-protection measure.'

'Voila!' Karan patted my bare back.

'Really!' Sandy chuckled. 'What about all my ex-girlfriends from the Music and the English departments, who had no hymen left in them?' There was pride in his voice.

'Sandy, in that case, your ex-girlfriends can easily ride and get off their bikes the proper way. The way men do,' said Karan. 'So, guys, the next time you see any girl getting off a bike like a man, be sure that she has been de-hymenized by Sandy. Ha-ha!' Karan hated it when Sandy boasted of his past victories.

Sandy grimaced and lunged toward Karan, who ran off, teasing him even more. Sandy ran after him, shouting abuses. I watched with disgust as my two semi-naked friends circled a lamp post that had a cluster of moths hovering around its flickering yellow bulb, scorching their tiny wings and showering the two semi-naked humans below with moth-wing-powder. A sleepy stray dog below the lamp post howled at them for creating such a ruckus at this hour. In the distance, beyond the dusty, moth halo of the lamp post and across the road, I could see the silhouette of the waiter at Omi Dhaba. Hands on hips, he waited for the underwear-clad gang to place its orders so that he could shove greasy food into our stomachs and go back to sleep beneath his blue plastic sheet.

Finally, I shouted, 'Hey stop it, guys! Or I will tell

Mallika first thing tomorrow morning about all the crap you guys keep talking about.' The threat worked and the two warring boys separated. Huffing, they stood gaping at the scooter. I pulled at my hair and cried out, 'Let's fix the damn tube and order food. I am famished.' My stomach growled in affirmation so loudly that for a moment, I thought that the scooter had re-started on its own.

The paranthas, with the repeated heating and frying, resembled deeply tanned leather. They were stale and to the two of us who had been seated behind Sandy, they smelled quite like the armpits of the front rider. We knew how the other's armpits smelled as we had just ridden the scooter bare-chested, stacked like spoons.

'The paranthas are not fresh,' I muttered.

'Yeah.They kind of stink of sweat,' grimaced Karan, emphazising each word.

'Come on, guys. They aren't so bad,' Sandy consoled us. He obviously did not have to smell an armpit on our way to Omi Dhaba.

'Hey, Omi!' Karan shouted to the weary dhaba owner, 'what is this? Rubber from a burnt tyre?' He held out a parantha and dangled it in the air. Omi stared at us, digging his ear for wax with his little fingernail. I was sure that Omi's ear wax was an essential ingredient in the paranthas.

'Forget it, Karan,' I said, 'No point cribbing about it. This is all we can get at this unearthly hour.' I chewed with effort and said, 'By the way, your mess food is worse. The rajmah we had for lunch yesterday was just gross. It was soggy and smelly, as if it had been ingested and puked onto our plates from the intestines of a street beggar. This is so much better.' I laughed meanly.

'Stop it, you scum,' Sandy yelled. He then yelled out to Omi. 'You know, tomorrow is the last exam, Omi! We will be free birds.'

Omi paused digging his ear and smiled at us.

'How can you say that, Sandy?' I said as I wiped my oily fingertips on the elastic of my underwear. I was chewing the last bite of the rubbery paranthas that had been decorated with some bright red spicy pickle. With parantha-slurry inside my mouth, I mumbled, 'It is only the end of the second semester. We still have another year to go after the summer internships.'

'Still, as of now we will be free birds.'

'You mean free-for-the-time-being kind of free?' Karan asked, lengthening each word, just to sound intelligent.

'Whatever.' Sandy shrugged, his hairless chest heaving in and out. 'At least we will be free birds for the next two months.' Sandy stood up and had a swig of water out of a cracked plastic jug. Then, swirling water in his mouth, giving it a quick rinse, and gargling out in the basin, he said, 'I am going home after the exams. Doing a summer placement at my uncle's factory in Ludhiana: the Smart Bra Co Pvt Ltd.'

7

'Hahaha, Sandy! You can even model for the product!' Karan jumped up, laughing hard, and pointing at Sandy's tender chest.

'Shut up, bugger,' Sandy sniggered. He was too tired to get angry.

'Seriously, Sandy. You are so fond of sex and you don't seem to be getting much of it as a guy. You better get a sex-change procedure done,' Karan guffawed.

I too laughed loudly and said, 'And, Sandy, before you go in for a sex-change procedure, do preserve your sperm, so that you can impregnate yourself as a woman later.'

'Holy shit,' Karan doubled up with laughter. 'Man, you will be the first human being on this planet who would be impregnating himself...err...herself, with his own sperm.'

'How intelligent!' Sandy said sarcastically. He did not seem to mind the remark though. He belched out the smell of parantha loudly and continued, 'Don't worry, dudes. No sex change for me.' He laughed, the dimples on his fair cheeks getting deeper. Pointing at the hoarding of the dhaba, he exclaimed, 'I just want to go to Punjab for the food. I don't care about my internship at the bra factory; learning about female assets will merely be an added bonus.'

'Good for you, dude. I am going to Faridabad. I managed to get a slot at Metal Bearing Company Ltd. They will even give me a place to stay,' I said. 'And Mallika is going to be in Delhi. Close by. She's doing her internship at GILT Industries in Connaught Place. Two months, me in Faridabad and Mallika in Delhi. And you guys far away in Ludhiana. Imagine that!' I twirled the ends of my moustache with traces of parantha grease.

I could see Karan and Sandy exchanging envious glances. I loved that look on their faces on such occasions. They were afraid that I might conquer Mallika by virtue of my geographical proximity to her. I yawned and said, 'And tomorrow, after the Business Economics paper, I am heading home. After almost a fortnight of staying with you two unclean buffoons.'

'Hey, come on. Take a look at yourself, Viraat. Never seen such long strands of hair sticking out of any armpit. Yuck!' Sandy frowned. Any hair, anywhere, repulsed him.

Omi came to take the aluminium plates away. He swiftly took out a filthy rag and swished it over the table. With every swish, dirt tads from the cracks on the table broke loose, and were spread uniformly over the table, even as customers felt gratified at the 'good' hygiene standards of Omi dhaba.

Sandy walked up to his Vespa and opened the dickey to count out a few soiled notes that looked as though they had been stolen from a temple donation box. For nine rubbery paranthas he counted out forty-five rupees, wiping his fingers on the soggy money. The Gandhi on the notes was totally smeared with oil from the parantha-greased fingertips. He gave the money to the stoned waiter.

A rickety truck rattled past us and its Sardar driver

gleefully waved at Omi. Sandy whispered to us that the truck driver was Omi's boyfriend. I scowled, but Sandy claimed that he had spotted them together on earlier occasions too. 'I swear. Look at the guy, man! You should have seen the way he whacks Omi on the bum,' he said.

'Shut up, Sandy! Give Omi a break.' I scowled as I generally mistrusted Sandy's judgment about hairy men.

Karan unhooked the scooter from its stand. Sandy kicked his Vespa thrice to rev up its engine and then mounted the seat from the front, delicately. As the scooter moved, six feet were raised up in perfect unison, three on either side.

'You know something? I am going rowing tomorrow evening after the exam. With Mallika, Vandana and Preeto.' The scooter had barely entered the university gate when I declared nonchalantly. 'I am going to take them to the Lake Club. My dad is a member, you see.' I upped my imaginary collars above my real collarbones.

'What!' Sandy pressed the brake pedal so hard that the scooter screeched to a halt. The three of us lurched forward and dug our feet into the ground to support the scooter. Six feet in flip-flops thumped the dusty road in sync, like oars of a wooden dhow. 'You can't go alone, all by yourself, with three girls!' Sandy screamed.

'Why not?' I smirked, straining my neck toward my right, across Karan's shoulder to glance at Sandy, who had turned around to scowl at me. Karan sat still between the two of us. He didn't seem to believe that I could possibly go with three girls in a boat, all alone, and still return alive.

'Why can't I go alone with the girls?' I grinned.

'Because...because we are friends. We do everything together,' Sandy blurted, trying to think of a good reason. 'Listen, dude. You guys are leaving today after the exams. And I live here and so do the girls,' I reasoned with them. 'That's why I thought of taking the chicks out for some fun.'

'What a coincidence! Bugger, you planned this out long ago! I know it for sure,' Sandy scowled.

'No way. Mallika called me yesterday. She said she wanted me to check them into the Lake Club as guests. And I said that I could be their boatman because it would be quite tiring for them to row.' I smiled deviously. 'Delicate species can't do that kind of labour, you know. So, I am just their boatman.'

'What rubbish!' Sandy exclaimed. 'Hey, Karan! Why aren't you saying anything? Tell him to go boating after we are back from our summer internships. He can be the boatman for all of us.' Karan continued to stick to his deadpan look.

'Relax, guys. I told you I am not going to touch Mallika. In fact, I wanted to go alone but she said Preeto and Vandana would also be coming. So it's all safe. No one has won her just yet.'

'Listen yaar,' Karan finally intervened, 'can he make out with all the three girls, that too in a boat? The boat will rock too much. It can topple over. So don't worry and let Viraat toil with the oars. He is a kid; younger than the girls. He is completely safe.'

'Me, a kid? No way, you buggers! I am not that safe,' I said, narrowing my large eyes. 'Now you watch out. I bet by the time we meet in the third semester, I would have done it with Mallika.'

'Look at him, Sandy! You have just provoked a sleeping lion! Ha-ha,' Karan laughed.

'Hey, come on now,' I was getting impatient, 'let's go and catch some sleep. It's 4 am. Jindal sir will come out for his morning walk any time now, and he will explode if he sees us like this!' I yanked at the elastic of my underwear and released it, creating the sound of a catapult. It was still dark but dawn would be breaking soon and our nakedness would be concealed for only a little more time.

Reluctantly, Sandy straightened up and rotated the gear-knob of the scooter. Little clouds of dust rose behind the rear wheel. Again, six flip-flops rose. The rickety scooter went past the paanwallah, his shop strategically located at the university gate. Sex and spirituality coexisted harmoniously on the shelves of his shop. He would ferret out condom packs with pictures of unreal, silicon-implanted white women, and display them in a neat array on his shelf that also stocked Osho trapped in key rings.

We entered the university gate and went past the English department, past the Psychology and

Anthropology blocks. Then past StuCee, the students' cafeteria. Our heads kept turned to the right, imagining the chicks on their scooters below the trees in a few hours. Dry leaves rustled upwards to match the symphony of the wind. Watchmen at entry points of various buildings snored on stools. Their wooden sticks lay still by their sides like tired mistresses.

At the end of the campus we came to the Shaheed Bhagat Singh Boys Hostel. The name on the hoarding had chipped in places so it read 'Sad Bhag Sin Hotel'. Girls called it the 'Sad Hostel' because its boys were generally so pathetic that they made the girls feel sad. They always cursed their decision of not going to another university that had better guys to offer!

'Bahadur, open the lock,' Karan hissed at the sleeping watchman. Bahadur was perpetually sleep-deprived, tired and underpaid. He always had a lazy smile spread across his face while he dreamt. Perhaps he dreamt of being the vice chancellor of the university. Or the hostel warden. We would never know.

The corridors were still and lifeless. We went up to the room which had 'Devils' Den' scribbled on its door.

We left the door ajar and slumped on our dusty beds, face down, and dozed off instantly.

2

FOUR HOURS OF SLEEP WAS NOT GOOD ENOUGH, BUT that's all we could manage. The exam was starting at 9 am. Unbathed, unshaven, with eye excretion intact, Sandy, Karan and I dressed and dashed off toward the B School with a ball point pen each in the back pockets of our jeans.

Hordes of students had started trickling in. Some looked worried but most of them appeared as though they cared little for the exam or the university. They were more concerned about their summer placements and were chatting about it.

Just then I saw Mallika standing at our B School gate. God, she was beautiful! Her Kashmiri complexion was fair, she had beautiful pink lips and that little gap between her front teeth made her appear even sexier when she smiled, as the tip of her pink tongue peeped out. She sported a ponytail that everyone found cute. She had almond shaped brown eyes and a little wart on her nose. She smiled, laughed, giggled and flowed like a wild breeze. She drove everyone crazy with her smile, even the professors. 'Hey guys!' she waved at us.

'Hi, Mallika,' the three of us bleated in unison. Jointly, we felt weak in her presence. It was strange how we instantly surrendered our male ego when Mallika was around.

'So, did you guys study a lot? The whole night?' Mallika giggled aloud, waving at Shivinder and Preeto who went past us. Girls knew how to juggle so many people at the same time. They could speak to one, wink at another, wave at the third and smile at the fourth at the same time, keeping an entire crowd motivated in anticipation of their turn.

'No, Mallika. Hardly,' Sandy broke into his typical smile, where his lips stretched from ear to ear, without revealing any teeth.

'Yeah, we were just loitering around,' Karan said.

'And hogging stale paranthas at 3 in the morning,' I laughed, trying to sound manly. I always modulated my voice in her presence. A deep, manly voice with a tinge of softness was the voice that I used when I spoke to Mallika. In the hostel though, I was generally hoarse or squeaky.

'So Viraat, we are going to see you at 5 pm at the Lake Club. Don't you dare ditch us!' Mallika was cute even when she was being stern.

Sandy and Karan exchanged envious glances.

'You guys are going to have fun…without us!' Sandy exclaimed.

'Why don't you join us for the boat ride?' Mallika looked at all of us with affection.

'Oh, Mallika! These poor things, Sandy and Karan. Unfortunately, they have to leave for Ludhiana this afternoon,' I said. I didn't want them to rethink and defer their departure. 'Their travel plans are confirmed.'

'Really! But summer placements start a week later. Why are you guys leaving now?' Mallika asked.

God, why did pretty girls have to dig into male issues and trouble their pretty heads?

'Sandy wants to model for a product in his uncle's factory, and I want to see him do that,' Karan said wickedly.

'Modelling? Wow! Which product, Sandy?' Mallika asked curiously.

'Uh… Nothing really! Karan was just joking,' Sandy was livid. 'Why should I be modelling? I am just going for my summer placement.'

The image of Sandy walking the ramp in his undies and a 'smart' bra flashed though my mind. Karan and I broke into a loud laugh.

Meanwhile, Vandana had walked over to us and joined in the conversation. 'What modelling, guys?' asked Vandana.

Vandana Vasudev was the daughter of an army colonel. She came to the university in an army truck with lots of vegetables, army rations, and a brood of clucking chickens. Each day the truck ejected her from its rear and roared on toward the cantonment. We were always amazed at the way she could jump out of the high truck, dust off her hands, straighten her clothes, blow hen feathers off her hair, and coolly walk into class. It was a daily sight that convinced the rest of us about the bravery of army men and their offspring.

'What modelling? Just kidding, yaar,' Sandy whimpered, covering his chest.

'Anyway, this boating thing is going to be fun, Viraat,' Vandana jumped in excitement. Vandana was very thin and had pimples that she kept scraping off with her delicate fingertips. Boys avoided shaking hands with her, fearing that some pimple-pus might rub off on them. She had sunken eyes, high cheekbones, a narrow but raised jaw, and a non-existent upper lip. Her profile reminded me of caricatures of prehistoric human skulls found in high school textbooks. She had short, unevenly cut hair that danced at her shoulders, swaying left and right like the leafy skirts of pseudo-tribesmen performing at cultural fests. Karan was her favourite but he kept running away from her all the time, moving toward Mallika whose trail was already overcrowded.

Karan remarked at times why a few girls had so many boys chasing them, while most of the others were always waiting with no takers. 'If only God made all girls equally pretty, things would be so much easier,' Karan always said. And Sandy would reply, 'I know. Then we could divide girls between ourselves and be happy. Instead of all of us running after Mallika.'

'Yeah! You could take Vandana if she had fewer pimples. Karan could have gone for Preeto if she did not have her extra-fine whiskers. And I would have been just content with Mallika,' I had said, chuckling.

'Shut up, Viraat. You mean to say that even if all girls were equally pretty, you would still have Mallika? How selfish!'

'Tell me one thing honestly,' I asked in mock seriousness. 'If all girls were equally beautiful, then what's the problem if you guys just left Mallika for me? Now aren't *you* chaps being selfish?'

'Stop this hypothetical argument, guys,' Sandy had said. 'The reality is that all girls are not equally beautiful, and so we three will have to work to get Mallika. She will be our common goal, our target, till one of us gets her.' Everyone had nodded. That had been our unwritten understanding right from the beginning of our course. Since then, we had competed for nothing else except Mallika. In other things—studies, summer internships, exams, term papers, assignments—we always collaborated. Only when it came to Mallika did we turn into squabbling hyenas.

Whenever I had tried to whisk Mallika away to the university canteen, the other two would jump in and break up our twosome. Once when Sandy had almost managed to stealthily take her to a film on his scooter, Karan and I had followed them in an auto-rickshaw to the multiplex, bought tickets and had managed to exchange seats, pushing out two sundry chaps, to be seated next to Mallika. The four of us were like tiny balls of mercury, always falling on one another, making sure none was left alone in the pursuit of Mallika.

This time, Sandy was unusually upset about me escorting Mallika and the girls for a boat ride. He pulled Karan by his arm and they started walking a few steps ahead, leaving me behind. I followed them, discreetly listening to their conversation. 'Let's postpone our tickets for Ludhiana to tomorrow, Karan,' Sandy said.

'I am not sure, Sandy. We may not get a bus for the next two days. The transporters are on strike because a poor driver was lynched by crowds in Gurdaspur for crushing a boy under his bus. Plus, train tickets aren't so easy to get this late in the day. Cabs are too expensive; I could use that money for better things in Ludhiana,' said Karan, winking at Sandy. He then smirked and murmured, 'You stay here, Sandy, and guard Viraat. I will go. Your uncle's Smart Bras can wait till you show up.'

I suppressed a chuckle.

'Shut up, bugger,' Sandy snapped.

Karan patted Sandy on the back and said, 'Hey man, don't worry. Viraat and Mallika are not going to be alone. The other two not-so-pretty girls will protect Mallika.

Girls who are not pretty are generally strong-headed; they won't allow any boy to act fresh with her in their presence.' Sandy nodded.

Reassuringly, Karan asserted, 'So let them go boating. Just make sure Vandana and Preeto go too, and the bugger does not manage to isolate Mallika and steal her away.'

'But, Karan, the lake is a very romantic place. If Viraat and Mallika manage to get away even for an hour, our battle is lost. Mark my words.'

I smiled hearing this and wished that Sandy's fears came true.

'I agree. Come, let's talk to Vandana and Preeto.'

I quickly joined Mallika, Vandana and Preeto. Sandy and Karan also joined us, unaware that I had overheard their conversation. Sharp ears, I patted my back in my mind and smiled at the duo. Sandy grinned cunningly and said, 'So, Vandana, you must teach Mallika how to row. You are so tough, you can jump off high trucks. It's good for girls to be strong. I mean, look at all the Hollywood chicks. The ones like Angelina Jolie, who are into action flicks, are the hottest,' Sandy sounded a bit silly and everyone laughed.

'Ha-ha. I am hardly any competition to Jolie but I learnt rappelling and rowing when dad was posted in Pehalgam,' Vandana said.

'Yeah. Look at our desi Bollywood babes. They may not be into daredevil stunts, but they are cool too, running around trees, mountains and lakes,' Karan said. 'Mallika, you must learn from Vandana.'

Obviously, they wanted Vandana to be in the boat with us, and be in close proximity to Mallika, instead of me trying to sit behind Mallika, hold her hand, and help her row. Devils, they always read my thoughts and saw through my designs. I was peeved. 'Hey guys, don't worry. Vandana is already too strong, so she doesn't need any lessons. She can dip her feet in the cool water and let little fish give her a pedicure while I teach Mallika how to row.' I looked at Vandana's feet and remarked, 'That will help you clean them up a bit.' The boys guffawed. That was a mean remark, but then everything is fair in love and war.

Vandana stared at me in disgust and said, 'Viraat, I won't go boating with a guy like you. You have strange, chauvinistic ideas about women and what they should do.' She slipped off her right shoe, curled up her foot and said, 'You can sniff my foot. I keep them clean, you moron.'

I smiled meanly and said, 'Oh yeah! At least your feet are good looking, Vandana.'

'At least!' She shouted and whacked me with her books. That was the last nail in the coffin; she was livid.

So, Vandana not going. One drop-out. Great! I thought. My own wickedness excited me.

Sandy stopped grinning and looked at Karan nervously. They seemed to have guessed my game plan. So, they decided to save the situation by saying nice things about me, just so that Vandana would not drop out. 'No, no Vandana. He is just kidding. Viraat has high respect for girls.' Sandy said kindly.

'Yes, Vandana. Viraat has great admiration for girls from Defence families. Whenever you jump out of that high army ration truck and dust off all those hen and cock feathers, Viraat always says that army girls are so tough and full of life!' Karan quipped, trying to veer the topic toward the glory of the army.

Vandana looked at me and seemed to be easing up. I was alarmed. Instantly, I drew out my innermost element of meanness and taunted her, 'Yes, Vandana. Army girls are great. The army is a great life, too. Once in school, I had gone to the Ambala cantonment to stay with my cousin, whose husband was a Major. It was so nice to sit in the army mess and observe people drink expensive drinks, cheaply. Uniformed jawans serving liquor with full discipline, instead of fighting the enemy. It was great.' I laughed. No one joined my laughter. Vandana withdrew into her shell. How desperately I wanted her out of the boating plan!

At that point, Mallika took control. She snapped, 'Shut up, guys! Vandana is coming with us,' she hugged Vandana as she spoke. Vandana smiled wryly at me. I winced. Somehow, pretty girls seem to have control over everyone else. Sandy and Karan looked at each other and heaved a sigh of relief. I was worried, but said nothing. How could I counter the princess of my dreams?

The Business Economics test went well. Sandy, Karan and I had studied together and so each one of us knew a bit of everything. While preparing for the exam, the three of us had passed on our notes to Mallika, individually, without the knowledge of one another, and so Mallika had accessed the best of each. We emerged from the exam hall beaming. We were free birds. The free-for-the-time-being kind of free; like convicts on parole. I folded my question paper into a tiny aeroplane and tossed it toward Mallika; Sandy made a shield of his question paper to protect her from my airborne assault; Karan made a sun shield out of his question paper and held it across Mallika's face. We were all using our best resources on the same girl. Mallika simply smiled at our desperation. The tip of her pink tongue peeked out of the tiny gap between her teeth, making us boys shiver in sheer excitement.

'What time is your bus, Sandy?' Preeto asked innocently.

I looked at Sandy's wrist watch. I wanted to be sure that they left. Sandy and Karan exchanged glances and then scowled at me jointly. I could read their feelings at that moment: they wanted to strip me down and put me on display in my dirty underwear that had holes, just to make the girls hate the idea of going boating with me. I smiled.

'The bus is at 4 pm, Preeto,' Karan said curtly, each word sounding stern.

'Oh! Then you guys can't come.' My voice was brimming with victory.

Sandy stared hard at me and I knew instantly that he was feeling all green and jealous. I looked away and found Mallika preening herself, looking into a little oval mirror studded with fake emeralds and real feminine pride. She adjusted her hair band and earrings, pouted and retouched her lips with a shiny gloss. Then she put the little mirror back into her overstuffed, chaotic bag and smiled.

Suddenly, Karan beamed and winked at Sandy and said, 'Hey, guys! Why don't we go to Viraat's place for lunch? I love the aloo paranthas that Viraat's mom makes.' I was very intrigued.

'But we have a bus to catch. How can we go?' Sandy was unable to fathom Karan's intent. I was getting suspicious.

'Doesn't matter, dude. Our bus is at 4 pm and it is only 12.30 now. We can pack and be at Viraat's place by 1.30, feast on the paranthas, and then leave for the bus station by 3 pm. We can easily make it in time for the bus.'

'Nice. I love Sudha aunty's paranthas,' Mallika said excitedly. 'I will come too.'

'Me too,' Preeto joined in.

'Sorry, guys, I can't come. I have to submit my last term paper by 3. I will see you guys at the Lake Club at 5,' Vandana said.

Sandy was gloating at the prospect of having his last meal with Mallika before he headed for Ludhiana. He felt as priviliged as the partakers of Christ's Last Supper!

But Karan had something else in mind. He patted Vandana and said, 'Fine, Vandana. You guys have a nice time at the Lake Club.' He cleared his throat and continued, 'And Mallika, I suggest you and Preeto also stay back. Otherwise there will be too many of us for Sudha aunty to feed. Sandy and I will go. We anyway have to triple ride Sandy's royal Vespa to Viraat's home to drop him off.'

I was quite puzzled. Karan did not want to have Mallika around? It didn't seem possible.

'Well, alright then,' said Preeto, who seemed disappointed.

Sandy was furious with Karan for depriving them of Mallika's company. To Mallika, it made no difference. She shrugged and purred, 'Alright, no problem guys. I will see you in the evening then. And Sandy, Karan, you guys have fun. And hey, Sandy! You better show me your pictures once you are back.'

'Pictures? What pictures?' Sandy was slow on the uptake and was left wondering what pictures Mallika was talking about. Once he had confessed to me that being the eldest among us, he often felt like he belonged to another generation. While the rest of the gang texted and chatted away, Sandy was always a little slow in catching up. I had once texted him in class—'Did you see that new QT?' and Sandy thought I was referring to some new car model. Karan and I were in splits when he later asked where the QT was parked as he wanted to drive her. 'It stands for "cutie", you dumbass!' we had howled back at him, while he stood there blushing.

Sandy seemed just as clueless right now, 'What photos are you talking about, Mallika?'

'Your modelling pictures, what else? Viraat mentioned that you were going to be a model during your summer internship? Make sure you mail us the pics. It'll be so cool to see you on the ramp.' Mallika was dead serious.

The image flashed in my head again: Sandy walking the ramp in the 'smart bra' and his undies, fair and hairless, wearing his typical grin. I was sure Sandy saw the same image too and it must have jolted him because his fair skin flushed a bright red.

'Come on, Mallika. Viraat was just joking. There is no such modelling assignment.' He pulled my arm, digging his nails into my flesh as punishment, and said, 'Viraat, Karan, we've got to rush now.'

We hugged perfunctorily and parted. The three of us walked to the tree under which Sandy's Vespa was parked. He scrubbed bird poop off the seat with his key. Karan sat behind Sandy. I was still confused as I climbed behind Karan. Why the hell would the buggers want to extract a lunch out of my mom? But I wanted them to do whatever they wanted and leave for Ludhiana, as soon as possible. The prospect of an evening boat ride in the serene, lonely lake, while holding Mallika's hand to help her learn the strokes filled me with euphoria. Let them have mom's paranthas and just get the hell out of the city.

As we whizzed past the building, we waved at the girls but they had already turned their backs and were walking toward the university library, chatting away. Mallika was in the middle, tall, wild and sexy, with Preeto and Vandana walking leisurely beside her.

3

MOM HAD PREPARED PUNJABI KADI FOR LUNCH. THOUGH it wasn't what the guys expected, they wolfed down the meal like famished refugees. Hostel food had made them appreciate any reasonably edible food anywhere, anytime. Yellow, homemade kadi with pakoras floating in it must seem like liquid gold to them.

Sandy kept glancing at Karan all through lunch. I was still not sure what Karan had in mind, though I had a sneaky suspicion that there was some sort of mischief cooking in his hairy head. Today, they seemed united, but many times in the past, Sandy had told me what he thought of Karan—some sort of chimpanzee, all hairy, itchy and smelly, that had managed to escape from his cage after somebody had implanted a few extra grey cells into his brain and turned him into a quasi-human being. Sandy had a strong belief that hairy men were sub-human, closer to prehistoric cave men, still undergoing the process of Darwinian evolution.

Karan winked at Sandy and this confused me further. Sandy raised his eyebrows. Mom was serving me rice, giving more to her son than the two hostel refugees. Dad sat at the other end of the table, reading the *Punjab Kesari*. He read aloud and exclaimed, 'Lactating bitch feeds a lion cub in Kapurthala. Unbelievable!' Sandy guffawed, while I was deeply embarrassed. Mom shot Dad a cold look and silenced him immediately. He slipped back into mute mastication.

'Uncle, do you believe in this kind of news?' Karan finally said. Even as he spoke, his lips were not discernible; his voice emerging from somewhere between the hair on his face.

'Oh yes, I think it must be true. And even if it's not true, who cares? It's pure entertainment.' Dad turned the pages of the newspaper. The fan above whirred lazily. One big fat fly with blue eyes glided in and settled on my lower lip. I spat out the food.

'Where are your table manners, Viraat! You can't spit food in your plate,' Mom admonished me.

'But, mom, the fly! It was a shit fly!'

'Oh God. Stop it, Viraat!' Mom was livid.

I smirked. She did not know the kind of friends I had; she did not know that Sandy and Karan were capable of comparing her yellow kadi pakoras with human excreta later, while on their way to Ludhiana. She did not know that very late last night, these two uncouth ruffians had prompted her son to ride a Vespa almost naked. She did not know that their undies had holes or that Sandy's Vespa boot was full of centre spread pages torn from *Playboy* magazines. She thought they were good, upright kids, the way most mothers think of their offspring's pals. Otherwise she would never have allowed me to go and stay with Karan and Sandy at the boys' hostel. So she was embarrassed.

'Don't say such horrible things in front of your friends, Viraat. Look at them, they are so decent,' Mom chided me again.

'Decent...ooh hahaha,' I doubled up, coughing out a mix of kadi, rice and saliva. The food fell on mom's sari and she became angrier. If she wanted to slap me, this was the moment. But she did not. She simply shot me a stare.

'Aunty, Viraat is a nice boy. It's okay,' Karan chuckled. Then he put his master plan into action. 'He is just excited.'

'Excited! Why?'

'Their exams are over, Sudha. It is natural for them to be excited,' Dad said in a soft, condescending tone laden with husbandly wisdom.

'Yes, Aunty. Uncle is right,' Karan smiled.

I was a bit alarmed by now. Karan's praise for me, defending me like this! It was indeed the most unexpected thing to hear.

'And Aunty...' Karan continued gently, 'Viraat is also excited and happy because he is taking the girls for a boat ride today. Mallika too.'

So that was it! The bomb!

There was complete silence in the room. The fan whirred. I could hear nothing but my own breathing, loud and clear. Everyone stopped chewing. The family froze. The journey of the food from the plate to the mouth was suspended midair.

'What?' Mom shrieked. 'Viraat! Are you going out with Mallika?'

I stared hard at Karan. Mom was very wary of Mallika. Last winter, she had caught me mumbling Mallika's name in my sleep one night. Just to wake me up, mom had pulled off my quilt with a jerk, my erection had embarrassed her. She had extracted a pledge out of me in front of Hanumanji's framed photo that I would stay away from the corrupting influence of whoever this Mallika was. Later, I had narrated the incident to Karan.

Today, Karan was taking advantage of my little secret. The pig! Son of an owl! I wanted to skin him alive and boil him in urine. Or take him to a taxidermist and have him stuffed, starting from the rear. But since I could not do all that right now, I simply sat there, dumbfounded.

'Mallika again?' A vein in my mom's temple throbbed.

'Mom, come on! There are other girls too, not just Mallika. In fact, Karan and Sandy were going to come too,

31

but they are to leave for Ludhiana for their internship,' I bleated, rising up in frustration. I felt like a sheep at the altar.

'But, son, you had promised your mother that you weren't going to let this girl influence your thoughts and deeds,' said Dad calmly. He always joined in to support all matters that mattered to mom.

'Dad, I am not going out with Mallika alone. It is not a date. There are two other girls too,' I stammered and looked at Karan, who was busy pouring kadi into his bowl with great gusto. Sandy looked at me sheepishly and shrugged.

My arguments with Mom and Dad continued, as Sandy and Karan polished off their food. Dad had joined in by then, sermonizing on the merits of brahmacharya. Dad even hinted at the growing menace of AIDS.

'Oh God!' I pulled at my hair and mumbled, 'Imagine! Poor me making out in a rocking boat with three girls, one of whom could be infected with HIV!' I felt pathetic, trying to suppress a burst of laughter.

Karan and Sandy polished off the rasgullas that were served as dessert and stood up to wash their hands. Motherly sermons continued non-stop in the tiny dining room, rising up and filling the air like helium balloons. At the end of it all, Karan and Sandy departed, with cunning smiles on their faces.

I stomped out and climbed the stairs to my bedroom, throwing Dad's Lake Club membership card on the dining table. The membership card got smeared with the spilled yellow kadi. Saddened, I texted Mallika: 'Hey Mallika. Sorry, I've got a bad stomach. No boating today.'

'Great! You're ditching us at the last moment,' she replied sarcastically. There was no smiley in her text.

4

THE BUS RIDE TO FARIDABAD WAS BUMPY. THE HARYANA
Roadways Corporation bus had a noisy engine and a
noisier staff. Yellow vomit rivulets streaked its windows.
Inside the bus, torn seat covers with gaping holes kept
passengers busy in their sponge-digging ventures. Some
passengers shouted away on their cell phones, trying to
make themselves heard over the din of the rattling bus.
Those who had dozed off leaning on the steel bars in front
of their seats had stripes imprinted on their foreheads. A
few rats scurried around the feet of passengers, while a
few fattened cockroaches watched them with quivering
whiskers.

The April heat was scorching. The high pollution
levels in Faridabad pushed the mercury higher. From the
bus stand, the industrial area was a good half hour away by
a rickshaw. I must have made a strange sight, seated with
my huge, black suitcase behind a lugging rickshaw-puller.

'How far, bhaiya?' I asked, wiping the sweat off my brow.

'Just around the corner,' the rickshaw-puller huffed in a Bhojpuri accent.

I looked at the bulging calf muscles of the otherwise lean man, as he rose up and pushed down on the pedal with each tug. I felt guilty. I wanted to become lighter instantly and so by foolish instinct, I lifted my suitcase and placed it on my knees, as though it might lighten the load on the rickshaw.

Soon we were there. Metal Bearing Co. had a huge metallic gate on top of which was a semi-circular, rusted metallic signboard that spelt out the company name. The enormity of the gate left me wondering if the company had used its entire inventory for manufacturing its own entry gate. I smiled at the disinterested watchman in khaki.

'I am Viraat Nijhawan, the summer intern,' I said softly and respectfully. I was surprised at my own tone. Seldom at the university had I spoken with such reverence to my professors or even to the Dean! The only other person who elicited such respect out of me was Mallika's father, Mr Mattoo. Even with my own parents, I was usually curt and irritable.

'You have a letter?' the watchman asked in a baritone voice.

'Yes, yes,' I fumbled and took out a crumpled envelope from my suitcase. The watchman was like a scowling immigration officer at the New York airport, scrutinizing visa papers of scared passengers. My entry into the haloed zone depended upon this goon.

The watchman pretended to read the letter, even as he held the paper upside down. I didn't have the courage to question his assessment of the contents of the letter.

The watchman seemed satisfied when he recognized the company logo on the letter. That was perhaps the only thing he was capable of understanding. The ability to recognize the company logo was all that was needed for his job, I mused enviously as I walked on, after depositing the suitcase in the security gate cloak room.

Inside the plant, noisy air sucked me deep into the vortex of manufacturing activity. Workers moved this way and that. Trucks with metals in various shapes ran here and there. Forklifts added to the chaos, noise and traffic. I crossed the road and entered the administrative block. It had an air-curtain at the entry and was air-conditioned inside. Nice and cool, I thought. I hoped that my own desk would be somewhere here.

'Thank god, I am not a forklift driver or a watchman,' I murmured and looked up at the ceiling where presumably God lived.

The receptionist was a dusky Keralite. Rosy—the little green badge on her large left breast read. She wore a long black skirt and a white top from under which her bra straps peered at me. For a moment I felt a pang of jealousy toward the badge but then quickly diverted my mind from the silly thought. Rosy smiled at me. It was the plastic smile of an air hostess. 'Yes, please. May I help you?' her voice was husky.

'Yes, you can,' I blabbered, sounding silly even to myself.

'Excuse me?' Rosy looked alarmed. The plastic smile melted away immediately, leaving behind a sheet of surprise.

'Sorry. I mean to say yes, I need your help in locating where to go.'

'As in …?'

'Well, I have come a long way to get here. In a bus and then a rickshaw. So excuse my stupidity. I am a bit tired and somewhat disoriented.'

Rosy kept looking at me blankly. I continued to mutter. 'Rosyji, you know we had our exam just yesterday. And all the midnight oil that I burnt. And all the oily paranthas that I consumed. All that. And the bus ride with people puking all around me. That's why I am a bit sick and tired.'

She looked sympathetic, 'Will you have some water?' Her badge bobbed up as she took a deep breath, stirring up excitement in my fatigued mind.

'Yes, please. Cold.'

She poured a glass of cold water from the water dispenser and gave it to me. I gulped it, still looking at her badge. Strange, I realized that for that fraction of a second, I didn't think of Mallika.

'So? Tell me now,' Rosy was really sympathetic.

I looked at her closely. She was sultry, and had short

hair that fell on both sides of her face. Her eyes were rimmed with kohl and a light lipstick further highlighted the pout of her lips. Her hands had the prettiest fingers I had ever seen. And there was no wedding ring.

The thought of Mallika tugged at me and I came back to the present. 'Rosyji. I am a summer intern. MBA student. I have got my summer placement here.'

She read the letter, this time the paper was held with the correct side up. Upside up, I heaved. Thank god, Rosy knew how to read!

'Follow me.' Rosy walked smartly.

I followed her dutifully into a corridor dotted with bright tubelights along the ceiling. The sterile, cold and bright white light was foreboding, and made me worry slightly.

Both sides of the corridor were lined with cabins. I looked around gazing at the small and large cabins that lined the corridor, occasionally stealing a glance at Rosy's posterior. Her swaying hips diverted my mind and neutralized the officiousness of the place.

At the end of the never-ending corridor, we reached the cabin that had the largest door. This door was made of solid wood. Transparency ended at the lower ranks, I persumed. The door had a glossy brass knob and a gilded name plate that read 'Ashok Kumar Nigam'. At the door, just before entering, Rosy pulled her top to adjust her bra. It made her figure more inviting and I presumed that would soften the General Manager. She broadened her smile, ran her fingers through her hair, looked at me as if to ask whether I was ready. Then smartly, she twisted the door knob and we both entered the room.

The room was needlessly large and boring, and also eerily silent. At the far end, seated behind a huge mahogany desk was a sombre, fat man. Nigam was short, bespectacled, with a pencil thin moustache and a jawline that almost disappeared into his ample double chin. He was smoking a pipe. His eyes appeared so magnified behind his thick glasses that they looked like attachments outside his eye sockets, like spherical objects placed from the outside, without a connection to his optic nerves. I had never seen such big pupils in my life.

'Yes?' Nigam said curtly through the smoke from his pipe.

'Sir, this is Viraat. The summer intern. MBA trainee,' Rosy spoke softly.

'Oh, yes. I see,' Nigam sized me up quickly, letting his eyes travel head to toe over me.

I thought of pulling a chair to sit down but Rosy's eyes advised me otherwise. I was reminded of my school prayer sessions.

Rosy spoke again, 'Sir, we can perhaps use him to redesign our new methodology for the performance appraisal formats.'

'Use him!' I murmured. Images of penguin-shaped municipal dustbins flashed through my mind; dustbins that had 'USE ME' painted on their broad chests.

'Sshh,' Rosy whispered impatiently to me as Nigam reached over to light his pipe with a mean dull gold bullet-shaped lighter. I looked at the lighter. It was very slick and smooth.

Nigam lit his pipe and looked up. His large, sleepy, red eyeballs scanned me from my head to my twitching toe again. Gosh, the bugger should have been in some spy film, I thought as I stood there silently, letting myself be examined.

'Can you do this project that Rosy is talking about?' Nigam cleared his throat. 'Or is it too complex for you?'

I was tempted to agree to the latter. I was there only because my B School made it compulsory for me to do a summer internship. I was there because I had to be, not because I wanted to. I just wanted the Fridays to roll in fast so that I could push off to Connaught Place in Delhi and meet up with Mallika, and by the end of the internship period, perhaps woo her into jumping into bed with me. I was there because I didn't want to stay with my parents during the summer, just to save my libido from being crushed. Exerting my grey cells was nowhere on my wish list.

However, I obviously couldn't let Nigam know of my real intentions. So I nodded dumbly and said, 'Of course, sir. I am here to learn.'

'Sir, we can assign him the work then?' Rosy asked.

Nigam looked at Rosy, lit his pipe again and took a deep puff. 'Fine!' Nigam rasped through the smoke and resumed his work, burying his head in his papers. The faint connecting line between his head and neck vanished with his forward tilt. Rosy knew that the meeting was over. Nigam seemed the kind of person who would use his voice only if it was most essential to do so.

'Gosh! He looks lazy and evil!' I muttered to Rosy as we came out of Nigam's chamber.

'Sshh, Viraat, this is not your university,' Rosy pinched my arm. 'This is the corporate world. So, learn to be respectful. Lesson number one.'

I liked the sting in her pinch. I nodded.

She took me around the plant. There were huge furnaces where sweaty labourers with thick gloves and red eyes shoved metal into gigantic machines, working in the sweltering heat and under very difficult conditions. I was reminded of the lesson on the industrial revolution that I had been taught in class XII. The Marx in me stirred and I started becoming sympathetic toward the proletariat, but Rosy's smile stifled the rising sympathy, the way pouring sugar settles down the froth in a cappuccino. I was instantly so filled with lusty excitement that no space remained within me for the likes of Marx.

The room I was given at the company guesthouse was sparsely furnished. The guesthouse was in a low-rise building, which was surrounded by better and larger buildings that housed senior company executives. My room had one single bed, so narrow that even if someone wanted to bring in a woman stealthily in the middle of the night, only one of the two could sleep on it, and that too sideways. The snores of occupants from adjoining rooms resonated through the thin walls; I didn't think I could even masturbate peacefully at night. The room had one wooden chair with a cane seat that was so brittle that no one could sit on it for longer than a few minutes without developing a pain in the posterior. There was a single door closet that was full of lizard eggs and sleepy spiders that fed on them. It was the only cupboard in the world where dirty clothes became irredeemably dirtier.

The guesthouse was meant for the lowest class of executives: the start-up management trainees as well as the senior-most watchmen on continuous night duty when they could not cycle back to their nearby hamlets due to long duty hours.

The grime-encrusted ceiling fan had one arm missing, so the air was rationed too. When I first walked in and assessed my humble living quarters, I was concerned about only one thing—the presence of a plug point. I scanned the damp and dirty walls, looked morosely at the cheap beige curtain fluttering by the window and continued to hunt for the switchboard. 'Ah, finally,' I heaved as I saw it near the toilet. I hurriedly removed my mobile and charger from my knapsack and plugged it in to test the point. The current flowed only when I rammed the charger in deep enough and held it delicately enough at just the right angle.

'Even sex is easier. You don't have to aim so much and for so long!' I mumbled. There was no place to keep the dangling mobile as it got charged, I realized. There was no counter and the cane chair barely managed to fit through the narrow passage to the toilet to seat my precious mobile or me. I had to keep the charger well-aimed deep inside the socket every time I wanted to revive my dying mobile battery. And while I did that, I could get a nice view of the bathroom that was so small and dingy that one could not bend down and soap oneself in all places.

In the evening, I sat wondering what Sandy and Karan were doing in Ludhiana. Tearing away at butter chicken, perhaps? Or drinking rum at the bar in Sandy's uncle's house? The image of Sandy romping around in made-in-Ludhiana smart bras made me laugh aloud.

Every morning, I would go to the factory on a cycle given to me by the big watchman whom I had met on the first day. The watchman now had night duty and so I would bring the bicycle back by the evening so that it could be used by him at night. During the day, it was ridden by me, its part-time borrower, very much like small investors' bank deposits being used by others for creating big wealth for themselves.

On my third day, I met the second intern.

'Meet Abhilaksh Tandon. From IIT Delhi. He is also joining as an executive trainee. They conduct their final internship at the end of all their semesters,' Rosy introduced the chap to me, as they walked into my cubicle.

The small glass-and-ply cabin was close to the reception counter, and I was quite thrilled that I could see Rosy from my desk, even though I could not hear her husky voice due to the glass partition in between. For the past two days, I had been watching her lip movements as she attended to phone calls and visitors and I was sure I would become very adept at lip reading by the end of my internship. Maybe I could then find a job as a newsreader for the hearing-impired on Doordarshan.

'Abhilaksh is joining today. For a two-month internship,' Rosy looked at Abhilaksh and said, and then addressing me, she smiled mischievously and spoke, 'So, Viraat, now you will have company and something to do.' Obviously she knew, I guessed, that the only thing I had done in the past couple of days at office was to leer at her through the silent airtight glass.

'Hi,' Abhilaksh said and smiled. There were dimples in his cheeks. He had curly hair and he was fair and delicate. He smiled coyly most of the time, but what bothered me was that he was going to share my cubicle. The two of us had two chairs and one computer between us. And we had only one Rosy to ogle at. Competition yet again, I thought.

I was unhappier because Abhilaksh was a fair Delhi boy, and I had heard that Kerala girls had a great fondness for fair Delhi boys. I was worried for Rosy. I hoped she knew that mere engineers got paid less than MBA graduates, and thus made a bad choice for romance.

Abhilaksh Tandon wore gold-rimmed glasses, a Rado watch and drove his yellow Zen to Faridabad every day. He was obviously from an affluent family and knew nothing of Haryana Roadways buses streaked with vomit. And, therefore, he was bound to be exclusive, reclusive and aloof.

'Hi, buddy! Nice watch. Rado?' I held his wrist and studied the jet black dial of his watch studded with four little diamonds. The diamonds stood out like sentinels on the dial. 'How much? I was too impressed to be polite and keep the question to myself.

'Don't know, dude,' Abhilaksh spoke softly, with a tinge of sadness layering his speech. 'It was just a gift from my father, who lavishes me with such things in place of his time.'

'Really! Wish I could trade a few of those for all the time my parents give me. My mom and dad are always sitting on my head. All the time!' I said.

'To each his own,' Abhilaksh cut me short. He wanted no sympathy from a stranger.

'So, Abhilaksh, where do you live?' I tried to change the topic.

'South Delhi. Vasant Vihar.'

South Delhi symbolized affluence. Other parts of Delhi stood far below. At times I felt that there were so many Delhis that it was difficult to fathom their inter-relationship. *Vasant Vihar is snobbish and rich. And Abhilaksh lives there so he is bound to be snobbish and rich*, I thought. I looked down at Abhilaksh's shoes. *Yikes!* My eyes momentarily widened in disbelief. *He's not only snobbish and rich, but eccentric as well.* Little bits of red peeked out from Abhilaksh's black leather shoes, and I saw that the bugger had a thing for colourful socks. *Who wears such colourful socks to work*, I wondered. My sense of style was far more conservative.

'You are wearing red socks!' I burst out, unable to contain myself yet again.

'Yes. So what? I love socks. I even have Mickey Mouse socks and day-wise socks, one for each day of the week. My dad gets them for me from his trips abroad,' Abhilaksh countered, unflustered. 'So tell me, Viraat, how is the scene here?' He diverted the topic. I noticed that Abhilaksh preferred to shift the focus away from himself.

'Come, sit down. Look there —Rosy! She is the only good thing in this place,' I invited him next to me, trying to be friendly.

'Yes, she is pretty smart.'

'And well racked!' I winked at Abhilaksh.

Across the silent glass, Rosy smiled at us. She always knew whenever she was being discussed. The badge on her left breast flashed even from a distance, through the glass. Later in the night, as I lay sideways in the guesthouse room, she was the subject of my fantasies.

'But she seems older to us by a couple of years,' Abhilaksh scowled.

'So? How does it matter? No one is asking for her hand in marriage. It's just time pass. Two months of this insane place.'

'A woman is never time pass, trust me. You either go the whole hog or stay away. They are dangerous creatures. Emotional and all. Not like us men.'

I looked at Abhilaksh. The boy made sense. There was a fleeting moment when Mallika's face flashed in my mind. Why did the thought of Mallika keep returning to me every now and then? I wanted to ask Abhilaksh. He surely knew a bit about women. But I didn't know him at all so I didn't ask.

In the evenings, I would pedal back to the guesthouse on the watchman's bicycle. The cycle had a cane—the watchman's stick—inserted below the seat and it was used to scare away dogs and to keep beat on the streets, which kept the ghosts away from the watchman's heart. But as it was still evening when I cycled back to the guesthouse, there was no need for the cane. So it lay inserted below the seat of the cycle, the way thin iron rods are inserted into grilled tandoori chickens. On the way, I would buy one fruit, a mango or a banana, and eat it in my tiny room. My mother had prescribed a list of vitamins, fruit-wise. So it was mandatory that I ate a different fruit each day.

Dinner would be at the canteen in the guesthouse. In comparison to what was dished out at Omi Dhaba, the canteen was like five-star service so I was fairly happy and satiated. Later, after dinner, I had mastered the art of sleeping sideways, to facilitate the act of masturbation. Each night Rosy's badge fired my imagination. Surprisingly, Mallika never came to fuel my fantasy at such times. Was that the difference between lust and love? I wanted to ask Abhilaksh, but did not quite do so, even when Abhilaksh had become relatively familiar, for the simple reason that I feared Abhilaksh might ridicule the fact that I had to lie sideways the whole night and do things that seemed impossible for any sane mind. So I kept that question unasked.

'This Nigam is such a wretch. Don't understand how he motivates his staff,' I muttered to Abhilaksh on a Friday morning. A week-full of fatigue had made me forget the lesson number one that Rosy had told me: to be respectful. But we were behind a silent glass and Rosy certainly did not read my lips the way I read hers. So, I felt free to say whatever I wished.

'In the corporate world, and in the real world, staff, subordinates and children are motivated by the stick, not by any of the leadership theories that they teach in MBA,'

Abhilaksh stretched out and yawned.

'So you mean to say the real working world is opposite of what they teach us in management schools and IITs?'

'Exactly! Management training is grandiose training in fiction. They charge you hefty fees and make you do tough projects to prepare you for a world that doesn't exist. The truth is that the guy who signs your pay cheques has supreme powers over you. He is never questioned.'

Suddenly, I said, 'Abhilaksh, you know something? The room that they have given to me is so pathetic that I can't even sleep properly. I have to lie sideways. Such a narrow bed. And here in office, I can't criticize the General Manager. This corporate world is so suffocating.'

'Right. But that's what life is like once you start working. That's why I never want to take up a corporate job. I will start my own business. Maybe deal in vehicles, or sell art,' he said.

'Then why did you join the IIT?'

Abhilaksh became silent. He looked sad. Not wanting him to feel low anymore, I had a brainwave and said, 'Abhilaksh, leave all this talk. Tell me, will you come with me to a cabaret tomorrow night? The Lido Cabaret at the Minto Bridge, Connaught Place? Saturday cabarets are topless. And cop-less.'

'Cop-less?'

'Yes. No cops on Saturdays, so I've heard. The guesthouse watchman told me about it. He lends me his bicycle every day so I've become friends with him.'

'But why did you suddenly bring up cabarets? We were discussing our future!'

'No! We were talking about the restrictions here and the restrictions that the future holds for us. And I suddenly felt the need to break free. That's all.'

Abhilaksh gazed absent-mindedly through the glass at the reception counter. Scratching his head, he muttered, 'Yes, I guess you're right. This place sucks. And the future is going to be like this for you, at least. I can imagine you sitting in a big cabin, like that Nigam guy inside. Serious, speechless, and perhaps senile.' The thought enlivened him and he broke into a smile and patted my shoulder.

'Whatever. Even I may decide to sell art or join a theatre company. But, as of now, I want you to accompany me to the topless cabaret at the Lido tomorrow.'

Abhilaksh looked through the glass again, this time more intently. Rosy was scribbling down her mundane tasks. It would have been nice to have Rosy join us at the Lido. But this was India and boys and ladies couldn't watch adult stuff seated together. Eventually he said, 'Done. I will drive us there. And you can stay at my place after the show. Our Vasant Vihar bungalow is so big that dad and mom won't even know if someone came in and left!'

The Lido was shady and dark. Jarring music hit us as we walked in, all perfumed and shaved. Swarthy, dark men in vests and track bottoms, some in lungis and a few others in kurta pyjamas, sat on foldable steel chairs at unclean wooden tables that were littered with glasses and ashtrays. Flickering bulbs dangled from the ceiling, and relayed insects into the Chicken Manchurian dishes that lay cold on tables placed below those naked bulbs. Red-eyed men sat there, staring into their dishes, as if expecting the dead chickens to sizzle to life once the cabaret started, while others stared at the red velvet curtain on the stage.

'Hey, the gentry is not nice,' Abhilaksh said, a bit wary of the place.

'That's why I was telling you to bring my watchman friend along. But you never let me,' I winked.

'Shut up and sit down.'

'Don't worry; it's safe. These people won't harm you. If at all, they will target the nude ladies. Not you and me.'

Just then a hoarse voice barked into the mike from behind the velvet curtain, 'Ladies and gentlemen, we present to you the world famous Lido Cabaret. Hold your hearts. Or whatever else you want to hold! Because here comes…' The music from the orchestra suddenly erupted with loud fanfare.

'*Ladies* and gentlemen! Ladies who?' Abhilaksh looked around. The place had only men seated all around. Drooling men.

'Ladies are coming. They are behind the curtain. Wait!' I shouted into Abhilaksh's ear over the piercing sound of the orchestra.

'But why should he address even the performing ladies?'

Before I could answer, the hanging bulbs above the tables dimmed further. I could see a thin, bald man twisting a fan regulator on a switchboard next to the stage. That was perhaps what controlled the bulbs.

The red velvet curtain opened and three dark, fat women jumped on the stage with a thud. One of them almost tumbled but the thin, bald man quickly left the light regulator and rushed to the edge of the stage to prevent her fall; he placed his hands against her ample hips and steadied her. She smiled at nobody and beckoned the other girls to start dancing. The three of them gyrated with such gusto that the whole stage creaked and trembled violently. The lusty drunk men cheered aloud. I was looking more at everyone else than at the three scary women. One of the women even had whiskers and hair in her underarms and drew the maximum whistles when she raised her arms and waved at the menfolk. With jerks, they removed their tops and skirts. I looked on. Sandy in a smart bra, there on that stage, gyrating and thumping away to that orchestra, would have been a more tolerable sight. I smiled at the thought, and Abhilaksh looked at me with surprise.

'How can you smile at these things, Viraat?' Abhilaksh barked.

I chose not to reply. I didn't want to ridicule my old best friend before my new best friend.

Two fat men, who looked like truck drivers, climbed onto the stage with wads of crisp ten-rupee notes and started showering it on the women. Then they whistled, and when the money had finished, the fattest of the three women pushed them off the stage with a swing of her hips. They looked like C-grade vamps from a Tollywood film, the kinds whose posters filled the fantasies of all the watchmen in all the factories of Faridabad.

The music by now had built up to a crescendo and had reached such a shrill pitch that it felt like steel utensils were clanging above our heads. The three women on stage unhooked their bras. Six voluptuous breasts swayed wildly for a split second before the thin bald man twisted the regulator fully to the left. There was complete darkness. The music stopped. The three women stumbled behind the velvet curtain. The thin, bald man turned the regulator again and the lights came back to life. The cabaret had ended.

I couldn't masturbate for a week after that.

5

SUMMERS IN FARIDABAD WERE UNBEARABLE. SLEEPING sideways was taking its toll on me, now more than ever, after the cabaret fiasco, I got weary of sleeping on my narrow bed so I decided to explore other possibilities. I managed to get hold of the key to the terrace, thanks to my friendship with the watchman and his clan. The guesthouse was housed in the narrowest of all the buildings in the vicinity. Not only did it have narrow rooms, but even its corridors, staircase and the lobby were slender like the waists of Awadhi concubines. And so was the terrace. No one ever went up there. A few sad discarded pieces of furniture lay there; dilapidated beds and chairs, a few useless taps, two cracked ceramic wash basins, and a few empty paint canisters that were dripping with rainwater and labourers' urine. Mosquitoes hovered over those containers, breeding in the putrid puddles of water and piddle. On the paint tin, some letters of 'Asian' and 'Paints' had been smudged and almost read like 'Ass Pains', my mind having added an extra 's' at the end.

Amid all those abandoned things, there was a clear and open area where I could spread my bedroll. Every evening I carried the heavy bedroll on my shoulder and took it up to the terrace. A few days later, I discovered a rejected dining table that could actually be used as a makeshift bed. It was convenient sleeping up here. If I happened to get up in the middle of the night to answer the call of nature I would just urinate over the low railing onto the backyard of the building where wild grass and moss grew in leaps and bounds.

Every day, some portion of the terrace got cleaned due to this human intrusion. Spiders ran helter skelter when I put a broom through their cobwebs. Vengeful mosquitoes buzzed and hovered over my head all night with their urine-smeared bites, but since I applied ample amounts of mosquito-repellent cream, they remained a frustrating distance away. Blind bats hung upside down near the railing, and got terribly warm and drenched whenever I pissed down on their dark abode. The lone human intrusion, me, had indeed created a totally unpleasant stir in that isolated, rooftop ecosystem.

Mallika visited me in my dreams occasionally. She smiled at my helplessness and then disappeared like early morning dew. I loved those dreams. They stayed on like a hangover even when I woke up, and gave me a nice, fuzzy kind of happiness. But generally the days passed without a sense of anything happening. It was all the same.

From the vantage point of my makeshift bed, I had a good view of the terrace across mine. On that other terrace, there was a clothesline that would be festooned with washed bras every morning, which were squirreled away as the morning progressed. Perhaps their owner was too shy to have her lingerie subjected to voyeuristic onlookers. The shame of public display that would creep in once the vegetable vendors and house maids started bustling around on the streets below. So, as the sun swelled in the sky, the lingerie got replaced with other clothes such as chunnis and churidars. I didn't know who replaced the clothes. I rubbed my eyes each morning to the sight of swinging bras on the rusted wire and I yearned to see the wearer of those lacey satins. I wondered how and when the mystery woman sneaked onto her terrace to embellish the rusted wire with her undergarments, without anyone being able to catch even a glimpse of her. Even when those garments were replaced with their lesser-shaming siblings, no woman appeared on the terrace. The bra-churidar interchange on the swinging metal wire happened imperceptibly, like the change of guard at the Buckingham Palace.

Under the trickle of the tiny shower, the mystery would rankle in my head. Prickly water jets from the clogged nozzles of my shower ran helter skelter like fresh sperm-tads going berserk inside a womb. By about 9 a.m., I would rush up to dry my towel on the terrace, and the dainty bras on the opposite terrace would have by then been magically replaced by more conservative wear. I hoped to catch the mystery woman during the changeover act someday. The mystery and the hope kept me excited, in the same way the fantasy of Mallika did.

By 9.15 am, I would set off on my rickety bicycle for the office. On the way, I would hungrily eat spicy bread pakoras and wash them down with extra-sweetened lassi at Pappu Dhaba. This was despite the fact that Abhilaksh had once told me that the ice put in those lassis came from left-overs of the ice blocks illicitly sold-off by the coroner at the hospital morgue next door. Many times I had chanced upon huge ice blocks being carried on hand-pulled rickshaws to the mortuary gate. The ice blocks preserved the corpses and saved them from rotting, since air conditioning was too expensive and of no use to the dead.

'Viraat, listen to me! After the relatives take away the dead body, the leftover ice gets sold off for a quick buck,' Abhilaksh had shouted at me. 'I am sure Pappu Dhaba also buys its ice from the same source. Imagine, ice with blood and sputum. They just wash off the surface and recycle it into the lassi. And you drink that lassi every day! For god's sake, stop drinking the dead, you stupid oaf!'

I had clenched my teeth and stared hard at Abhilaksh, but hadn't said anything. Every morning at Pappu

Dhaba, I would first examine the lassi, looking for hair or a relic of the dead. Then I would shake the tall, thick glass delicately, the way the French swivel their fine wine glasses, and sniff attentively to discern the aromas. No deathly aroma ever wafted up. To me, the lassi always smelled creamy and fresh. It was only after that initial sniffing that I would proceed to gulp it down. I drank it day in and day out despite Abhilaksh's strong advice.

Back in my guesthouse room, the thought of the mystery woman played on my mind persistently. In my office, thoughts of Mallika and her unattainability kept me agog. In between, the glint of Rosy's breast-badge charged me up. That was how my summer internship progressed.

'Abhilaksh, what do you think? A ghostess. Or spirit. Invisibly shuffling clothes on the line.'

'I don't really think she is a ghost. Or ghostess as you say.'

'Then?'

'I think she is a very ugly woman who doesn't like coming out on the terrace when you are around.'

'Or a very beautiful one, who is too shy to acknowledge the fact that someone as good looking as me knows her bra size!' I chuckled.

'Shut up, Viraat. What do you think of yourself? Someone whose shit doesn't stink?' Abhilaksh snubbed me.

'Come on, dude. Why the hell are you jealous?' I patted

Abhilaksh's back and remarked, 'I attract women all the time.'

'Oh really? You are just an over-confident clumsy asshole.'

'Oh, I can see you are really very jealous.'

'Jealous, my foot.' Abhilaksh scowled, paused, stared at the ceiling for a few moments and then said in a hushed tone, 'Okay! What's your score then?'

'Score?' I raised my eyebrows, not liking where our conversation was headed.

'How many girls have you screwed, you idiot?'

'Well, I exercise self-restraint,' I said self-righteously and then fell silent. My ears reddened and my face flushed with the lie. That happened to me often, particularly when someone reminded me of the impotence of my fantasies. I vowed that someday I would earn a score that would impress buffoons like Abhilaksh. Then I thought, why some day? I might as well make a start during this internship. I clenched my fist tight. *And I must do it with none other than Mallika. I bet she likes me too, and I can turn her on if I try a bit harder. Plus, she is in Delhi, while Karan and Sandy are in far-off Ludhiana. This is my one big chance*, I thought. My knuckles went white and beads of sweat broke out on my forehead.

'What are you mumbling? Say it loudly,' Abhilaksh taunted me.

'Come on, Abhilaksh, I will show you!'

'What?' Abhilaksh snarled.

'This Friday, after lunch, we will drive to Delhi. To Connaught Place. Inner circle, M block.'

'Why, what's there, huh?' Abhilaksh sounded disinterested.

'I want you to meet my girlfriend, Mallika Mattoo.'

That made Abhilaksh sit up and look at me intently. For the first time, Abhilaksh looked interested in something that was happening within our glass cubicle. 'Really! You never told me you had a girlfriend. Is this a fact or is it going to be another one of your fiascoes? Like the Lido cabaret!'

'No, no, no, no!' I protested. 'It is a reality. She exists. My GF.'

'She works in M block, CP?'

'She is also doing her internship. She is actually my classmate in Chandigarh. We have been going around for a while.' I blushed once again, like a shy bride. Colour rose in my ears yet again. I hated my ears for being antennas that could catch lies and convert them into red hues of shame.

'And you two have done it?' Abhilaksh persisted in his interrogation of my supposed love life.

'Of course, man. That's a done thing. Normal. What's the big deal?' I blurted. My mouth had gone dry too. The lie was enough to make my heart pound and dry out my tongue, so that it felt like a rough, scaly lizard between my teeth.

'How many times have you done it with her?'

'Oh! I have lost count. She is crazy about me, you see. We make love every day.'

'Hey, come on! How is that possible? You aren't married, nor are you living together. Are you?'

'In Chandigarh, we go out rowing every evening. She loves to do so. And then, once we're in the middle of the gorgeous and desolate Sukhna Lake and the sun is setting, she goes down on me. And then rides me. We have a rocking time, literally,' I boasted, smiling wickedly. 'And I am so grateful my dad's a member of the Lake Club!' I went on and on, babbling uncontrollably.

Abhilaksh was stumped. He had always thought I was a virgin, but now I had suddenly been elevated to the level of a maestro in the art of screwing. Envy gripped Abhilaksh.

'But how is that possible?' Abhilaksh growled. 'How can you do it daily in a boat? In a bloody boat!'

'Hey, don't shout, stupid. Rosy will hear you. This glass is not really soundproof!' I lowered my voice, winked and whispered, 'And Rosy is my next target.' I suddenly felt far superior to Abhilaksh: more accomplished, seasoned and powerful. I noticed Abhilaksh's pupils dilate so much that he almost looked like a wax statue at Madame Tussauds.

'You are solid, dude!' Abhilaksh uttered in awe.

I smiled, despite the fact that my ears were blood red. Rosy looked on with curiosity; she could tell that there was something fishy brewing, but I ignored her prying eyes and the glint of her breast badge.

Friday came after two painfully long days. For two days, I had been trying to figure out how to impress Abhilaksh and prove my sexual proximity to Mallika to him. The challenge of turning a lie into reality was as heavy as the burden of 'corporate social responsibility'. Abhilaksh did not stop quizzing me even for a moment in those two days. He was still a virgin and was overawed by the knowledge that I had already tasted the forbidden fruit. Abhilaksh's questions ranged from romance to biology. Anatomy particularly attracted him, and those queries stumped me and left me groping for answers. Yet, with evasive eyes, reddened ears, and deliberate vagueness, I handled Abhilaksh's questions. The MBA course had honed my skills of evasion.

Abhilaksh's yellow Zen carried the two of us to Connaught Place. Traffic floated around us amid the sounds of road rage, creating drama along the way. Rickety State Roadways buses farted fumes right into the noses of two-wheeler riders with precision. So much so that I imagined that the buses might have been manufactured by using a two-wheeler as a measuring unit—the shop floor supervisor at the bus factory would have perhaps designed a one-scooter-high exhaust-pipe, two-scooter-high windowpanes, three scooter-high wipers and a four-scooter-high roof, atop which, during peak hours or for breeze, commuters could travel. A scooter could almost be like a peg measurer. There could be no other reason why the exhaust outlets of moving buses were so perfectly aimed at the noses of hapless scooterists.

I hadn't told Mallika that I was coming to see her and that I was also bringing along another friend, to show her off to him. I had planned to surprise her. Perhaps I was hoping to choke Abhilaksh's expectancy by a chance possibility that Mallika might not be there in her office since she was unaware of our visit. I could then make an excuse to Abhilaksh that she had to leave suddenly due to some important work related to her project. That would smother Abhilaksh's curiosity.

Abhilaksh was almost drooling on the way. It amused me how boys could presume that a girl was available to to all boys if she had slept with one. On more than one occasion, Abhilaksh had confided to me that whenever he saw a couple kissing behind the bushes in Lodhi Garden, he got excited. Abhilaksh's lapping libido had been annoying me for the past two days.

We were nearly there and my heart drummed out a prayer—I hoped Mallika would disappear, vanish into thin air for just that moment when we were to barge into her cubicle to surprise her.

Abhilaksh drove rather recklessly, and I felt I was being roller-coastered around the strangely shaped park

that housed a cramped market of fakes and duplicates—
Palika Bazaar. Swerving to his left, Abhilaksh drove into
an empty parking slot with the suddenness of a newborn's
urination. A small band of beggars had gathered in the
parking lot. A girl clad in jeans and a sleeveless top
had just parked her Maruti 800 and was walking away
without giving the beggars any money and they hooted
and whistled at her.

'Look there,' I shouted excitedly, hoping to distract
Abhilaksh and slow him down. 'Here, even the beggars
eve-tease.'

'Yes. They have a right. After all, they work so hard at
begging and she didn't even give them a five-rupee coin,'
Abhilaksh smirked.

I guffawed in feigned disgust. I knew I was making a
vain attempt at distracting Abhilaksh. We walked briskly
toward M block. Under the parapet, a new shoe store
had opened up, seemingly the same morning. Garlands
of marigold flowers fluttered on the shop's door in the
warm afternoon wind, and the thin owner seemed to be
haggling with a bunch of eunuchs who were blocking the
passage of his shop. The owner seemed hassled. A tiny
bemused crowd had collected around the shopkeeper the
way ants gather around a dying cockroach. The eunuchs
were threatening to strip if they were not paid the goodwill
sum, the shagun. Their masculine sari-clad bodies and
their bawdy singing and shouting accompanied by crude,
loud clapping spooked the poor owner. He was cringing,

but the beads of sweat on his bald head further fanned the eunuchs' aggression.

'Your city is strange, Abhilaksh!'

'Why?'

'There are beggars who eve-tease and shopkeepers who beg hijras!' I said. 'Why the hell is he so scared? He should just tell the eunuchs to take off their saris, run naked on the streets, do acrobatics and go to hell for all that they are worth. Why is he trembling and cringing before them?' I yelled over the din. I actually hoped that the trembling shop owner would hear me.

'Viraat, the belief is that if you see the private parts of the eunuchs, I mean whatever they have or don't have, you too shall be born a eunuch in your next birth!'

'Oh, how silly! Really! I mean do people in this great big city still believe in all that nonsense? In Chandigarh, we don't care two hoots for such bullshit.'

Abhilaksh refused to be detracted. He kept charging ahead, looking up for the hoarding of 'GILT Industries'. I felt pangs of guilt at having brought Abhilaksh along. I was almost running, trying to keep up with him. The hijras' claps and goading faded away. Abhilaksh's body-language was making me very concerned. It was as if he was salivating with lustful expectancy.

'Hey man, cool down, she is my girlfriend, not yours. Why the hell are you in such a hurry to get to her office?' I wanted to ask Abhilaksh, but somehow could not.

We walked past a red-and-yellow mascot outside

the McDonald's outlet, past a vendor selling fake herbal aphrodisiacs on the pavement, past a madari whose ape looked happier than him, past a herd of scabies-ridden dogs wagging their tails, past a supposed blind beggar who had the ability to count currency, past a small betelnut shanty that displayed condoms and cardamoms in a single row, past a stick-wielding red-eyed cop looking for helmetless riders, past a large garish jewellery store whose gun-toting moustachioed guard looked prouder than its whining owner, and past a bunch of cab drivers scratching their crotches at a tea stall that was suffused with the aroma of stale tea. Delhi unrolled before me like the sequential unveiling of clothes by a bride on her first night.

The stairs to the first floor of the GILT office were narrow and reeked of betelnut spit and urine. Any place that is owned by the public is owned by no one, and so such spaces are usually unkempt and filthy. But the glass door of the GILT office shone and stood out like ivory on a tusker. I raced past Abhilaksh and pushed open the door. At the reception, a decked-up, obese woman sat lazily filing her nails and yawning. She smelled of a sweet perfume that had mingled with her sweat to give out an odour that guaranteed a headache. She wore a bright blue polyester blouse that ensured that she perspired more profusely and revealed her bulges more eloquently.

I went up to her and said, 'Excuse me, Ma'am. I want to

meet Mallika Mattoo. Intern at the HR branch.' Abhilaksh had never seen me so humble; it was as though I was ashamed of my own existence and was overwhelmingly apologetic about having interrupted her stupor.

The woman looked at us with expressionless kohled eyes. She scanned me and blurted through her red lipstick, 'Why?' She never stopped filing her nails for even a minute. She was decidedly curt and stared at me with a strange expression on her face. 'Why do you want to meet Mallika?' She asked again, blowing nail-powder off her filer.

'Well...just like that. I am her class fellow, Ma'am,' I pleaded.

'But this is not your classroom, boy. This is an office. There has to be a good reason why you would want to meet her.'

'But, Ma'am, I know her,' I squirmed.

The image of the shoe store owner pleading before the hijras flashed in my mind. Just ten minutes ago, I had scoffed at that scene, and now, here I was doing exactly the same thing. Abhilaksh was probably thinking along the same lines because he said, 'Everyone has to beg, cringe and beseech at some point in life.'

In a few minutes, I was almost prostrating before the fat receptionist. 'Ma'am, we have come all the way from Faridabad, just to meet her,' I whimpered.

'So what? Boys come all the way from Bhopal and

Jhumari Talayia to meet girls here. No big deal! Faridabad is just next door.' She began filing her nails again. Strangely, most fat women that I had seen had nice, slender fingers and pretty nails. It was as though their entire prettiness had been sucked up by their nails.

By then, Abhilaksh had decided to take control of the conversation. He pulled at my shoulder. I was completely out of ideas so I let Abhilaksh do the talking despite my own feeling of jealousy toward him at that moment. Abhilaksh, just like Sandy and Karan, had in that instant, joined the category of my adversaries who were out to woo Mallika.

There was no doubt that Abhilaksh, the cool rich dude, knew how to deal with the receptionist. He bent over the reception counter, put his elbows on the glass, looked left and right, and whispered in a conspiratorial tone, 'Ma'am, you see it is something very sensitive and personal.' Abhilaksh came so close to her face that I could see her twitch at the whiff of his foul breath. 'Ma'am, it is about...err...a marriage proposal,' he muttered, 'I have come to check out this girl, Mallika, for my brother who is coming down from the US just for a week, tomorrow, on a bride hunt. He is a Green Card holder, you see. I have to inform him what she looks like as soon as he lands. If she is good, he will rush straight to CP; if not, then he might go to Ludhiana where all the pretty and fair girls are.'

'Ludhiana!' I suppressed a laugh.

'Oh!' The receptionist said, suddenly melting the

way a big frozen fish thaws at the touch of a button in a microwave oven. She looked into Abhilaksh's eyes and said, 'Yes, I understand how sensitive these matters are! Even I have been on the lookout for quite some time.' She paused, lowered her eyes and said, 'For myself.' A comical sadness engulfed her big mouth as her large jaw bones sunk in frustration into the layers of flesh on her neck. She patted Abhilaksh's forearm gently and said, 'Just go in, boys. Go, go. Quietly. Turn right. Third cabin. She is there. Alone!'

'Thank you, ma'am. You are really so understanding.'

'And sensitive too,' I added, trying not to chuckle as we rushed toward the corridor.

'And, Ma'am, please do one more favour,' Abhilaksh turned back at the corner of the corridor and said in a hushed tone, 'please don't tell Mallika the purpose of our visit. Because in case we reject her, she will be very hurt.'

'Yes, yes! I know what you mean. I know very well what rejection means,' she said, on the verge of tears.

Inside, there was a long row of small cabins, so tiny that it was difficult to imagine how people worked in them. Acute shortage of space in a prime area like CP ensured that offices were tadpole-sized. I felt sad that Mallika was working in this environment; it would have been nice if she had done her internship in Faridabad with me. She could have been sharing my air-conditioned glass cabin instead of smart-ass Abhilaksh. If that had happened, I would never ogle at Rosy, Abhilaksh would have vanished from the scenario, and I would have had a clear field to woo her on sultry afternoons and possibly play with her feet under the table. The imagery was so vivid that it made me quiver. Abhilaksh noticed my quivering, looked at me with wonderment and scowled.

'Hey, Mallika, it is me!' I shouted as soon as we barged into her tiny cubicle.

There she was, seated at her small desk, typing out something on her laptop. Her fair pretty fingers glowed under a lampshade and stood out against the black keyboard. She looked up and broke into a smile—a smile that warmed my heart and caused it to skip a beat. Mallika was pretty; so pretty that I was certain that Abhilaksh must have been gobbling her up with his eyes. I could feel Abhilaksh's eyes piercing right through my back and delving straight into the third button of Mallika's white top.

I felt proud and jealous at the same time. Jealous for the obvious reason: because every boy who saw Mallika wanted her; and proud because Abhilaksh thought that she was my girlfriend with whom I had been copulating every evening in a boat at the Lake Club. That would certainly be a matter of great envy for any boy to imagine, something that made me mighty pleased.

Mallika sprang to her feet and shook my hand warmly. 'What a pleasant surprise, dude!' she exclaimed. I expected a hug, but then I was happy that she had totally ignored Abhilaksh. I was now sure that I was better looking than the fair Delhi IITian. The exhilaration gave me enough confidence to introduce Abhilaksh to her.

'Meet my friend, Abhilaksh. From IIT. He is also interning with me at Metal Bearing Co.'

'Hi, Abhilaksh,' Mallika murmured, and I was happy that she did not shake his half-extended hand.

We chatted casually about various subjects. I wanted to tell her about the Lido cabaret and my other strange experiences, but I saved it for another day. Abhilaksh feigned decency and looked like a priest who had escaped from the Papal kingdom. *What a scoundrel*, I mused. *The cunning chap knows how to cast the best first impression on chicks and present himself as the most well-behaved guy on earth*. Abhilaksh caught my eye and smiled at me, perhaps reading my thoughts. The exchange of our glances was like the instinctual competition between jungle beasts when they were on a quest for a mate.

'Viraat, tell me, how do you pass your time? I find this internship very boring,' said Mallika, looking at me and then at Abhilaksh. I was not sure whom she wanted a reply from.

'I feel the same, Mallika. It is very boring. No work. The company bosses don't take interns seriously,' I blurted.

'Well, I am sure that won't be the case with Mallika,' Abhilaksh said gently.

'Why? Which company takes their interns seriously?' I demanded somewhat angrily. Why did he have to defend Mallika? Why the hell couldn't Abhilaksh accept that she was my girlfriend and not his?! My face flushed with anger, although I still tried to smile to keep Mallika in good humour.

'Viraat, come on! Abhilaksh is just joking,' Mallika chuckled, 'and perhaps he is complimenting me. Right, Abhilaksh?'

Abhilaksh beamed. I could sense his confidence swelling up like freshly baked pizza crust.

We chatted a little while longer. Small talk, most of it by Mallika. We boys listened and nodded our heads. She talked about films, college, and her internship. I wanted to tell her about my lie. The urge was strange and inexplicable but I managed to suppress it quickly. Seated there, I just drank the sight of Mallika in—her pink lips, the little gap between her pearly teeth through which the tip of her pink tongue peeped intermittently, her chipped nails that she kept nibbling on, the little wart on her nose, the third button of her top that would yield to my fantasies later at night, the arch of her neck, her chuckle that put those Kashmiri cheeks in blossom, the abruptness of her talk and the sweetness of her voice, her painted toe nails, a pencil twirling between her fingers... the room and everything in it that was so overwhelmingly suffused with her that it drove me crazy.

Abhilaksh was quiet too, smiling idiotically, and laughing at her girlie talk and jokes. *If I had cracked the same jokes he would have called me a clumsy oaf,* I thought.

Suddenly, the thought of the mysterious woman on the

terrace and her bras crossed my mind and momentarily distracted me from Mallika. I felt it was time to leave. We had already spent over an hour and that was enough for Abhilaksh to be sufficiently impressed with my 'girlfriend'. It was enough to give me an upper hand for our future interaction. If we sat any longer, Abhilaksh might guess that perhaps Mallika and I were not intimate.

'Mallika, we must push off now. We'll leave you in peace,' I spoke quickly, breaking through her non-stop chatter.

'What? Hey, I was telling you about this latest Hollywood release,' said Mallika.

Abhilaksh seemed a bit disappointed but he smiled and said, 'Listen, Mallika, the receptionist outside is very strict. She wasn't even allowing us to come in. So we don't want to get you in trouble. She could be rude to you if we stayed any longer.'

I thought that was unnecessary. Why was Abhilaksh trying to play the good guy? Why couldn't the bugger just stay silent?

'Oh, yes. I was going to ask you that,' Mallika said, 'how did you guys manage to get past that bitch? She is like a matron of a girls' hostel!'

'Well, nothing much. We told her we are classmates, and she was nice to us,' I was lying to Mallika, again. It was beginning to dawn on me that I wasn't very imaginative in cooking up believable lies. My rich, jealous IITian colleague seemed to be smoother and more suave.

'Come on, that's not possible. You tell me, Abhilaksh, how did you guys manage to get past the female James Bond?'

I shot him a serious don't-tell-her look. It would be disastrous if Mallika found out the truth.

'Tell me, Abhilaksh. How did you guys convince her?'she insisted.

Girls! I thought.

'Nothing, Mallika,' Abhilaksh said softly, 'Viraat is right. She was really nice to us when we told her that we are your friends. "Mallika is a very sweet girl," she said, as soon as we mentioned your name. And she gave us directions to your cabin.'

I raised my eyebrows. I knew that Abhilaksh had scored yet another brownie point by paying her a compliment.

'Really? I am surprised. I thought she hated me,' said Mallika.

'No one can hate you, Mallika,' said Abhilaksh very gently.

I hated him and wished he'd disappear. I cursed myself for having brought him along in the first place.

'Nothing of that sort happened, Mallika. This is just another of Abhilaksh's jokes,' I wanted to quickly erase the impact of all his sweet talk and so I quickly said, 'Actually, the fat bitch at the reception counter was quite difficult. It was I who ultimately convinced her that I had to see you for your internship term paper.'

'Oh, I see. Then you guys better leave. One hour seems

a decent enough time to discuss a term paper,' she winked and gave out a hearty laugh. 'And come by on a Sunday, we can go for a movie or something. I am staying at the YMCA Working Women's Hostel in GK I.'

'Sure. I will call you and come,' I said.

'And, Abhilaksh, you should come too,' she said.

Now that was too much! I cursed under my breath. Boys knew that if you were having sex, you would want privacy. But since Mallika was inviting a third person to accompany us to a film, it could make Abhilaksh a wee bit suspicious of my amorous claims. Abruptly, I tugged at Abhilaksh's arm. As we rose to leave, Mallika shook hands with Abhilaksh for a split second longer than with me. Abhilaksh was smiling like an idiot when I pulled him away from Mallika's grip and pushed him out of her cabin. Briskly, I led him through the narrow corridor. The receptionist raised her eyebrows to inquire if the matrimonial thing had worked out. Abhilaksh simply smiled at her as we left the building. I hoped she would not tell Mallika.

We walked toward the parking area. The parking lot attendant, a filthy man with unwashed hair and clad in a vest and loose pyjamas, snatched our parking ticket. Just as we got into the car, a beggar came lumbering toward the driver's window and thrust an amputated limb inside.

'Go to the other side, to my friend. I have no money,' said Abhilaksh, but the beggar wouldn't budge, making it difficult for Abhilaksh to roll up his window. 'I say, go to the other side,' he shouted this time. 'My friend here has a lot of money. And he just saw a girl. He is soon getting married to her. He will give you money!' Abhilaksh was shouting at the top of his voice. He desperately wanted the beggar's disgusting limb out of his window so that he could roll up the glass and drive off.

Suddenly, the beggar stepped back from the car and hastily ran away in the opposite direction. I looked at Abhilaksh in surprise. He shrugged back at me. What had scared away the scum? But before I could come up with an answer, someone grabbed my arm with such pressure that I thought my arm would turn into pulp.

'Badhai ho! Getting married, eh?' A familiar, cracked voice startled both of us. The same group of eunuchs who had been annoying the shoe shop owner an hour ago surrounded us. Me in particular! They had probably overheard Abhilaksh shout to the beggar that I was getting married! The entire gang of eunuchs descended upon the car like bees from an agitated beehive.

Out of the gang of goons, it was the biggest and the most grotesque eunuch who had caught hold of my arm. Apparently, he (or she) was the ringleader. I cried out in pain and shouted at Abhilaksh to start the engine and speed off but Abhilash sat frozen in the driver's seat.

'Congratulations on your forthcoming marriage, our dear boy. Hai-hai!' The eunuchs started clapping around the car. The tiniest eunuch sprang up on the bonnet of the car and started dancing.

'Abhilaksh, start the engine. Quick!' I said frantically, quivering with disgust. I tried to free my arm from the ringleader's grip, but the eunuch was much stronger than me. I felt ashamed that I was weaker than even a eunuch! In any case, I was too scared and disgusted to fight back. All I did was bleat, 'No, no. He was just joking. Let go of me. I am not getting married. Let me go. Please!' I desperately tried to free my arm so that I could somehow roll up my widow, but by then, another eunuch had inserted his (or her) bangled arm through the window and had opened the door. With a jerk, both eunuchs yanked me out of the car. I fell on the ground, got up, dusted my backside and stood still, trembling in humiliation as the bunch of eunuchs encircled me and started dancing and clapping loudly. They broke into a boisterous, crude item-number type Hindi song.

It was such a pitiably funny sight. A few small-time vendors and some passers-by had started gathering around us. All this while, Abhilaksh sat, still and did nothing to help me. He even seemed to be enjoying the cruel entertainment that was taking place right there at the expense of his pal.

I had never felt so helpless, disgusted and humiliated in my entire life. Just over an hour ago I had scoffed at the shopkeeper for cringing before the eunuchs and now the same band of thugs had trapped me. The eunuchs kept clapping and singing in an eardrum-piercing pitch for a long time. They even performed a garba around me. The crowd of bystanders had started enjoying themselves thoroughly and were clapping along. Some people guffawed, while others shouted mock congratulations. I felt so grossly violated that I yearned for the earth beneath my feet to part and gobble me up. My face turned crimson with disgust. With trembling hands, I took out my wallet and counted the money. All I had was a mere eighty rupees. With shaking fingers, I took out the meagre money and thrust it into the face of the ringleader.

'What is this? We are not beggars!' The ringleader shouted, pretending to be insulted.

The others started clapping even louder in anger. The whole drama sickened me and I felt like throwing up. 'This is all I have,' I said helplessly.

They checked my wallet, rummaging through all its nooks and crannies. One eunuch even inserted his (her) hand inside my pockets and felt around my undies, but at the end of the search they found nothing. They turned toward the car but by then Abhilaksh had managed to roll up both windows and also lock the doors. He had even started the engine. I feared that Abhilaksh would drive off, leaving me behind. I feared that perhaps the eunuchs would then kidnap me and take me away with them. When I was a child, my grandmother told me stories about eunuchs who abducted small children and castrated them to turn them into little eunuchs. Even though I was not a child anymore, the fear of being kidnapped and castrated scared me to death. Instinctively, I covered my crotch with both my hands. The eunuchs continued to clap and dance in a frenzy for some more time.

In the distance, a PCR van passed by. I shouted for help. The eunuchs snatched my eighty rupees and my empty wallet. Then the ringleader caught hold of me from behind, while the rest of them stood in front of me in a row, like concubines on display before a Nawab. Suddenly, in one single synchronized motion, they lifted up their saris and petticoats in unison. I was utterly disgusted by what I saw. I was almost about to collapse; I felt sick and feverish beyond anything I had previously experienced. The PCR van crawled toward us like a slithering centipede. The cops seemed to be in collaboration with the eunuchs. The thugs sang and danced a little longer. Then, when the police van was a stone's throw away, the eunuchs shouted abuses, pinched my ass with their red painted nails, and ran away screaming, 'Shaadi Mubarak! Shaadi Mubarak!'

For many days to come after that incident, I would puke out the lassi at Pappu Dhaba. Finally, I had paid heed to Abhilaksh's advice about the lassi.

6

WE WERE IN THE LAST WEEK OF OUR SUMMER INTERNSHIP. The monsoon was knocking at the southern-most tip of India, as declared by a dusky weather reporter on TV. It was the only segment of news that I watched. I sat at the long dining table that had as many legs as a centipede's, which made it impossible for people seated there to insert their legs into the womb of the table and sit with some comfort. The table was smeared with dal and the stained steel containers made sharp, noisy clink-clank sounds as people served themselves food from those vessels.

Back home in Chandigarh, I used to sneer at even the most scrumptious paranthas layered with a mound of yellow butter and motherly love that Mom fed me every Sunday. But here, in this wretched canteen of the guesthouse, I polished off even half-burnt-half-cooked rotis on a first-grabbed-first-eaten basis. After everyone had eaten, I would wipe my washed hands on my trousers and my face with my shirt sleeve, and then sit at one end of the table to type out my term paper on the laptop.

I had started doing this because the assignment had to be submitted to the General Manager, the despicable Ashok Kumar Nigam, before the company could grant me a certificate of successful completion of my internship. It was the last week and if I did not submit the assignment on 'Redesigning of Performance Appraisal Formats', my own appraisal would get screwed up beyond recognition. As a supposedly smart, young, soon-to-be MBA, the appraisal formats redesigned by me had to be smart too. They had to be peppered with enough management jargon, innovative formats, simplicity and complexity. Something I had no clue about.

I discussed my concept with Abhilaksh during the day. 'Abhilaksh. Can you guess what the concept of my performance appraisal is?' I asked him in all seriousness.

Abhilaksh looked at me blankly. He never expected me to talk about work. I patted his hand and said, 'Buddy, frankly, if left to me, performance appraisal should be measured on what I would like to term the "Rosy-index". The index ranks employees on their ability to get things done.'

'I think I have some idea about what you mean, but can you elaborate?'Abhilaksh asked with a smirk as we both ogled Rosy, who was shuffling about her desk.

'It simply means that every employee in the Metal Bearing Co. can be measured against Rosy and graded on a continuum that runs from ZR at the lowest end to TR at the highest: "ZR" standing for "Zero Rosy" and "TR" for "Ten Rosy"—the highest score that only Rosy can earn.'

'Haha. Sure, why not!' Abhilaksh coughed up a laugh. 'On such a scale, Nigam would never slither up past "OR" or "One Rosy". What do you say, Viraat?'

'Only if either of us happens to mark him. But, unfortunately, we don't have the privilege of evaluating him. It is only Nigam who has the right to assess us and everyone else. So sad.'

'Maybe you are right. Rosy is not only attractive and beautiful, she is even…'Abhilaksh left the words hanging in the air.

'Even what? Hard working?'

'No. Sexy!'

Both of us laughed aloud. 'So, under this new performance appraisal system, work will have no value?'Abhilaksh asked me with a laugh.

'Not work, but results. Results alone will be of value. Which means you score points for being sexy if that helps you get your work done,' I whistled.

'Now what is the difference? Results and achievements will come your way only if you work hard. Right?'

'Not necessarily.'

'But that's what's been ingrained in us since our childhood by everyone—our parents, teachers, and elders. Those who work hard get the best scores.'

'Abhilaksh, I said results. Not scores. Scores are no

measure of success. Brilliant minds with great scores can still be losers. Look at the world. Most of the successful people—entrepreneurs, celebrities, all those filthy rich blokes—did not have great scores in college. In fact, many of them were drop-outs and did not even go to college.'

'So basically our parents have been feeding us nonsense—work hard, study hard!' Abhilaksh was trying to contrast my philosophy with his parents'.

'From Ambani to Milkha Singh to Govinda to Giani Zail Singh, even Bill Gates and Steve Jobs. Most of our ministers, too. They all did so well in life; not by getting great marks in schools and colleges, I am sure.'

'That's fine, Viraat, but coming back to your concept, what is this Rosy Index? You mean looks? Smartness? Sexiness?'

'Of course! All that and more. She is sincere and reasonably hard working, but more than that she has her other trademark skills that make her so popular and sought after. So whatever job she wants out of people gets done pretty easily.'

Abhilaksh was nodding. I guessed he had started perceiving me as some sort of a management guru. We both kept eyeing Rosy through the glass. She really got work done out of people. Except perhaps the unmovable Ashok Kumar Nigam; that's why Nigam deserved the least score in my assessment index.

But what I fervently typed that evening was just plain bookish knowledge. I thought it sensible not to reveal my findings, which proved that charm, sex appeal and a sense of humour mattered more when it came down to getting the job done across different levels of the office hierarchies, lest others should steal my concept and get the idea patented. To me, Rosy was the embodiment of all that was right in the corporate world. Having her around din't make the adage 'all work and no play' sound like such a bad thing. Despite all work and no play, Rosy in our midst charged Abhilaksh and me up.

'At some later stage in life, perhaps, I will declare it as my intellectual property right; this concept of the Rosy Index,' I murmured, while feverishly typing out the report. My template rated workers on ambiguous aspects like 'how much they participated in the company's decision-making processes' and rated their efficiency based on 'how much over-time they put in'.

In office, I was always distracted because of Rosy, so I could never type out the damn assignment during the day. She floated around us and suffused the air with so much sensuality that office no longer appeared to be a place for work. Pretty women could turn work places into chambers of fantasies.

'What are you doing so late in the night, Viraat?' Tej Singh shouted from the other end of the corridor leading up to the dining room when he saw the dim light flickering late at night. He was the GM's chauffeur and stayed in a small room right below mine.

'Typing out something to please your GM sahib,' I

muttered. I wasn't interested in conversing with drivers and watchmen or any other similar inmates of the place that the company had so graciously allotted to me for the two-month period.

'Then you are trying something impossible. Nigam can never be pleased,' Tej Singh burped helpfully.

'Yes, I know. He doesn't even smile at Rosy,' I whispered. I hoped Tej Singh did not hear me say that.

'Look at me, Viraat. I have never tried to please him, even though I have worked with him all my life. Then why the hell are you trying to impress the dead rock?'

'Tej Singh, you've got such a wonderful, secure job. You are the chauffeur of the highest ranking person in the company. I still have to start my career,' I teased him. I wanted to be in Tej Singh's good books. I would have even toilet-trained his pet dog in the hope that both the driver and the dog barked in my favour.

Tej Singh smiled and twirled his whiskers that were as pointy and spiky as a porcupine. 'Maybe you are the only one who can impress the rotten pumpkin.' He came around and squeezed my shoulder. 'Anyway, all the best. I have to go to his house now. He has to go on a surprise inspection of the plant. And I have already given the night supervisor a heads up.'

I smiled, nodded and went back to typing. I wanted to finish it as soon as possible. The flickering bulb hanging over my head scorched a dozen more moths by the time the first gentle sun rays crept through the windows. I had been bitten by mosquitoes through the night and it had made writing the assignment more painful than it already was. Repellents too had given up on those little winged demons. So I decided to keep a nightly vigil on them as I typed, and killed each buzzing creature as it landed stealthily on my hand and made a meal of me. Then I neatly lined up all the dead mosquitoes on the table. There were about fifteen of them. My logic was that eventually the mosquitoes would see their dead comrades and would cease their attack on me. I had no idea if mosquitoes could see or not, but my tactic worked and they stopped biting me.

Soon the sounds and smells of daybreak floated in through the three triangular crevices between the blades of the defunct exhaust fan on the wall across me. I had actually worked through the night. I got up, stretched my back like a lazy cat, broke an early morning wind, belched out last night's dinner, and dizzily climbed up the narrow stairs that led to my room. 'Another night and I should be through with this painful assignment,' I muttered as I shut the laptop that was weighing down my left hand. I walked up the stairs, dragging my flip-flop clad feet. I could perhaps take a short nap before leaving for office. I turned the key to open the large, rusted padlock that dangled outside my door like the testicles of a stray bull, when suddenly, the thought of the mystery woman flashed through my mind. I glanced at the last stretch of the winding stairway that led all the way up to the cluttered rooftop. The thought made me stop. The possibility of catching the mystery woman at dawn crossed my mind and instantly revved me up the way a hungry hyena gets excited by the prospect of digging into the leftovers of a lion's kill.

Normally, I am not an early riser. It was generally the buzzing of flies that woke me up on the rooftop, and it was always well after the sun had turned angry and yellow. At times, I was drummed out of sleep by the war cry of the scrap-vendor in the street below, or by the honking of school auto-rickshaws, or the bicycle bells of night watchmen returning from duty. Such were the sounds of the day that usually jolted me out of my slumber. Sleep would otherwise not let me escape from the lusty wet dreams that it wove around me every night. That was why by the time I woke up, the bras would have already been wrung, spread and hooked to the wire with bright yellow plastic pegs.

But today was different.

It was the first time I was awake at such an early hour, and so I could perhaps unravel the mystery that had been haunting my thoughts all this while.

'Today I shall find out,' I muttered, 'whether she is young or old, pretty or ugly, human or a ghost, or simply a spirit of some washerwoman.' I placed my laptop on the narrow bed, squatted, and took out the terrace key from the low, wooden drawer of the bedside table. Along the edges of the drawer, there were tiny, prickly wooden splinters that stubbornly hung on, the way commuters stubbornly hang out of Mumbai Metro. They jutted out in the drawer as specimens of inferior carpentry, and more than one splinter pierced my thumb. But by now, I had got used to the pricks, just as beggars get used to receiving abuses.

Quietly, I tip-toed up the last flight of stairs and noiselessly turned the key to open the lock of the terrace door. Stealthily, I pushed the door slightly to create a slit that was just enough for me to peer through. From that crack, I peeped out.

There I saw her—pretty, fair, slim, with hair in a bun atop her head. She had a towel covering her dainty breasts. She seemed on the threshold of exiting her teens. I opened the door a wee bit more and stretched my neck out to look at her better. Her pretty arms held a bucket. She smiled at no one in particular as she walked by the wire, spreading undergarments meticulously on it. Below the towel, she wore a magenta salwar that rustled in the early morning breeze. All the while, she kept looking around, particularly in my direction, perhaps to make sure that there was no one around. Finding my make-shift bed empty, she appeared relaxed and went about her task with abandon.

I, on my part, kept gaping. I drank in the lovely sight of her as much as the weak light of dawn permitted. I was storing her up, the way camels on long desert journeys tank up on water from an oasis.

'*What timing!*' I thought, rubbing off the last bits of my

eye secretion. *If I was late even by a few minutes, I would never have discovered the mystery girl!*

She took out the last bit of her clothing from the bucket, rinsed and spread it and upturned the bucket to empty out the water. Then she turned back. Oh god, she was beautiful! I ogled at her and suppressed my early morning erection. My bladder was so full that I would have gladly jumped on to the terrace and relieved myself the way I usually did. But this wasn't a gentlemanly thing to do as she was there, right in front of me. I feared that even if I went down to the toilet in my room downstairs, she would vanish. *What pain a girl can give you!* I thought and kept watching her with sensuous excitement despite the excruciating pressure on my bladder.

She slowly walked toward the door of her terrace with the empty bucket dangling in her hand. Her towel was fluttering behind her to reveal a smooth back and a slim waist. Suddenly it dawned on me that perhaps I would never ever get to see her again. It was my last week in Faridabad, and I didn't want to go back without speaking to her. Such regrets, I had heard, lingered much beyond youth to nibble away at one's happiness. I didn't want to be left with the regret that I had missed the opportunity of speaking to her. I did not want another failure lurking and growing inside me, apart from my failure to woo Mallika: a feeling that already haunted me like the echo of a drowning child's wails in a village well. I knew what I had to do.

I jumped out from behind the door and shouted, 'Excuse me. Hi!'

She stopped in her tracks, startled. I imagined that although she had seen me asleep many a times from a distance, she had never imagined that I would one day come out of my slumber to suddenly catch her in a towel. For a moment, I thought she would turn away and run inside. But she did not. She froze. She was perhaps too stupefied. I could not understand why she looked so shocked at my simple 'hi'.

'Hi! My name is Viraat Nijhawan,' I said softly as I walked to the edge of the terrace. My own politeness felt odd to me, like jeans on an Indian priest.

The girl did not answer. She instinctively held her towel tighter around her. I made a conscious effort not to gaze below her chin as I spoke. 'Hi. I am Viraat. I've been in Faridabad for a few weeks. I'm a Management Trainee at the Metal Bearing Co. You may have heard the name?'

She nodded and some life came back to her. 'Yes, I know!'

'You know?' I was surprised. I never knew that I was so famous even in Faridabad! 'You know about me!' I exclaimed.

'Not about you. About the company.'

'Oh!' I felt silly.

She looked at me, and said, 'I have seen you many times, sleeping on that table there.' She pointed to the pile of broken furniture.

'Oh! This is just a temporary arrangement. Back home, I have a nice bed.' Gosh, why was I talking about my bed to a pretty girl in my first meeting? 'So, what's your name?' I asked.

'Vasundhara. I study at Home Science College here.'

'Home Science!' I exclaimed. Another dangerous girl, someone just waiting to be a wife before she could be slept with or so Sandy would have advised me. But something about her still kept me interested. Very interested.

'Yes, Home Science. Why? Is it a bad thing?' she said.

'Oh, no, no! I mean, not at all,' I stammered. 'If all girls study computers or medicine, who will run homes?'

Vasundhara put her bucket down. A breeze stirred a bra making it fly off the wire. Vasundhara looked at it from the corner of her eye but was too embarrassed to pick it up. I wished I could jump on to the other terrace like Tarzan to rescue the bra from the floor, dust it, and hang it up for her. All for her.

Though I did not jump across, I did something sillier. I shouted, 'Vasundhara, that thing has fallen. Pick it up and put it back on the string!'

'That thing! How cheap!' Suddenly, she turned livid. She hastily picked up the bra and hung it. Then, she turned back, picked up the bucket, and swiftly rushed toward her terrace door.

'Listen, Vasundhara...I...' I stammered. I didn't expect her to react like that. 'Just listen. I didn't mean for it to sound like that. I was just trying to help...thought you had not seen your clothes fall off.'

'My clothes falling off? You sick rascal. My clothes are downstairs. I am wearing a towel. Doesn't mean my clothes have fallen off, you moron.'

She ran toward the door and was gone. I was dumbstruck. She was gone. I stood there for a long time. The bras on the string were almost dry. I presumed that she must be waiting for me to go before she could emerge to interchange her smaller garments with bigger ones. There was no point waiting any longer, so I staggered downstairs like a lost gambler.

In office that day, I did not talk much. Abhilaksh spoke about Rosy, but it did not interest me. I was so angry with myself that I wanted to get out of my body and slap myself.

'What is wrong with you today, Viraat?' Abhilaksh asked.

'Nothing.'

'Then why this silence? Never seen you so quiet.'

'Abhilaksh, I found out who the mystery girl is,' I broke my silence.

'Oh really! Is she actually a ghost?'

'No, stupid. Why do you say so?'

'Because you are so quiet and bloodless like you've seen a ghost.'

'No! She is a beautiful girl. Very pretty. Dusky and petite.'

'Wow, really?'

'Yes. She is studying Home Science!'

'Home Science! So now you can propose to her straightaway, get married, and start procreating!' Abhilaksh chuckled. 'You've already used Mallika to her full potential. In the boat. Everyday. Remember?'

'Shut up, Abhilaksh. This is not a joke.'

'Then what is the problem Viraat? Why are you so quiet?'

'I made a fool of myself in front of her.' I narrated the entire incident and Abhilaksh laughed his guts out. I had never seen him laugh so hard.

'Abhilaksh, stop it, man. It's bad.'

'Go and apologize. Find out where Vasundhara lives. You know her name. So you can go to her flat tomorrow, or even in the evening today after work.'

'How can I apologize, Abhilaksh? I mean, what do I tell her?'

'For god's sake, I am not going to tell you that. You are my senior in the art of lovemaking. Just go and clear it all up, and then take her to the Lake Club in Faridabad, if there is one here. Or to Surajkund Lake. And rock a boat with her too!'

'Shut up, man!'

It was evening and as we rose to leave, Rosy beckoned me from a distance.

'Lucky chap!' Abhilaksh murmured as I made my way to her.

'Oh come on, Abhilaksh. She just wants to talk.'

'Well it always starts with small talk. Best of luck, buddy. I am pushing off. See you.' Abhilaksh picked up his brown leather bag and as he reached the door he turned around and said, 'And call me if you need directions to the boat club at the Surajkund Lake, you boat-rocker!'

I scowled at Abhilaksh. After he left, I walked toward the reception counter where Rosy stood with her eyebrows raised like the arches of Ramlila bows.

'What is it, Rosy?' I sounded distant and curt.

'It is about Mr Nigam. He wants you to see him,' she said, without any expression on her face. 'Now!'

My heart skipped a beat. A call from Nigam for someone at my level was indeed an unusual thing. It sounded like the death knell. Why did he want to see me?

7

I HAD NOT MET NIGAM EVEN ONCE AFTER THE INITIAL courtesy call that had left me detesting the arrogance of the man. I had not even seen him walk in or out of the office, or move around in the corridor or the canteen, or for that matter, anywhere else. At times I wondered if Nigam ever left his chamber; it was as if he was born in that room.

I dragged my feet toward the corridor on the right side of the reception counter, which led to the cabins of all the senior managers. As usual, the corridor was suffused with a sense of gloom that is usually associated with age and seniority. It smelled of exclusivity. Even the sounds and noises of the world beyond the corridor did not dare to tread in. It had a carpet that bore no foot marks and bracket lamps that emitted sad, dispersed light. Its ceiling had no lizards and its emulsion did not dare to even peel off at the corners and nooks. At the end of this corridor, where even sunlight did not enter, there was the familiar large door with a name plate in golden letters that stared in my face.

Ashok Kumar Nigam

'Ashok the Nigam,' I murmured. 'Sounds like Ashoka the Great. The guy who needs no introduction!' I hated that I had to present myself to the Don Number 1...alone. His scowl could make even dead wood jitter and his voice could freeze steam. I entered his vast chamber gripped with fear.

As usual, Nigam was smoking a pipe, seated behind his large mahogany table, his big pupils magnified through his thick glasses.

'So how is your internship going?' Nigam spoke with the pipe in his mouth. The tobacco-laced voice sounded like the gurgling of a hookah.

'Sir, it is going to be over next week. Was nice.' Images of the Lido cabaret and the hijras flashed through my mind. And the mystery girl on the rooftop, the company of watchmen and the breast-badge of Rosy. Years down the line, this was about all I was going to remember of my internship.

'Good.'

Nigam lit his pipe with the bullet-shaped lighter. The click of the lighter resonated in the silent chamber.

'Good,' Nigam repeated. It seemed as if he was being

generous with his voice. It was rare for him to repeat himself.

'Sir, I need to submit my term paper to you. Will you please mark it for me?'

Nigam smirked. 'Do you expect a General Manager to read reports of interns?'

'Sir, it is a good report. I am sure you are going to find it useful when the company decides to revise the performance appraisal system.'

Nigam sucked the end of the pipe, which had a round golden tip. Tiny clouds emanated from his thick lips. I gave out a little cough because of the tobacco stench.

'I like your self-confidence,' growled Nigam. 'Come home in the evening. You can dine with us. And have a beer too!' he added magnanimously.

Now, I was pleasantly surprised. I was already counting the number of pints I would guzzle and had almost started counting them on my fingers, behind my hips, where I held the wrist of my left hand with my right one. Clasping one's hands behind one's buttocks and standing stiff were signs of feigned respect and genuine servitude. 'Thank you, sir. It would be an honour,' I said and waited for further instructions.

Nigam sucked on his pipe a few times and said, 'And you will also get to meet Mini, my only daughter. Mini is studying in college. She is very nice. In a year or two, I am planning to marry her off.' He looked up at me and smiled.

That was decidedly unusual. 'We are a very conservative family, you see. My daughter and I, we don't believe in love marriages. The only things I have inculcated in her are good Indian values.'

I kept nodding stupidly until I realized I needed to respond to what he had just said. Thinking that it might improve the score on my term paper. I said, 'Indian values? That's nice, sir. But I read somewhere that even in Indian mythology, the concept of gandharvavivah or love marriages actually existed.'

'Where did you read all that crap?' Nigam tore away his eyes from the swirling smoke and looked up to scowl at me.

'Sir, in one commentary of the Kamasutra.'

'You've read the Kamasutra!' His jaw twitched, but I decided not to chicken out.

'Very often, sir. It is a bit comical. Funnily impossible poses and weird herbal concoctions and other aphrodisiacs!'

Nigam looked shocked. A moment later he smiled. He seemed relieved when he realized that I did not take the Kamasutra seriously. 'Hope you did not read that thing in office?' He gave out a deep chuckle.

'Not at all, sir. It is useful only at night.'

Nigam's smile evaporated. He lit his pipe again and sucked at it in fits and said, 'Come tonight. Mini is going to cook mutton roganjosh for you.' His invitation sounded like a warning.

'That is so gracious of her, sir. I will be th-there,' I stammered.

There was silence. I stood there for some time, waiting for him to say something but I realized it was time to exit his chamber. I turned back and slowly walked toward the door. As I reached the door, Nigam spoke again, 'And Viraat, I would be glad to hire you as a Grade I executive next year, after you finish your MBA.'

I turned back, bewildered. I could not fathom what it was that had turned an oversized recluse like Nigam into an angel, when all that I had done in that office for the past two months was ogle at Rosy and bitch with Abhilaksh.

'That is really so very kind of you, sir. I would love to work under your guidance. I have learnt so much from you, sir.' I came up to Nigam, held his limp hand and shook it. His thick, damp fingers and large palm felt like slithery whale skin.

'And one last thing. Hope you don't have a girlfriend?' Nigam whispered suspiciously.

Flashes of Mallika in an imaginary boat went through my mind in quick succession. 'No, sir.' I spoke the truth this time. 'No girlfriend. In fact, I stay away from girls. Can't even talk to them freely. My dad believes that romance, love, and such stuff are a waste of time.' And ogling at cleavages or leering at gross cabarets was a good utilization of time, I wanted to add but did not.

'Good. I am also on the lookout for a good match for

my daughter,' Nigam muttered and lowered his chin to light the pipe again.

I knew what was coming but strangely, I felt neither happy nor worried. It was the first time I had got a matrimonial offer and that too from a person who was so high up in the corporate world. Nigam lit the pipe and looked up into my eyes to gauge my expression. I didn't know what to say.

'But I am too young, sir,' I tried pleading in an unsure voice. 'And I still have a lot to do before I get married.' Lot to do ? Like what ? In my head, I could faintly see a rocking boat with Mallika lying naked in it. 'What is your score?' Abhilaksh's words came back to me.

'You have to do a lot before you get married! What does that mean?' The scowl returned to Nigam's face. 'You are already in your final year of MBA. And I am assuring you a job straightaway in Grade I, where we take only IIM chaps. While you are just an MBA from a tiny town.'

I swallowed the lump in my throat and bleated, 'I mean, I have to work for a few more years and save some money before I raise a family.' In my mind, the target of achieving a respectable score with girls was flashing like a 'Sixer' on a cricket scoreboard. 'At least six!' my libido nudged me from deep inside.

'Don't worry about money. We will set up everything for you. After all, I have just one daughter and all I have is going to be hers,' he said.

'But that shall be after you kick the bucket!' I wanted

to say but obviously could not. Instead, I said, 'But, sir, your daughter needs to like me too!' My liking her was immaterial.

'Oh, don't worry. Mini will do whatever I tell her. We are not in a hurry. She is also studying. And the wedding can happen two years down the line,' he said dismissively.

I stood still for some time, holding the brass door knob. I had never expected this when I had walked into his office. As I opened the door to exit, Nigam's words chased me, 'We will be going home at eight, when I leave office. Stay at your desk till then and refine your term paper.'

Back in the glass chamber, I felt benumbed and yet strangely, I was exhilarated, perhaps due to the faint realization that matrimony would earn me the right to the freedom of daily fornication. I opened my laptop and did a spell check on my term paper, since that did not require deployment of the grey cells. Rosy had already left. The sweeper was scrubbing the floor and the watchman was checking if all the doors and windows were locked. Nigam was perhaps lighting his pipe for the last puff in his chamber before he left for the day.

Time moved excruciatingly slowly and the minutes hung heavy on the gigantic wall clock. Tej Singh strolled in and went toward Nigam's chamber and in a few moments walked out carrying Nigam's brown leather briefcase that shone and reflected exclusivity and authority. Behind him, Nigam strolled out with his hands in his pockets. His gaze beckoned me. I scurried out of my cubicle. Like a stray pup trailing behind his mother, I followed Tej Singh and Nigam in a queue. I rolled on mindlessly, like a ball of wool rolling behind a sweater-knitting housewife.

As we approached Nigam's parked car, Tej Singh waved at me, asking me to sit in the front. But Nigam was kind to his future son-in-law; he permitted me to occupy the seat next to him. I glanced at Tej Singh with pride to make him jealous. I felt proud with the realization that after all these weeks, finally, I had risen above the ranks of drivers and watchmen. Tej Singh's eyes narrowed at me in the rear-view mirror as I lowered myself into the seat next to Nigam. I sat stiffly and still, stifling the urge to adjust my underwear.

The car had velvet curtains and white seat covers. Soft music was playing. Tej Singh donned a crisp white cap that concealed all the lice and dandruff in his hair that I was aware of. He drove the car carefully and silently without seeming to move a limb. Even Nigam did not move much. I imagined that he was meditating with eyes open and so I also sat still, in a meditative state, thinking of Vasundhara. The air conditioner purred out cool air that whirred past Tej Singh's armpits and brought some of his faint stench to me. I was sure that the armpit odour must never have bothered the boss, since he smoked all day long and it probably snuffed out his sense of smell. The car and its immobile passengers moved in silent unison through the darkness.

The car entered the portico of a neat building and stopped. All that while, I had kept myself busy observing the interiors of the car, imagining that a few years down the line I too would be travelling in a vehicle like this one; perhaps with Tej Singh as my very own chauffeur. The thought engrossed me so much that I did not notice where we were. I never realized how quickly we'd reached.

The watchman of the building opened the door for Nigam and saluted. I came out of the other side and both of us walked into the building to the elevator. Not a word was exchanged and the sombre ambience of my surroundings made me shudder. It was still as a graveyard, even though we were going to be discussing matrimony. I wondered if Nigam's daughter was also as serious and scary and maybe as fat and arrogant as Nigam! A feminine replica of Nigam flashed through my mind and I grimaced. The elevator stopped and I shuddered the way pavement dwellers do on wintry nights.

It was a penthouse, simple and not too gaudy. We were ushered in by an old maid servant, someone who had probably been with them for ages. 'This is our family maid, Shantabai, from Nasik. She is the one who brought me up when I was a kid,' Nigam gurgled, 'and now she is company for my daughter. She is like family.'

Oh, so this old hag had brought this specimen up, I

mused, and smiled at her. 'And your wife, sir?' I asked respectfully, as we walked into a corridor and entered the second glass door to reach the drawing room that was large but relatively empty.

'My wife passed away when my daughter was born,' Nigam said matter-of-factly. 'And since then Shantabai is the one who took charge of my daughter. There are no other servants. You know how it is in Delhi, Gurgaon, and Faridabad. These days servants have become killers. Killers whom you harbour. It is hara-kiri to keep too many servants. It is like feeding milk to a snake that will ultimately bite you some day.'

We sat down. It was certainly a very simple room, and bereft of a feminine touch. I felt sad for Nigam. I had imagined Nigam's apartment to be swanky and aloof just like his office chamber, but the rather simple home filled me with a sense of ease. I allowed myself to slump a little bit on the sofa and let out a breath of relief.

'Shantabai! Call Mini,' Nigam shouted. 'Mini is a very nice, homely girl. She does all the household work since Shantabai is very old and we don't keep other servants, as I have already told you.'

I nodded. I kind of liked the idea of marrying a girl who had been raised to be a housewife and nothing more. Someone who had no ambitions, wasn't high maintenance, and displayed the least possibility of going astray; and then perhaps I could still chase Mallika or Rosy and rock many a boat. Such prospects filled me with evil joy and I was now eager to see her, fervently hoping that Mini Nigam would not be a mini Nigam.

The sound of wind chimes drifted in from the balcony adjoining the drawing room as Shantabai held the glass door open and Mini walked in with her hair neatly braided and her long earrings swinging to and fro as she moved. A sudden stillness filled the room and everything froze before my eyes. I couldn't stop the words that came out of my mouth, 'But this is Vasundhara! The bra girl!'

'What?' Nigam screamed. In an instant, the still air around us sprang to life and the empty space in the room was filled with nervous energy. Nigam became so angry that I feared he would get up and throttle me to death. 'What are you talking about, boy?' he shouted.

'I will tell you!' Vasundhara said, her lips twitching. 'I have already met this buffoon. He stays in your company guesthouse in the next building and sleeps on a broken table on the rooftop where no one ever goes. He tried to act fresh with me one morning when I was drying my washed clothes on the terrace.' Vasundhara paused for a moment to see the impact. Her father's face turned red with anger. His pupils had widened so much that I feared his eyeballs would pop out of their sockets. His fists were clenched so tightly that if he were to die of a heart attack, it would be impossible to free them from rigor mortis.

'But, sir...' I interjected meekly, 'she is Vasundhara, not Mini.' I was also preparing to run if Nigam was to attack me. I was quite sure that I'd be able to outrun the obese man whose lungs were filled with tar from a lifetime of smoking.

But Nigam chose not to attack me. Instead, he screamed at the top of his voice, 'You idiot! Mini is Vasundhara's nickname.'

'Sir, I am sorry. It was unintentional,' I stammered.

'You lecherous fool!' Vasundhara shouted at me, 'All you used to do was to stare at my undergarments! You are sick and disgusting!' Then she paused and said to Nigam, 'And father, you keep getting home any Tom, Dick or Harry to wed me off to. Am I such a burden on you?' Tears welled up in her dark pretty eyes. I felt sorry for her but there was little I could say that would pacify her.

Slowly I rose, bent forward and whispered, 'Sir, I apologize to you and to Vasundharaji. There was a misunderstanding. I was nervous and foolish. In fact, I was an idiot.' I paused and stood still for a long moment. Then slowly and remorsefully, I turned toward the main door and said, 'Really sorry. That is all I can say.'

That night, I lay hungry and resentful on the narrow bed inside my room. I knew that for the rest of the nights in Faridabad, I would not have the courage to sleep on the terrace. So hereafter, the spiders and bats on the terrace could sleep peacefully without the fear of getting drenched in jets of human urine.

8

JULY 15. THE UNIVERSITY REOPENED.

Students came in hordes, happy and carefree. Disinterested professors, weary readers and lecturers were ready to repeat themselves for yet another term. The cooking at Omi Dhaba resumed; stale oil bubbling in rusty frying pans to churn out paranthas that smelled like burnt tar. Illegal video parlours reopened their midnight porn shows in dark, smelly cubicles.

StuCee had pasted a new menu card on the peeling round pillar near the cash counter. The new menu screamed out a new price list with enhanced rates, and also added seemingly healthier options alongside samosas and French fries. Burgers were made healthier and pricier by wedging the fried cutlet draped in mayonnaise between two whole wheat buns, so that only your heart was in danger and not your bowels. There were healthier options for drinks too—tetra packs of sugary juices in addition to the bottles of sugary colas. But more or less, the food at StuCee was still the same. The continental fare still had more white sauce and only an occasional piece of pasta floating in it, and the chhole bhature was still the dependable favourite for any young, tired diner looking to bombard his taste buds with spice and grease.

Familiar stray mongrels would linger around the cafeteria in twos and fours to pant for food and mate thereafter, as if to entertain the leery students sprawled on the chairs in return for the food thrown at them. Most of them had also been appropriately named by students, making the entertainment almost complete. So Basanti was the bouncy, yelping mongrel and Whisky the dazed brown canine that had trouble walking straight. Rambha was the seductress, capable of melting the heart of even the stoniest and most studious of students, and Rambo was the large, hot-blooded mongrel that was eternally ready to fight for Rambha. Rambo and Rambha were a pair, with Rambo guarding her wherever she went.

At times it rained, making girls run for cover, while a few stubborn Romeos ogled at their drenched, bouncy torsos. It was the time when the university bubbled and brimmed with exuberance that surged past libraries and classrooms and immersed many a rendezvous with its vivacity and joie de vivre. The big campus had indeed sprung back to life after a long slumber. Even the lizards in the classrooms had stirred back to life behind the photo frames of disfigured leaders, and the cobwebs in bookshelves were finally releasing worm corpses that had remained trapped in them for a full quarter-of-a-year.

The trio—Sandy, Karan and I—were back together again, triple-riding the Vespa on our way to the B School. Karan looked startlingly different. He looked less ape-like, having shaved off his beard. I stared at him in amazement and before mounting the two-wheeler, had asked, 'What is with the new look, dude?' He smiled sheepishly and said, 'Those guys at the internship wheren't taking me seriously. I though maybe letting go of my beard would earn me more respect! Don't get excited though, I may just decide to grow it back. I miss it! Feel too naked without my hair!' We burst out laughing but as we rode the Vespa, we were again our smitten selves. Each one of us harboured individual plans of how to get Mallika in the course of our third semester.

Sandy parked the Vespa below a tree which had the least number of birds perched on it to minimize the quantity of bird poop on it. We got down, tucked our shirts in, and straightened our collars. I combed my hair with my old dandruff-lined pocket comb, and asked, 'So buddies! How was your internship at the Smart Bra Co.?'

'Just time pass, man,' Sandy said and smiled. 'I just rested and slept, had paranthas in the morning and had my fill of booze and joints at night. And lots of butter chicken too.'

'Marijuana! Drugs?' I was aghast. 'When did you start?'

'Oh, come on! Marijuana is organic. Even Lord Shiva used it. So smoking marijuana is like going back to our roots kind of thing,' Karan preached me. He made such a virtue of smoking weed that even I began to look at it in a better light. After all, if Lord Shiva thought cannabis holy, who were we lesser mortals to question it? But my good sense prevailed and I realized with a certain dread that Karan was indeed very good at packaging vices. Why the hell doesn't he become a lawyer, I wondered, and side with the criminals?

'So, that's what you did during your summer internship in Ludhiana,' I scowled. 'I don't think it's a good idea. Don't screw your life up,' I said worriedly.

But Sandy had a smug look on his face. And with Karan backing his misdemeanour, I might as well have been trying to reason with a blank wall.

'Anyway, it is your life, who am I to stop you?' I said. They were silent.

The whole marijuana thing suddenly made me feel a little lonely. I had always thought that the three of us believed in the same things but this was a territory that had sinister undertones to it, and I had no plans of stepping there. I realized that my friends were turning out to be different from what I had imagined them to be, and this realization saddened me.

We walked toward the main building of our department, where we sighted nice looking girls perched on a tree branch next to the sign that read 'University Bus School'.

Someone had clumsily knifed away the other letters of the word 'Business'.

'So, did you happen to catch up with Mallika in Delhi?' Sandy asked me matter-of-factly.

I knew that this was a loaded question so I said, 'Oh no! She was in Delhi, I was in Faridabad. It is far away.' Then, to skirt the issue, I chuckled, 'And what did you two do for sex in Ludhiana?' I wanted to shift the focus away from my non-existent sex life to their sexual adventures. It worked. Karan laughed aloud, patted Sandy on his back and said, 'I wanted to do nothing but Sandy got a whore to our room one night.' His whisper was conspiratorial. 'It was good fun, buddy,' he continued. 'She spoke only in Punjabi and generally pandered to half-literate NRIs—taxi drivers from South Hall or plumbers from Sharjah. It was off season for her when we were there and she was without work. So we thought of creating some employment in the lean season.' He winked at Sandy.

'Bloody hell! Are you guys mad? First marijuana and then whoring around with local women. Aren't you dudes scared of HIV and syphilis?'

'When lust boils within you, there is no room left for thoughts such as these.' Sandy looked at Karan and smiled.

'Plus, we had protection,' Karan guffawed, 'but that was never used. First, she sang a few Punjabi songs for us, some kind of wedding songs, and then she removed her kameez. She was so hairy that Sandy ran to the bathroom and puked!'

'It was horrible. It must have been her trick. So, we paid her the dues and returned her to her pimp.'

I felt sick. The image of half-naked hijras in the Connaught Place parking lot flashed through my mind. I said nothing and looked the other way.

Inside our department, we walked past the reception, past the Dean's office, and across the courtyard that had a little water lily pond buzzing with mosquitoes. We went past the fee window and entered Seminar Room 1. Mallika was not there as yet, and I was content with saying 'hi' to Vandana and Preeto. The internship had done Preeto good. The corporate world had got her interested in grooming herself, so that her more feminine side came to life. Her nails were neatly filed and painted, and she wore a light lipstick and had even applied some mascara, and her keds had given way to low heels. *That girl has potential if only she tried a bit harder,* I thought. Vandana, on the other hand, had taken to puffing cigarette after cigarette. She looked dull and tired, but she didn't seem to think so.

'So girls, how was your summer training?' Sandy smiled.

'Nothing much. I was in Bangalore and Preeto was in Chennai. Both with tyre companies, far away from this place.' Vandana shrugged, showing little interest in us.

I wondered if she had figured out what we called her behind her back. I noticed that Vandana had less acne than before. I was well trained at arriving at the negatives of any girl. My mother had trained me well. 'You must always look at a girl's feet to know her real complexion,' Mom had once told me. 'That is their real colour. The rest of her could be layered with make-up.'

We noted the schedule of classes for the third semester and took a cursory look at the mark sheet of our second semester exams that had been pinned up on a notice board in one corner of Seminar Room 1. Around that notice board, a group of students hung around. I was quite surprised to see that my term paper at the Metal Bearing Co. had earned me a respectable B+. 'Nigam has been quite generous,' I told Sandy, narrating to him the story in brief. 'Even after the fiasco, a B+ is good enough.'

'Nigam must have feared that one day he might be left with no other option but to marry off his daughter to you, since you are the only man in this world who knows her bra size,' Sandy chuckled.

'Hey guys!' Mallika came from behind and thumped me on my back. That made Karan and Sandy very jealous instantly, I could see it in their eyes. 'It was so nice to meet you in Delhi, Viraat,' Mallika said, giving up my secret.

Damn! I cursed silently. *Why can't women keep their mouths shut!*

Sandy was already staring at me. He whispered in my left ear, 'Bugger, you said that you never met her in Delhi.'

I feigned amnesia, and pretended to read text messages on my cell phone.

'So? Back to studies, guys? Another year to go!' Mallika patted Vandana on her back.

Preeto smiled and before Mallika could pat her, she remarked, 'I swear, Mallika, another year of listening to the drone of professors. I am dying to finish college and be the master of my own destiny, ASAP.'

'Oh, come on! We are such a nice group of friends, never mind the professors. I missed hanging out with all of you during the internship. The people at work can be so rude and bitchy, and they certainly don't teach you about these things during our boring lectures. Ask Viraat, he knows the kind of receptionist I had to deal with every day. I can bet you we are going to miss our days here,' Mallika said, caressing the cute wart on her nose. Boys thought it enhanced her sex appeal. As for me, I fidgeted with my cell phone again to avoid the topic of me visiting Mallika in Delhi.

After taking down all the information such as the schedule of classes, lectures and seminars, the abbreviations of our subjects, the professors' names, timing of breaks and vacations, and other such sundry things that made up our academic drudgery, we headed to deposit our fees for the third sememster. Attending classes was just the price we had to pay for being able to loiter around the campus and enjoy the real pleasures of university life—checking out girls, fantasizing, riding naked on the rickety Vespa, and generally gossiping about anyone we wanted.

114

Once we were done, our gang of six strode out of the building to do the real things like hanging around StuCee. We crossed the lawns littered with students.

'Let's check out the latest coffee rates at StuCee,' Mallika waved her pretty hand and all of us followed her like mice stalking the Pied Piper.

'And Sandy will treat us today,' I said.

'Why me?' Sandy stammered. He was the oldest, richest, and stingiest of the lot. He counted his pennies all the time, even while photocopying notes and buying stationery, so he usually had the least number of photocopies and the cheapest of pens. He even preferred tea over coffee at the cafeteria, because it was cheaper.

'Because you are the senior most. Almost a big bro,' Vandana giggled. It was a victory of sorts to extract a treat out of him and all of us knew that.

'I am not the big bro. It is Karan who is the brother material,' Sandy objected.

'Hey, cool it guys,' Karan quickly intervened, 'we can go Dutch.'

'No, no! Come on! You guys have no sense of chivalry. Not once has Sandy treated us. Won't you treat us, Sandy?' she asked, batting her lashes playfully at him.

He watched all the drama around him, unmoved and quite stoic. 'Mallika, I think we should break the tradition. For a change, you girls should pay for the boys,' Sandy responded seriously.

We boys found it a phenomenal idea and jumped at

it. 'Why not? Let's have "gentlemen first" today. And you ladies can be the hosts,' I suggested, smiling shamelessly from ear to ear.

'No problem, then,' Preeto looked at Mallika who gave a reluctant nod. Preeto was the independent sort, and didn't mind footing her own bills. It gave her a certain sense of empowerment and kick that she could pay for the boys too. Mallika clearly preferred chivalry so that she could save up more for her manicures and pedicures. Vandana just shrugged at Preeto's suggestion.

'Okay, guys. Fine,' Mallika announced, 'but on one condition. You boys will have to rag a bunch of freshers first.' She pulled me by the arm and dragged me. The rest followed meekly. She led us toward a quiet, deceptively subdued group seated at a distance around a long stone bench by the water lily pond. Three boys and a girl sat there, looking lost. One of the three boys sat on the grass and had his back facing us. His head was bowed to reveal a fair neck.

I stopped at some distance and freed my arm from Mallika's grip. The gang looked at me in surprise. 'First tell me, Mallika, what do we do to them? Ragging is banned, don't we know that?' I was worried.

'Don't whimper, you weakling! We'll just do some masti,' Mallika smiled. 'Think of some decent way to rag them.' She dug her nails into my arm.

But I was still tense. I did not want to be thrown out of university for ragging juniors, and in the process leave

Mallika alone to become prey to these two hungry wolves.

'Why are you tense, buddy?' Sandy whispered, trying to pull me away from Mallika.

'I don't want to rag anyone, man.'

'Come on. Ragging is like sex. If you are tense, you will not be able to perform,' Sandy made sure the girls heard him. But the girls didn't even giggle.

'I don't want to rag and be buggered in the process,' I protested.

Mallika and the rest pushed me toward the group. I finally gave in. We walked up to the group. 'Hey there, freshers!' Sandy initiated the ragging, trying to sound stern, but failing because of his effeminate voice. The boys on the bench, except the one sitting on the grass, looked up, unimpressed.

The fat lad who sat on the granite bench munching a Five Star bar, looked up and mumbled, 'So, you guys plan to act fresh with freshers, eh?' The rest of them laughed cheekily. I felt embarrassed and looked at the silent boy who continued to squat on the grass. He had curly hair and from where I stood, I thought I could see dandruff. The other two boys in the group looked bemused. They looked at us as if we had descended from the Planet of the Apes.

I whispered into Preeto's right ear, 'Seems like we're the ones being ragged by the freshers rather than the other way round!' Preeto didn't pay any heed to my words.

'Let us just go,' I said. 'I don't think ragging the juniors is a good idea.'

Mallika looked at me disappointedly, the way a jockey looks at her horse after losing a race.

'Yes. Let us just get the hell out of here, guys,' Vandana also joined me. I was sure she was happy that Mallika's plan had boomeranged.

'No way!' Mallika quickly gathered her wits and grimaced at us. 'We can't chicken out at this stage. How will we face the juniors for the rest of the year?' She dug her nails into my forearm again, this time leaving marks. I surrendered but moved to a safe distance.

The freshers seemed to be looking at us in pity. All the while, the boy on the grass stared listlessly at one spot as though he was counting earthworms and black ants. Nothing seemed to matter to him—seniors, girls, dogs mating, scurrying professors, fluffy squirrels playing, floating tufts of cloud and fighter jets that ruffled the calmness in the skies at this time of the day. He just sat there pulling at blades of grass. There was something very familiar about him. Then I caught sight of his bright green socks with Pokemon on them and it seemed like déjà vu.

But just then, Mallika resumed her leadership of the gang and I turned my gaze back to her. She exhorted, 'Okay, let's just do one thing. Let's ask them to introduce themselves one by one and we'll see how it goes.'

We nodded in unison. There was nothing else we could do. We just couldn't afford to annoy Mallika. We approached the freshers again.

'So freshers,' Sandy said, 'we are your seniors. Now stand up and tell us about yourselves, one by one.' He sounded apologetic. His voice was soft and raspy, and had little effect.

The girl in the group looked a bit jittery. She glanced at the two boys on the bench, but they seemed to have taken for granted that the ragging would begin with her. It seemed like an extension of the ladies-first syndrome.

'Errr...well...my name is Ranjeeta. I'm from Hoshiarpur,' she stammered and managed to reply with some degree of coherence. As she spoke, she looked at Mallika and Preeto for help, perhaps looking for some feminine camaraderie. But the senior girls seemed determined to prove to the boys that even they could act tough.

'So you are from Hoshiarpur!' Mallika laughed out loud. The rest of the gang burst into a guffaw as if on cue, like circus animals responding to the ring master.

Preeto did not join the laughter because she herself was from Bhatinda, and instead looked at us with disdain and growled, 'Why? What's wrong with Hoshiarpur?'

The laughter stopped.

'Nothing! We like the name. So Ranjeeta, you must be hoshiyar being from a place called Hoshiarpur,' Karan spoke with a hiss.

Everyone laughed again. Ranjeeta was now decidedly nervous. She looked at her classmates, but the two boys maintained their stony countenance. No one seemed to be coming to her rescue, till suddenly the boy on the grass turned slowly to look up. A strange expectancy gripped me, the kind that comes to an adolescent lad accessing a porn site for the first time. When he finally got up and faced us, I was shocked.

Mallika squinted her eyes to stare at him, and then she shouted, 'Hey is that you? Abhilaksh Tandon! What on earth are you doing here?'

Sandy and Karan gaped at us. Preeto looked at Mallika. I looked at everyone and then screamed, 'Hey man! Is that you?'

'Yes.' Abhilaksh dusted the buttocks of his frayed jeans and bear-hugged me. 'It's me!' He beamed at Mallika and exclaimed, 'And Mallika! We met at your office in CP. Remember me?' He shook her hand vigorously.

'Yes, I remember clearly. Viraat had got you along all the way from Faridabad to meet me,' Mallika purred. She had suddenly turned soft and friendly.

Karan and Sandy took turns to shake hands with Abhilaksh, and he waved at Preeto and Vandana.

'But you were doing your internship with Viraat at Metal Bearing Co. How come you are here?' Mallika chirped aloud.

'I want to do a Master's from a good B School after IIT. Wanted the double advantage of both degrees,' Abhilaksh said matter-of-factly. 'And when I met Viraat he told me a lot about this B School. It seemed cool so I thought why not. Also, I wanted to get away from the comforts and luxuries of home. My dad would have interfered with my career decisions too much.'

I smiled at him. What was I? A mascot for my almamater? Abhilaksh knew too many of my secrets. We had been together through the fiasco of a disgusting cabaret and molestation by eunuchs, and so I could not afford to treat Abhilaksh as a junior, nor could I ever dare to rag him. Quickly I shouted, 'Guys! It's great to have Abhilaksh here. He is a really cool dude. And he is going to be part of our gang, even though he is a *junior*.' I emphazised the word 'junior' but my emphasis lacked the impact.

Abhilaksh smiled. I was wondering why he was being so cordial. The seven of us—Mallika, Sandy, Karan, Vandana, Preeto, me and the new entrant, Abhilaksh Tandon—headed toward StuCee. *This gang is going to rock*, I thought, looking up at the sky. A crow released its dropping, cawed and flew on. No one else noticed, but the bird shit fell precisely on my nose. I cursed silently and wiped it with the back of my hand. Suddenly it started to rain and the smell of earth rose to fill the air.

9

THE MONSOON HUNG HEAVY OVER THE MORNI HILLS, casting streaks of creamy lightning across grey clouds. On the other side of town, puddles gathered on the campus lawns, which the girls skirted, raising their skirts a bit more than needed, making the boys love the rains more than necessary. Sometimes the rains annoyed me, as they made getting around a messy affair, but then guilt and patriotism would grip me, and I would will myself to love the rains for the sake of the Indian farmers. The raising of skirts also reinstated my patriotic fervour. The drone of lectures often got drowned in the thundering rain.

'Viraat, listen…' Mallika whispered to me from behind when Prof. Abhyankar had turned his back to draw an indecipherable graph on the blackboard. I usually sat in the first row, insulated from the mischief brewing at the back. There was also another bigger benefit to sitting in the front row. I got to look out into the corridor and check out any pretty girl who happened to pass by. I guessed Mallika must have had to move forward several rows so that she could whisper to me.

'Listen, Viraat,' she hissed again, 'we are making a plan to bunk two days, combine it with the weekend and go on a trip to Kashmir.'

I turned back slightly and raised my eyebrows. The professor was still struggling with his graph, trying to draw the right curves. 'When?' I muttered.

'Talk to Karan after the class. He has planned the entire trip,' she whispered and then fell silent.

Prof. Abhyankar had turned around and was scowling at me, as if I was conspiring to elope with his daughter. He paused his monologue, stared at Mallika, and asked in his nasal voice, 'Tell me. Do you know what this curve means?'

I had to stifle a chuckle, and would have been only too happy to describe all the other curves that were not on the blackboard. But I said nothing. Prof. Abhyankar had the face of a pig—the white man's, well-bred pink pig, not the Indian scavenger-swine with its dirty snout. In an eerie way, Prof. Abhyankar's pink face, his snout, his protruding teeth, his sunken eyes and his long parted hair all ganged up to lend a mysterious aura of authority to his persona. So much so that even troublemakers like Karan and Sandy could not confront him when he pierced them with his glance.

'Mallika, you heard what he said?' Preeto remarked

after the class was over, as they munched steaming hot samosas in the canteen. The samosas had stale potato paste in them that oozed out in a thick trickle from their crisp corners. The canteen-wallah had the uncanny ability to turn staleness into repackaged crispiness. At times such people gave me fresh ideas on how to repackage and market myself to Mallika.

'What about that?' Sandy quipped.

'Prof. Abhyankar asked Mallika about curves. You heard that?'

'So what? He was just asking about the graph. He is too stupid and dense for anything else. Old man!' Mallika wiped samosa morsels off her lips with a white tissue, imprinting it with her pink lip gloss. How I wished I was the tissue that those lips had delicately caressed.

'Mallika, I am sure Prof. Abhyankar was being lecherous.'

'Oh shut up, Preeto,' said Mallika.

'I mean it. You should have seen the look on his face,' Preeto said as she gulped down the last sip of her sweet cappuccino. 'In fact, I feel most of the professors, lecturers, and even the Dean, all have a crush on you.'

'Hey, come on!' Mallika said, clearly embarrassed.

Abhilaksh jumped at the opportunity to butter her up. He said, 'I don't blame the professors for having a crush on Mallika. See in B School, where candidates come in through a tough selection process with a written test, group discussion and interviews, it is rare to find someone as pretty as her.'

'Beauty with brains is rare to find, eh?' Karan hissed sarcastically, trying to join the bandwagon.

'Just as difficult as finding brawn with brains,' Preeto retorted. I had to give Preeto some credit; she was indeed intelligent and could stand her own ground.

I got worried about the way the conversation was turning out to be a debate over beauty and brawn, but thankfully Mallika just ignored the three of them. So, I interrupted, trying to sound as matter-of-fact as I could, 'By the way, Mallika, what were you saying about the trip to Kashmir?'

'Oh yes! See, I was just telling Viraat about the trip to Kashmir. It was Karan's brainchild.'

I stared at Karan. Why the hell did the moron not confide in me first? These buggers can't be trusted, I grimaced.

'Yes, Viraat, I was telling Mallika in the morning. Let's just bunk two days before the coming weekend and go to Srinagar,' Karan said sheepishly.

On the FM station in the canteen, an old song played, 'Dost dost na raha, pyaar pyaar na raha.' How true! I nodded seriously into the air, thanking the soul of Rafi for reminding me about the reality behind so-called friendships. What a wretch Karan was, I swore silently.

'So, what do you say?' Karan asked everyone.

'Just four days? Won't be enough,' I said bitterly.

'It is,' Karan said emphatically. 'There is an overnight train to Jammu. And an early morning flight from Jammu to Srinagar. Costs just four thousand bucks. We can visit Srinagar, Pehlgam, and Gulmarg. On day four, we fly back to Jammu, catch the train back to Chandigarh, overnight again, and come straight to the classroom. Unbathed and refreshed!'

So the bugger had planned the entire thing, and had not told us anything. I looked at Sandy, who also looked a bit surprised. He was more preoccupied calculating the expenses.

The die had been cast. On Wednesday evening, we climbed into the running train and found seats in a stinking second class compartment.

'Why did railways remove the third class?' Preeto covered her nose and said. 'They should have actually added a fourth class, a fifth class, and no-class compartments.'

We sat through the night on two unreserved berths. Sandy consoled us saying that making last-minute reservations was usually more difficult than finding a free whore. He winked at Karan, and the image of their hairy encounter with the Ludhiana call girl flashed through my mind, sickening me further. En route, we haggled with the TC to reduce the bribe on account of 'student concession'. The TC was quite amused at first but agreed when Mallika showered a dozen smiles upon him. By the mercy of the TC, we were allowed to spend the night on the unreserved seats.

The twin lower planks accommodated the six of us: Mallika, Preeto and me in one berth; and Abhilaksh, Sandy and Karan on the other one, facing ours. I had managed to grab the slot next to where Mallika's thigh lay quivering. Preeto was on the other side right next to the window. She was sleepy and continuously looked at her wristwatch. 'Eight hours, guys!' Preeto growled.

Abhilaksh sat opposite me and he scratched the dandruff off his scalp. Sandy sat next to Abhilaksh, trying to touch Mallika's unsuspecting knee with his own, as he sat right across her. A jealous Karan sat next to Sandy, keeping a watch on the space between Mallika's thighs and mine. The train whistled its way through darkness.

'Let's get some sleep guys,' Mallika leaned against Preeto and Preeto leaned against the rusty iron grill of the large train window. By morning, Preeto would have the grime from passing stations choke the pores of her skin. In a way, she was doing Mallika a favour by shielding her from the soot and dust. On the other hand, if Preeto had not been seated by her side, Mallika would have perhaps leaned against my shoulder and dozed off like a newborn hare. Slowly, with sleep weighing down my eyelids, I leaned back and fell asleep.

We passed by myriad stations during the night. The train halted at half of them, ushering in the smell of stale pakoras and clanking sounds from tiny tea glasses. The scurrying boys held four glasses in each hand with their blue, grime-filled nails dipped inside. To facilitate holding as many glasses as possible, the tea-maker always sent out lukewarm tea. Also, the tea was always lukewarm because trains stopped at stations only for a short time, so if the tea was hot, the customers would be unable to finish it in time and could leave with the tea maker's precious little glasses. Due to such practical reasons, the tea had to be sold lukewarm and had to be drunk like shots of tequila in a couple of large swigs.

The next morning, no one except Sandy could defecate in the train toilet. I tried my best, squatting and balancing myself for quite some time but the sight of dark earth from the hole in the shit pot dissipated my efforts. The hole seemed so big that I was scared of slipping through it. I tried clutching onto the rusted iron bar in front of me that had a leaking metal mug chained to it. The metal mug had such sharp rusted edges that I was afraid of peeking off my scrotum if I used it for ablutions. In addition, the train lurched violently making it impossible for me to be still. It was a chamber of horrors from the Dark Ages: I felt like being seated atop a scaffold, ready to be castrated. The entire experience was too scary and repulsive for even my waste to venture out of me.

The train arrived at the Jammu station early in the

morning. Our flight to Srinagar was at 10 am, but since the airport had better toilets than the trains, the six of us jumped into the first cab we found and headed straight for the Jammu airport.

'I am never going to travel by train again,' I muttered, as we stood in the check-in queue at the airport.

'Why?' asked Preeto.

I shrugged and said, 'You won't understand, Preeto. You should have seen the train loo!'

'What's the big deal?' Preeto smirked.

'She is right, Viraat. Why did you have to use the loo inside a moving train?' Mallika laughed.

At that moment, I hated her.

'Guys think they can piss anywhere, Mallika,' Preeto said laughing loudly. 'They pee behind bushes, in street corners. So you see, these train loos are meant to reform guys and teach them the art of self-control.'

I was annoyed. I looked at Sandy and Karan, and they too weren't looking amused.

'So, dude, there's a lesson for you. Excercise self-control and in the future, never pee in the open,' said Abhilaksh laughing.

I was mad with rage that was exacerbated by squirming bowels and inadequate sleep. 'Shut up, you girlie she-man,' I said and caught Abhilaksh by the collar. I had enough grudges against him from my internship days and now I couldn't stop myself.

In that instant, Karan held my wrist and snarled, 'Stop

it. It's okay. No one will use train toilets again.'

'And no one will ever pee behind bushes and in street corners again,' chuckled Preeto.

The journey was nice and short. The air hostess was plump and old, and the plane was quieter than the train. I must have been the first one to doze off. An overnight train journey in a sitting position had tired all of us. When the plane landed with a thud, I was shaken out of my slumber. The weather in Srinagar was pleasant. The drive from the airport to the town was a good three-quarters of an hour. There were security check posts with fair, bearded policemen who looked too delicate to be cops. The taxi driver had gracefully allowed all six of us in the cab, with our luggage in the carrier on top. He sang Kashmiri songs all through the drive.

The cab driver dropped us off at Dal Lake Shikara Point. To our right, we could see Pari Mahal on the hill. Across the road, vendors were selling char-grilled mutton. Large, fair, smiling men welcomed us everywhere we went.

A shikara took us to our houseboat. It was a low quality houseboat and the area around was filled with poor, stoned hippies. Wealthy Indians stayed on the other side of the lake.

In the houseboat, we were given a hot welcome drink called Kahwa which was served in round, handle-less cups with green roses painted on them. 'Never knew a rose could be green,' Mallika whispered.

'Sshh…green is the colour of religion here,' Sandy snubbed her.

We drank our Kahwa and then went in. The houseboat had two rooms. The two girls grabbed the bigger and better room, while we, the boys, were consigned to the second cubicle at the end of the corridor from where a wooden staircase led to the roof of the houseboat.

'Let's quickly shower and eat. It is almost lunch time!' Preeto shouted from the other room.

'Great idea,' said Karan. 'Kashmiri food is so yummy. Goshtaba and rishta and biryani. My mouth is watering just at the thought of it.'

'Go and empty your stomach out first, dude,' Abhilaksh taunted him.

Karan scowled at him and before either of them could emerge as a winner of the argument, I occupied the toilet. By the time I came out, Sandy had already shaved in the small dressing table mirror, while Abhilaksh had used the common loo outside. I smiled: travel did strange things to people—it altered natural body cycles.

Half-an-hour later, we were all at the dining table in the front hall-cum-lobby that also served as the TV room, and the sleeping space for caretakers. Sandy whispered to me that a few of those houseboat attendants, particularly those who descended from far off hills, indulged in sodomy when there were no guests; but I ignored him. I was engrossed in observing Mallika who slurped and chewed on meat balls and licked her pretty fingers after dipping them into thin Kashmiri curry. The sight turned me on.

We had just three days. We had to catch the Sunday afternoon flight back to Jammu. So, we finished our lunch quickly and hopped into a single *shikara* to get to the Dal shore. This time too, it was Mallika's smile and a few words of broken Kashmiri that won the heart of the shikara-wallah. Her smile and the fluttering of her eyelashes saved us money all along. In the train, it got us 'student concession' in bribing the TC; at the airport, it was the taxi driver; and here another shikara. Again at the shikara-point, she managed to seduce the driver of a dilapidated cab. He agreed to ferry us around and then proceeded to show us all the must-see spots: Mughal Gardens, Char Chinar, Charar-e-Shareef, Pari Mahal, and Royal Spring Golf Course. We managed to see all the famous sights in day one.

'Wow, Mallika, you certainly know how to capitalize on your charms,' Preeto commented at the end of the day. 'You had everyone eating out of your hands!'

'No harm in using your resources, especially if they happen to be naturally endowed ones,' Mallika said and winked. 'Makes life so much easier.'

'Jeez, Mallika, that's being so cheap,' said Preeto.

'Come on. Loosen up. It's fun to watch everyone dance to my tune. Besides, all of us ended up saving some money,' Mallika retorted, and walked off.

After dinner, the girls went to bed and us boys drank

a bottle of cheap rum that we had made the boat guy get for us. It cost a mere one hundred and fifty rupees. Just before sleeping, Karan dug out a small bit of marijuana from his pouch, rolled it into a soggy joint, and took a deep drag. He gave a puff each to Sandy and Abhilaksh. I refused and asked the trio to go to the rooftop if they wanted to smoke.

'This chap smoked most of it. My whole joint is finished!' fumed Karan, when they came down the wooden stairs. I had already occupied the best side of the bed.

'Don't worry, we will find some more tomorrow,' consoled Abhilaksh.

'I never knew you smoked up, Abhilaksh!' I scowled at him, 'You never did in Faridabad.'

'Depends on the company, buddy!' Abhilaksh's eyes were red and watery and he smiled from ear to ear like a buffoon. 'You must try it once, dude. Here, want to try this?' He extended his hand in which there were bits of paper. I looked at him quizzically.

'It's acid, dude!' he laughed. 'Try it. You'll have fun.' And saying this, he popped some in his mouth. Karan decided to give it a go.

'What nonsense!' I snubbed them. 'I won't accept this invitation for the shortcut to death. You guys are killing yourselves. I will never consume drugs, *ever*.' I pulled myself up, trying to stand tall to acquire stature among my drug-addict mates.

In the meanwhile, Abhilaksh and Karan waited for the acid to take effect so that they could feel the kick. Both waited and waited and nothing happened. 'Let's have some more,' Karan suggested, and immediately they popped more pieces of paper into their mouths.

Just then the first round of acid hit them. What followed next was a riot. They were so freaking high that they both sat on their haunches on the creaky wooden floor, smiling foolishly.

'He's being such a sissy,' Karan giggled softly, careful not to wake up the ladies in the next room. Sound, in the wooden houseboat, traversed fast. The 'sissy' was supposed to be me.

'Heee heeee heeee! Heee heeee heee! He is a sissy, he is a sissy!' giggled Abhilaksh as stupidly as Karan, swaying back and forth on his haunches. He stuck his tongue out at me, and started flapping his hands over his head.

I was losing my temper very fast. I curled my hand into a fist to punch the daylights out of him, but Sandy intervened.

'Cool it, guys. You're both being stupid. Go to sleep now,' Sandy pushed the two lightly and they fell on their backs. At least he was not on a double dose of narcotics!

'Shhh!' Karan said, putting his finger to his lips. 'Careful how you talk to holy men! We wear holy undies and live a holy life! Om Namah Shivay!

'Om Namah Shivay! Om Namah Shivay,' gurgled Abhilaksh lying flat on his back.

'Holy, my ass. They have totally lost it!' I was still furious but decided to walk away. 'To each his own. All of you go to hell if you wish to, for all I care. Goodnight,' I mumbled in a pissed voice. I was more upset because I was the minority in a room full of drug addicts. It was hard being the odd one out, even if it happened to be drugs.

The next day, all was forgotten and we took a cab and visited Pehalgam. We tried our hand at angling in the Jhelum river. The river gushed too fast and the fish turned out to be too smart for us. It wasn't a very eventful day, except for the fact that Sandy sat between the two girls in the back seat of the car with Abhilaksh seated next to Mallika. Karan and I sat in the front next to the driver. I had never felt both jealous and bored at the same time. I kept a watchful eye on Mallika in the rear-view mirror. After Abhilaksh had fallen asleep, Sandy was making futile attempts to elbow Mallika's breast from under her armpits. But to my great relief, he didn't succeed. Mallika seemed to revel in her beauty, but didn't appreciate being taken advantage of. I scowled into the mirror and Sandy quickly reformed himself. He then seemed to be trying his luck with Preeto, who was seated on his other side, but quickly gave up the attempt. Perhaps she was too strong-headed for him. For once, I was grateful to god for manufacturing girls differently. The cab rattled and zigzagged its way back to Srinagar. We were all in a trance, half-stoned by the stench from the driver's clothes, half by the weariness of continuous travel.

In the evening, we had a shot of Kahwa each at Lal Chowk in the heart of Srinagar. Sandy and Karan thought of shopping for walnuts and some fake pashminas for their mothers. But even the fake stuff was so expensive that they didn't end up buying anything. They needed the money to buy their month's stock of marijuana. So they just bought tiny packets of saffron and we returned to our houseboat. Since I did not need to save up for marijuana or anything else, I splurged on a nice black cashmere pullover. Its snug softness was comforting, especially since I still didn't have a nice girl who would have the same effect. At the end of the day, we were exhausted, and so we ate our dinner quickly and hit our beds. I went into a deep slumber, something that I hadn't done in recent times.

On the last day, we headed for Gulmarg. The rickety J&K transport corporation bus took three hours to cover the journey. The girls went to sleep almost instantly. On the way, we saw pink damsels in the fields, orchards and on hilltops; some tending to their apple trees, others de-weeding their paddy, and some tending their woolly sheep at impossible slopes. They all seemed to stare back at us with amusement.

'Kashmiri girls are the best,' Sandy postulated. Karan nodded and winked at Sandy. Abhilaksh, not to miss a chance to flatter Mallika, spoke aloud, almost so as to wake her up from her slumber, 'We know, pal! Look at Mallika. She is Kashmiri too. That's why the whole of Chandigarh is trying to woo her all the time.'

What a wretch!

Karan clenched his teeth and replied, 'Of course, Abhilaksh. We know that, well before you joined the university.'

'And don't forget, you are still a junior. So look for beauties within your own grade,' Preeto was annoyed too. 'And Punjabi girls are hot catches too.'

'Of course,' Karan muttered. 'But there are exceptions always.'

'What the hell do you mean, Karan?' Preeto was livid. 'You mean to say I am not a good looking Punjabi girl?'

'Guys, take it easy,' Mallika stepped in. 'We are on holiday. This is the time to enjoy. And ogle at the real Kashmiri dames. Not to discuss me.'

All of us fell quiet. We were all subservient to her desires, even Preeto. There was no other way for her to go, in that brute majority of Mallika-admirers.

The winding road took us up to Gulmarg. Snow-clad peaks gleamed all around us. I looked at those towering mountain peaks and tried to imagine how militants could cross over such desolate, impossible peaks where even sheep couldn't graze or shit peacefully. It seemed so unlikely. The place seemed too pristine, too mysterious, too silent. Militancy did not seem to belong there. I shuddered and put away such troubling thoughts.

In Gulmarg, we decided to go on a short trek to Khilanmarg. We walked past the poles of the cable car and beyond the midpoint BSF chowki. A sentry stood there, slouching and bored. As we passed him by, he ogled hungrily at Mallika. Even at Preeto, I felt. Perhaps he was tired of flirting with ruddy Kashmiri girls. The temptation was different for each one of us. While we craved the carefree, salwar-kameez clad rural belles, the BSF jawan lusted for taut urban posteriors wrapped in tight jeans.

On our last evening in Srinagar, we sat on the roof of our houseboat listening to Kashmiri songs sung by the young houseboat attendant. Sandy and Karan lit a joint and took several deep drags. They smoked too fast and got stoned much too quickly, and in no time they were asleep right there on the roof. Both the girls also looked sleepy and wanted to go down. It was getting a bit chilly but Abhilaksh said that he loved the nip in the air and wanted to stay back a little longer. He slumped into the lumpy cushion on the rooftop.

I stared at him and asked sternly, 'You aren't sleeping as yet, Abhilaksh?'

'I want to look at the stars for some more time. They are beautiful here,' Abhilaksh said, looking into the vast inky sky. Dreamily, Abhilaksh blabbered, 'You take these two downstairs and go off to sleep. I will come downstairs when I am bored of the stars.'

'As you wish. You and your weird star gazing,' I said and woke Karan and Sandy and took them downstairs. The girls followed us.

The attendant boy and I put Sandy and Karan to bed. The girls in the adjoining cubicle had already fallen silent. I took off my shoes, yawned loudly, and lay down.

The wooden floor would creak at the slightest movement, and it was getting annoying. Someone or the other would shift sides, break wind, or masturbate and I could hear everything. Since Sandy and Karan were fast asleep and Abhilaksh was upstairs, I hoped to enjoy the unbridled, pre-sleeping ritual of self-pleasuring. Silently, I switched off the flickering light and got busy.

A lot of time had elapsed. I had finished quite some time back, washed up, and had even slept for some time. But a lizard fell from the roof, very close to my face and I jumped out of bed. I hated lizards.

I sat up and looked around in the darkness. Abhilaksh had still not returned! What the hell! It was past midnight and nobody could be gazing at stars for so long, especially in the chill of Srinagar. 'Damn!' I cursed, and rubbed my eyes. The lizard had disappeared. Sandy and Karan were snoring loudly.

Still cursing, I stood up and walked out, past the corridor, up the stairs, softly, so that I didn't wake the girls. I was most considerate when it involved Mallika. She meant the whole world to me. Almost!

A silent fear lurked inside me and I suddenly felt quite concerned about Abhilaksh. I hadn't been able to find my shoes in the dark so I padded up the stairs in socks. The door to the rooftop was ajar. By now I was really worried about Abhilaksh. My heart was pounding and in that silence, I could hear the sound of my own heartbeat. I pushed the door open softly.

Two shadows lay entwined on the cushion. Sounds of soft gasps filled the air. One of them was definitely Abhilaksh. Obviously, Abhilaksh had not been star gazing. Instead, Abhilaksh was rolling on the cushion with someone. Passionate kissing sounds were clearly audible from where I stood. Suddenly, I felt weak in my knees and my head started reeling. I felt as if my head had been dissected and thrown into the Dal Lake and was being chafed and pounded by the oars of moving shikaras. Even though it was dim, there was enough light for me to recognize the couple that lay there kissing passionately, groping and rolling on that dirty cushion.

They were Abhilaksh and Mallika.

10

THE SUNDAY AFTERNOON FLIGHT TOOK US BACK TO Jammu. We got the last row, near the stinking toilet. Sandy and Karan scurried to grab the seats next to Mallika, and in the process sandwiched her between themselves. Preeto sat on the other side of the aisle, Abhilaksh sat in the middle seat, followed by me at the window. Abhilaksh was quiet and composed.

'The bastard seems too satisfied!' I cursed silently, and then looked out of the window. Throughout the journey, I felt Abhilaksh's overbearing presence next to me. Preeto and Abhilaksh talked a little as the flight took off. A fat, gaudily dressed airhostess managed to reach us just in time before we landed and handed us a box each that contained stale curry and burnt naan.

'These chicken pieces are the size of bird droppings!' Abhilaksh said to me, trying to be friendly, but I ignored him and continued to look out. Budget airlines always seemed to have plumper airhostesses, whereas expensive airlines had slimmer, better looking staff. On the other side of the aisle, Sandy and Karan were vying for Mallika's attention. Their banter irritated Preeto. For a change, I didn't feel jealous. I knew the reality. And I was probably the only one who knew. Last night, I had quietly withdrawn from the terrace, tiptoed back to my bed. I had lain awake on the bed, eyes gaping, chasing the lizard on the roof and it was a long time before Abhilaksh came back from the terrace, as stealthy as a panther and slipped into his quilt. They had probably made out for a while, and maybe even made love. I had imagined this scene the whole night, and had only fallen asleep in the early hours of the morning. And so, it was only I who knew that Mallika had been claimed; the trophy was gone, annexed by Abhilaksh, the one person who was the quietest, had tried the least, had spent minimum time with her, and who was still a bloody fresher! To add to the insult, he had been introduced to Mallika by me! What a fool! I cursed myself. I wanted to slap and kick myself.

I looked out into the clouds below. I could never imagine in my wildest dreams that while the three monkeys—Sandy, Karan and I—fought over Mallika, someone entirely new would steal her away. Had the other two won this battle, I wouldn't have minded so much. But Abhilaksh! The traitor! Someone whom I had groomed, saved from ragging and introduced into our own gang of seniors. I was hurt, stunned and angered beyond words. I got up to use the loo.

As the plane began to land and the seat belt sign blinked, I went back to my seat elbowing Abhilaksh on my way. He looked surprised at this, but quietly removed his arm and turned to talk to Preeto. He was very silent, but in a happy way. 'I wish I could hurl this bugger out of the plane window,' I muttered, my nose pressed against the glass.

'If we had more time, we could have gone to Vaishno Devi,' Abhilaksh said to me, trying to break the silence.

I could read no guilt in his face, which annoyed me even more. 'Since when have you become so religious?' I retorted, encroaching Abhilaksh's leg space. How I wished I could crush him to death right here in the aircraft! His presence was unbearable.

'I'm not religious. I simply like the trek to Vaishno Devi,' Abhilaksh said in a cold voice, his good humour gone. 'Helps me assess my level of physical fitness.'

'I love climbing hills too,' Preeto joined in.

Mallika, seated on the other side of the row, bent forward to listen in to our conversation and nodded. I was scorched with jealousy; Mallika had never paid so much attention to anyone in the past as to respond to a remote conversation that was not about her.

'I know how fit you are, Abhilaksh. You're a Delhi dude! You can't have the strength and fitness of a real, pure-bred Punjabi boy from Chandigarh,' I remarked bitterly, brandishing my bulging biceps. I could no longer contain my disdain for the chap who had stolen my love.

'Ha! Why not! Who else, apart from me, would know how strong you are, Viraat?!' Abhilaksh was beginning to lose his cool too. He bent down and whispered into my ear, 'The eunuchs of Connaught Place scared the shit out of you, buddy. And I was a witness to the whole scene! Should I tell the gang about that?'

I was livid. My jaw twitched, my temples pulsated violently, and my face was flushed. I was trembling with rage, and just to prevent myself from hitting the moron, I got up, passed by them and rushed into the toilet again. The airhostess gestured at me from the front end of the alley, pointing to the seat belt sign, but I ignored her and bolted the door. The plane was tossing through the low clouds of the Jammu sky, making a steep descent. I pressed the tap on and splashed my face with water that came out in a trickle, like government's generosity. I took a paper napkin and wiped my face. When I looked down, there was a sign that read, 'As a courtesy to the next passenger, may we suggest that you use your towel to wipe off the wash basin.' Courtesy my foot! I cursed and dirtied the basin further. I gargled and spat on the commode. Then I took out lots of paper napkins and threw them around. I stared at the sign and showed it my middle finger. I took off my wristwatch and with the edge of its metal strap vigorously scraped at the sign. I looked down and smiled wickedly; the sign now read, 'As a courtesy to the next passenger, may we suggest that you use your *bowel* to wipe off the wash basin.' I smirked at the sign, and murmured, 'Bowel. That's what you will get. Oh my next passenger! You suck!' Surprisingly, I felt better, having drained my frustration into the basin and its sign.

The fat airhostess was screaming into the mike, requesting all passengers to be seated for landing. Her screams were meant for me, of course, and they managed to drum me out of the toilet. I came out, carrying the stench of the loo with me, and settled down in my seat. The plane landed with a thud and pushed me and my rage back against the seat.

In Jammu, the gang roamed about the streets and markets. The girls bought rajmah, promising to cook for the boys someday. Sandy and Karan continued to fuss over Mallika; they're such fools, I thought. My own coldness toward her seemed odd to the other boys, but Mallika, as usual, was least bothered by it. She stirred only at the occasional voice of Abhilaksh, looking at him with smiling eyes, turning her back on everything else.

'Can we find good stuff here?' Karan whispered to Sandy.

'What stuff?' Preeto had overheard.

'Grass,' Karan winked.

'Hold on, Karan,' Preeto snapped, 'only cattle eat grass.'

'I mean our kind of grass.' Karan hissed at her through clenched teeth. 'The dopey stuff.'

'I know that, you skunk,' Preeto retorted. 'I was trying to dissuade you guys. Why can't you stay off that muck?'

'Forget it, Karan,' Sandy calmed them. 'We will get our stock from Mohali.'

'But you get better stuff at hill stations. No?'

'Not really. And this is Jammu, not Manali. It's more of a religious place,' said Sandy. 'You can buy incense sticks here!' He guffawed in his soft, feminine voice. Sandy had this quality of turning almost motherly.

'Yeah! We will buy it in Mohali,' Abhilaksh whispered, as we walked through the bazaar, gaping at the countless small shops.

The fresh mountain air and the milling bazaar crowds jostled for space in my consciousness. Plastic toys, little gods, women's petticoats, and men's underwear alternated with exquisite Kashmiri embroidery. Bored shopkeepers sat cross-legged on cushioned platforms inside those shops, digging their noses and reading vernacular newspapers. A maze of electric wires criss-crossed the street in front, hither and thither, without any design, scheme or logic. Faded hoardings of cooking oils, toothpaste brands, unheard of foot creams, and slogans on keeping the city clean filled our sight. Below a slogan on the government's sanitation campaign, a naked child squatted and shat in impossible proximity to the traffic. Scooters, mopeds, bikes, rickshaws, and a few cars zipped around in such a disorderly manner that it seemed as though all those things, objects and humans, had been sprinkled by the devil himself in that landscape, and that he had ordered them all to go berserk just for the heck of it. Everything seemed to defy logic and nothing followed a plan.

'Don't you dare smoke grass, Abhilaksh!' Mallika ordered.

She was already the girlfriend, I knew, and would perhaps soon be the wife.

'I don't really. Do I?' Abhilaksh looked at Sandy, begging for deliverance.

'No, Mallika,' Sandy replied. 'This kid is too pure. We are yet to corrupt him!'

'Come on, Sandy,' Abhilaksh nodded his head furiously. 'I am not that pure.' He was stuck between wanting to be the macho friend and the boyfriend. He looked at Mallika and they smiled together for a split second. 'I just take a drag sometimes, for the heck of it. I am not a regular smoker. Ask Sandy.'

Mallika's eyes were probing his for the truth. Girls, when in love, become maternal, their instincts growing like wings of the monsoon moth, almost overnight, becoming overly concerned about their boyfriends' health. They try to own every breath of their lover.

'Leave the kid alone, Mallika. He is still in the first year,' Karan yawned.

Kid! I wanted to jump, climb atop the huge hoarding

of 'Victor Underwear' where a herd of langurs rested, and shout on top of my voice that last night I had caught this first-year *kid* smooching and groping this girl here, his senior. Kid, my foot! Even God couldn't have guessed how and when this nincompoop seduced her. Such sacrilege deserved the severest punishment: perhaps the gang should forcibly make the rogue smoke so much grass that he chokes to death. I wanted to shout and scream about all of it. And here, Karan, the ignorant idiot, was calling the bugger a *kid*.

Despite such emotions, something held me back from revealing the reality to others as much as it hurt me. Quietly, I turned to look at Mallika for the first time since the morning. She looked amazingly pretty as she walked along leisurely in an off-white skirt and pink top. I sighed and looked away. Just to divert my attention, I scowled at the defecating child squatting in the middle of the street as we walked past him. The squalid street urchin had hopped from the corner to the middle of the street, just to prevent the growing shit pyramid from touching his butt. Only a disgusting sight like that could take my mind away from the overwhelming feeling of loss.

At the end of the street, just before the taxi stand, we gathered around an ice cream vendor. 'I will buy you all ice cream today,' Preeto announced generously.

I was amused in a bitter way: did Preeto also find someone to kiss her? Generally the lady was a scowling-and-growling type.

'Good news, guys. Preeto is giving us an ice cream treat!' Karan announced, as though speaking from the podium.

I scowled. Why did he always speak like that: with such eloquence and effort? I was angry, and everything irritated me. The girls bought ice lollies, sticky and colourful, while the boys preferred milkier options. The boys ate their ice creams fast while the girls licked at their ice lollies, showing off their tongues and lips.

A bunch of beggars floated toward us like drifting clouds, including a shabby woman with knots and lice in her hair. She had a small infant, who cried incessantly, balanced on her waist. She looked like she would pinch him if he stopped. Snot was flowing down his nose and upper lip, spreading like little streams. It was disgusting. Accompanying the clan was a little girl with gas balloons in her hand. She was wearing a torn vest and her skin was alive with an infection that she scratched with her other hand. The older woman begged with her outstretched hand that had amputated fingers. She tried to touch Mallika with her infected knuckles, begging alms.

'Disgusting! Go away!' Mallika shrieked in horror.

But the beggar woman stood her ground. 'God will give you a good husband, sister! Give me some money to eat and feed my children.' The naked infant on her waist looked like he was stolen; he was fair and foreign looking, while the beggar woman had a dark complexion with completely different features. The woman and her infant begged in unison, and their racial differences seemed submerged in a common curse of poverty. Did the beggar woman steal a Manipuri infant, I thought for a moment. Or maybe even a Japanese one? Such inane thoughts kept oscillating in and out of my mind like waves on a sea coast.

'Shoo! Go away!' Everyone shouted. Karan had lit a cigarette and was puffing away at some distance.

'Please give us money for food. For medicine,' the rant continued, as they kept trying to touch Mallika. It was blackmail via disgust.

'Get lost!' Abhilaksh shouted at the top of his voice. He was suddenly very furious, far beyond what the situation warranted.

I watched with some degree of amusement, almost waiting for the beggar woman to set him right in some way. How I wished that the beggar woman would get really angry and slap Abhilaksh! Even better would be if she smooched him. 'That would be the right punishment for the skunk for kissing the girl of my dreams,' I blabbered to myself and smiled for the first time in several hours.

'Rogues! Will you go away or not?' This time Mallika's shout was full-throated. Her smile had fallen off her face like ash from cigarette.

'Give them something and get rid of them,' Preeto blurted, digging into her garish yellow bag, a fake Gucci.

'No, Preeto. We should never succumb to their pressure tactics,' I held her hand. The image of the Connaught Place eunuchs demanding money flashed before my mind. The thought made me shudder.

'These beggars are social parasites, Preeto,' Sandy joined in. 'They can work and earn a respectable living but they want easy money. They're the scum of the earth!'

'But who will give them a job?' Mallika asked.

'At least they can work at some road construction site, break stones and earn two hundred rupees a day, Mallika,' I said. 'Besides this is a big racket. These beggars abduct kids, cut their limbs off, or blind them. Then they make them beg forcibly.'

'And Mallika, many of them are drug addicts too,' Abhilaksh remarked.

'That even you guys are!' Preeto giggled, fishing for the most soiled and crumpled notes inside her fake Gucci. 'You and your grass!' She looked evil when she smiled. I was happy that she had at least snubbed Abhilaksh.

'Shut up, Preeto. These rogues are into deadly addictions. Some of them even eat shoe polish and drink nasal drops,' Abhilaksh said.

Karan too shouted from a distance, puffing away on his cigarette, 'Beggars disgust me. They are a burden on earth. They should all be herded to one place and exterminated, Nazi style!' Surely, Karan, the ace debater, was at his rhetorical best.

Yet, the beggar wouldn't give up. 'At least buy a balloon. Just for ten rupees.' The beggar girl, who held the gas balloons, bleated.

Suddenly, I walked up to Karan, snatched away the lit cigarette from his fingers, and walked up to the beggars. I extended my hand to the little beggar's gas balloons. The simmering cigarette butt smoothly sheared into a balloon. It burst with a whimper and shrivelled up, apologetically hanging like a flag at half mast. The beggar girl shrieked in horror and jumped away, wailing aloud, while the older woman backed away mouthing profanities. They were aghast. Nobody would have done a thing like that to a beggar.

The angry devil in me was appeased and I barked, 'You rogues! Go and earn a respectful living. Get lost. Shoo!' I looked at the gang; everyone looked equally shocked. I turned back to stare at the beggars and snarled, 'And if you don't leave right away, I am going to snatch away all your coins and buy myself some ice cream.' I lunged forward, feigning to flick away grimy coins and crumpled notes from those outstretched eczema-coated palms. I could feel Gandhi on those notes scowl at me, for my act of violence against the clan of filthy beggars, but I ignored the reproachful look. My actions actually helped vent my pent up anger. I felt much lighter.

The beggar clan fled the scene, and my chest swelled with pride. I looked at the gang, most of them appeared amused. There was a smile on their lips, and the girls were giggling.

Sandy guffawed and said, 'Wow, Viraat! It was like

shooing street dogs away, by pretending to pick a stone up from the ground.' Karan too laughed meanly.

'Hey dude, thanks,' Abhilaksh said, 'You prevented those filthy things from touching Mallika.'

Gosh! Abhilaksh had once again jumped in to take advantage of the opportunity to show his concern for Mallika, though it was me who had gotten rid of the pests.

'You are so cheap, Viraat,' Mallika burst out laughing and said, 'How could you do a thing like that—bursting the beggar girl's balloon!'

'Mallika, there is no other way of getting rid of beggars, dogs, and eunuchs,' Abhilaksh said, winking at me.

His words hurt. Why the hell did he have to remind me of eunuchs repeatedly? Why the hell did he have to jump into my situation like an idiot and start blabbering nonsense? It was I who had shooed away the beggars, it was I who had saved Mallika from them, it was I who cared for her more than anyone else, and it was I who had been burning in silence since last night. Yet, this rogue had to interject, just to score a point over me. His words, his intrusion, his irritating mannerism, everything about him burned a hole in me like the cigarette butt had burnt a hole in the beggar's balloon.

It was getting late, and so we shoved ourselves into one cab and persuaded the driver to take us to the train station. When we got there, we found that our train had already arrived. The second class compartment was already too full to welcome any new entrants. We managed to grab four seating spaces into which the six of us squeezed in like sardines in a can.

Noisily, the train chugged out of the Jammu station, while the smells and sounds of the platform, its tea vendors, its stray dogs, all lagged behind. I took a deep breath and closed my eyes, cutting myself from the gang. It comforted me.

Every now and then, the train would stop at unknown stations. At Harami Pahadi station, just when people had emptied their dinner tiffins and were gargling out of windows, a vendor of herbal aphrodisiacs entered the compartment and started chanting about the magical qualities of his products. I opened my eyes, irritated. Sandy looked at me and winked.

'Listen, boy!' he shouted at the vendor boy, beckoning him. Surely, he wanted to play a prank. 'What do you have?' he asked the vendor.

'Sandy, you surely must need them, considering your age,' Mallika giggled.

'I am just acquiring product knowledge and learning his selling techniques,' Sandy smiled.

Nothing seemed to enrage him, I thought. 'Oh really! You specialize in learning from odd people,' I bellowed. Everything continued to annoy me. Meanly, I whispered into Sandy's ear, 'You even did your internship at the Smart Bra Co.!'

154

'Shut up, silly guy!' Sandy snubbed me and mumbled, 'Don't discuss secrets here!' He didn't want his internship secret to be known by the girls or Abhilaksh. Though the girls had not heard the conversation, Abhilaksh, as expected, had overheard.

'Smart Bra Company!' He chuckled softly, and then patted Sandy's shoulder. 'Don't worry, dude. I am not going to disclose anything. I am not like Viraat. And, I know more about Viraat's secrets than he knows about yours.'

Gosh, he was going to spill the beans to the gang! My heart skipped a beat and I gave him a cold stare. 'Shut up, you sodden piece of scum! This is gang talk. No one is talking to a junior. So, you better stay away!' I shouted. This time our conversation reached the girls.

'Why have you been so angry, Viraat?' Preeto tried to pacify me.

All this while, the aphrodisiac seller stood there, laughing in amusement and peering down Mallika's cleavage. Perhaps he regularly consumed his own herbal aphrodisiacs, I guessed

Abhilaksh stood up. 'What crap! I am no junior. I am the same age as you guys,' he growled. 'Stop treating me like a kid. I am older than Mallika.'

He glanced at her and a meaningful smile spread across his face.

'Of course, your would-be fiancée has to be younger

than you, I know that, you bugger!' I shouted. 'You thankless thug! *I* saved you from ragging. *I* brought you into the gang. And *I* introduced you to Mallika.'

'And you took me to a rotten cabaret in Delhi. And you ogled at your boss' daughter,' Abhilaksh burst out, folding his sleeves menacingly. His face was red with anger.

'Shut up! Just shut up!' I was livid. My heartbeat pulsated in my ears.

'Mallika, this guy is a creep,' Abhilaksh continued. 'All he did the whole day, during his entire internship, was to ogle at the office receptionist's boobs.'

'That's so sick!' Mallika gasped.

This was humiliating. Finally letting everything out, I screamed, 'One word from you and I am going to crush your dirty face, you bastard,' I shouted, stood up and clutched Abhilaksh's collar, towering above him.

'Don't you dare lay your hands on me, you moron!' Abhilaksh was hysterical too, shaking and mumbling. 'You can't do a thing, you weakling!' He screamed. 'Remember? You couldn't even save your skin from those eunuchs in Connaught Place!'

That was the last straw.

'You son of a bitch,' I clenched Abhilaksh's throat and gave him a blow on the nose. He was smaller and thinner. The blow hit him real hard.

'Stop it, you ruffian!' Mallika shrieked and held my wrist before I could hit him again. Abhilaksh was bleeding profusely from the nose. He sank down into his seat.

'And you will obviously protect this scum, Mallika!' I shouted, trembling with rage and embarrassment at being laid bare of my dark secrets in front of the gang. How would anyone know that the eunuchs of Connaught Place were so muscular and big that they could get together and disrobe even the Great Khali.

'What the hell, Viraat!' Karan shouted at me. 'Why did you have to hit him so hard?'

'Karan, Sandy...you guys don't know...this wretch here is going around with Mallika,' I blurted. I was a man possessed and didn't realize what I was saying. The vendor boy searched through his sling bag, took out a pimpled piece of wood and offered it to Preeto. 'This is a herb to stop the bleeding. I am sure your friend will need this now,' he said smiling.

'Shut up, you idiot. Go away!' Preeto shouted. The boy scratched his balls, whistled, and started to walk away. Halfway down the corridor, he turned back and waved a piece of tree bark at Preeto. 'And this tree bark here can transform pimpled girls like you into pretty ones like this other one here.' He pointed a finger towards Mallika and then showed his middle finger to the gang.

Karan ran after him but the vendor boy quickly made his getaway through the cramped corridor and crossed over to the next bogie through the connecting walkway. Karan came back and held Abhilaksh's face against a piece of cloth that Sandy gave him, and which, he realized later, was a used underwear. Sandy had taken it out of Karan's handbag.

'Sandy, you asshole! Couldn't you find any other piece of cloth to stuff into my nose?' Abhilaksh wailed in pain. But the crumpled underwear, now soaked crimson red, managed to stop the blood.

'Viraat, what have you done? Have you gone mad?' Sandy admonished me, raising his squeaky voice. It was rare for Sandy to shout.

'You don't know, Sandy. This guy here has been humping Mallika,' I shouted, clenching my fists. Abhilaksh, holding his nose, tried to lunge at me but Mallika held him back. She looked at me in disgust.

'What nonsense are you talking, Viraat? Have you gone completely out of your mind?' Karan hissed.

Preeto looked the other way. Ah! So, she knew!

'I am telling the truth, Karan. I saw them last night, making out on the houseboat rooftop. Ask them if you don't trust me,' I said, still agitated.

Sandy and Karan slumped into their seats. Disbelief was written all over their faces. Sandy looked like he was about to puke. Karan scratched his beard and looked at Mallika in disbelief. Abhilaksh buried his face in Mallika's lap while she held his head. We had been feeding a snake, after all.

'Listen, guys,' Mallika spoke after what seemed like

eternity, 'I was going to tell you all. Preeto already knows. Abhilaksh and I love each other.'

There was complete stillness. The kind of stillness that comes after a storm.

'So, you guys hooked up quite some time back? Or did it happen during this trip?' Sandy asked gently.

Abhilaksh raised his head and looked up at the gang. 'Why else would I join your B School, guys? That too as a junior,' he bleated.

'So you were actually dating earlier?' I snarled, feeling calmer now. Things were slowly falling into place. For the hundredth time, I cursed the day when I had taken Abhilaksh to introduce him to Mallika.

'Yes. We met the very next day at Nirula's. It was a Sunday. And then we kept meeting almost every evening in various cafés in CP.' Abhilaksh smiled at Mallika, who blushed.

Oh God! What a fool I have been! I thought. 'And you guys never told me,' I said.

'It was on my insistence that Abhilaksh came from Delhi to Chandigarh even though he had got admission in Delhi University. He could have stayed at home and could have studied at a better B School but he sacrificed all of it for me,' Mallika said, looking at him fondly.

Damn! I could sacrifice anything for you, I thought. *Even my notes, my test papers, and my CDs. Anything. You just had to ask me!* But now, it was too late.

None of us spoke. The train had gained speed. Night had progressed. The others had ceased to look shocked. We sat still and allowed the night to pass. It was dawn when the train roared into the Chandigarh railway station. The gang's dynamics had been altered forever.

11

OUR CLASSES WENT ON IN FULL SWING. SEMESTERS CAME and went. My grades slipped a bit. But I still managed to top the list at the end of the third semester, even though Preeto scored close. Since the trip, the gang rarely hung out together. Most of us got more serious and put ourselves through the grind, busy completing assignments and term papers. The third semester before the final exams was very crucial for campus recruitments. Big men from small companies and small men from big companies came to the campus to gauge, analyse, and finalize their picks; just the way cattle are purchased at the Pushkar Fair. Till that happened, we had to finish the mindless term papers, cut-paste and plagiarize the assignments and cram our way through the semester exams (Sandy called them sinister exams). In the entire two-year MBA course, this was the most crucial phase for those who wanted good jobs.

Mallika didn't fall in that category. She was easygoing yet clear about her life; she didn't want a job. She just wanted to get married and rule the household. Earning and yearning was for men, she often preached to other girls. And thus, outside, on the sprawling green lawns, Mallika would bask in the winter sun all alone and watch the dogs mating. The bugger Abhilaksh was in first year and had another year to go. He was somewhat busy in applying for his summer internships, though that wasn't much of a concern.

'Don't worry, dude! I will get you one in my uncle's firm, the Smart Bra Co. in Ludhiana, if you don't get in anywhere else,' Sandy had assured him.

Sandy couldn't remain angry with anyone for too long. In any case, he was too experienced to be fixated on one girl. As of now, he was busy enticing the wife of the librarian. The librarian was a staid, serious, statuesque Sardar whose shift extended into late evenings. His wife Harwinder Kaur had met Sandy in the corridor one afternoon when she had come to beckon her husband and wean him away for a post-lunch session of sex in their staff quarters at the other end of campus. But the Sardar was too committed to his job. He couldn't bunk. What if some student tore some pages out of an encyclopaedia? No, he couldn't leave the library unattended even for a minute. So, newly married but unsatiated, Harwinder would stand at the library door, waving, smiling, beseeching, and finally scowling at her husband. Sandy instantly knew that she was good bait. The possibility excited him, so he focussed all his energy on the task of seducing Harwinder Kaur.

'Did you actually take her buddy?' Sandy asked Abhilaksh one afternoon when they were in the library. He pointed at Mallika who sat reclined on the lawns outside.

'Shut up, Sandy,' Abhilaksh snubbed him. 'We love each other.'

'Yes, I know. But who says people who love each other do not make love?'

'But it's true love, man. Not the dirty type,' Abhilaksh scowled.

But Sandy was confident that Abhilaksh would fall into his trap. 'And true love prohibits sex. Is that your theory?' Sandy had asked, winking.

'I don't know, dude. But I don't feel the need to.'

'Then there's no attraction between the two of you, Abhilaksh. Have a re-look at the whole thing. Because without attraction, love is not possible.'

Abhilaksh nodded and said, 'I mean I am physically attracted to Mallika. And she is indeed very beautiful. Irresistible, at times.'

'Yes, I know that. Even I have similar feelings for her,' Sandy had winked.

'Oh, shut up, man.'

'Hey, I am just supporting what you are saying. Don't be angry, dude.' Sandy had patted his back like a master patting his pet. 'Tell me, why do you feel sex is out of bounds when you love someone?'

'Because I am going to be with her all my life. So why hurry?'

'You silly man! All the more reason to do so. Don't we test drive a bike before buying it? What if you don't like her after you have done it with her...maybe her legs are too rough or something and you may like to change your mind? At least test drive her once.'

Sandy narrated his conversation with Abhilaksh to me the same evening, and it made me giggle. We were scanning a few finance magazines in the library to pick up some random material for our term papers. Sandy chuckled too. I loved bitching about Abhilaksh.

'Come on, Sandy! I am sure he has already test driven her several times over,' I had muttered. By now, the Sardar librarian was staring at us, gesturing at us to not chat in the library. 'Even distant whispers don't escape the bugger,' cursed Sandy.

'And yet the idiot always fails to be there for legitimate post-lunch coitus with his young and new wife,' I whispered.

Sandy winked and whispered back into my ear, 'That's why I have decided to take care of Harwinder Kaur's needs.' His wide, innocent smile belied his carnal intentions.

I stood up and pulled Sandy toward the book racks. Once we were away from the librarian's prying eyes and sharp ears, we got talking again. I held a fat brown book, turned its pages, and asked Sandy, 'Tell me more about your discussion with Abhilaksh about Mallika.'

Sandy looked around and spoke softly, 'I had told Abhilaksh that if he wanted, I could manage a room for him here...you know, about five kilometres from here, my uncle has a one-bedroom flat. And I have the key. It's adequately furnished for the purpose. I mean it has a mattress on the floor and that's enough for the job.'

I frowned. So, Sandy had indeed incited Abhilaksh. Rogue! Why the hell was he so keen for Mallika to make out with someone else? Shutting the fat brown book, I looked at him with suspicion. What if Sandy also made blue films in that flat, dubbed them in Malayalam and sold them off in flea markets in South India? Was it the reason why Sandy was encouraging unsuspecting friends to visit his apartment, bugged with tiny mikes and concealed cameras? But on second thought, when I looked deep into Sandy's eyes, it didn't seem possible that he was capable of monetizing other people's sexual escapades.

'So what did Abhilaksh say? Did he accept your offer?' I asked doubtfully.

'He was noncommittal. Maybe someday he will ask me for the key. And I will know,' Sandy yawned and stretched like a dog stretching after defecation. The Sardar librarian had walked in around the alley, arranging books. Sandy tugged at my shoulder and said, 'Let's get out of here. I feel claustrophobic.'

I smiled, 'Yes, let's. I can understand why you're feeling suffocated. After all, he is the ferocious husband of the woman you plan to screw.'

Sandy smiled and we walked out of the library.

Outside, tiny groups of students were loitering in the corridors with rolled-up posters and large cans of gum and brushes. Karan stood near the veranda, smoking. Sandy and I walked toward him. Abhilaksh passed by and he smiled at Sandy and Karan, but avoided me.

'What are these guys doing with those posters?' Sandy asked in his high-pitched voice.

'It's about Rangoli, the upcoming youth fest,' Karan hissed like a serpent. 'Last year, I won the Best Debator trophy there.'

'Yes, we all know that, Karan. It's common knowledge that the first prize is always reserved for you,' I was irritated.

'Why are you so pissed, man?' Karan was hurt.

'We all know that you are the best debater. Why do you have to rub it in?' Sandy chided him, looking at me in motherly sympathy. Nowadays, anything that anyone said hurt me. I was still fragile and caught in the aftermath of Mallika's betrayal.

'Anyway, Viraat, you must also participate in Rangoli. You write so well. You must take part in the story writing competition,' Sandy said.

Karan held my hand and patted the back of my wrist, 'Viraat, join me. We will be a team and win the debate.'

I wasn't sure of what to say.

'And Rangoli starts next Saturday,' Karan continued.

I smiled, and tried to look generous. We shook hands and parted.

It was Friday and the weekend seemed uneventful so I went home. Mom tried her best to excite me with paranthas but I remained listless like a cold soggy dosa. I went through my notes, but mostly I watched TV, surfing endlessly, between maddening advertisements and mindless programmes. Nothing excited me at home. I missed the Kashmir trip, even its pain. By Sunday night, I was already sick of sitting at home and was looking forward to Rangoli.

The youth fest commenced with lots of excitement and fanfare. Hordes of students roamed around trying to look busy. Everyone felt as if they were organizing the fest. Girls paraded around the campus, walking aimlessly just to excite boys with their smiles and their short skirts. Flags and posters depicting various events dotted the entire campus. Even the wretched Omi Dhaba had a poster announcing the events and schedule of the cultural fest.

'Why do they call it a cultural fest? They should call it the fashion parade or the grand bazaar of consumerism or something,' Sandy had opined, ogling at the busts and backsides passing by.

The sponsors had a field day. Bright Pepsi banners were interspersed with at least a dozen other FMCG ad posters. The fest taught us more about marketing than our lectures ever could. We had to plead and beg sponsors to contribute to Rangoli. In the end, it was the power-packed combination of Preeto's hard sell, Karan's eloquent rhetoric, and Mallika's beauteous presence that had wooed the sponsors to sponsor our event. And they turned the campus grounds into a veritable bazaar, advertising everything from colas to shoes.

Karan succeeded in roping me in for the debate. We paired up to participate in the debating competition and the JAM session. The topic of the debate was 'Pre-marital sex is Western culture and not for us!' Karan spoke against it and I was debating in favour of the topic. Images of Mallika and Abhilaksh rolling on the cushion on the houseboat egged me on and I was at my furious best, with a lot of punch in my arguments. I spoke with passion.

As the audience clapped and I descended from the podium, Sandy smirked and muttered, 'Hey man! You spoke like an angel. And the entire thing was for Abhilaksh and Mallika. Wasn't it?' I nodded. I looked to my left, five seats down Mallika was seated next to Abhilaksh, smiling with meaningful bashfulness. She raised her eyebrow at me and gave me a thumbs up sign. I ground my teeth to keep it together. She nudged Abhilaksh and made him wave at me. She was sweet. Even after I had beaten up her lover boy in the train and had publicly argued against pre-marital sex, she was still nice to me and had made Abhilaksh wave at me. Grudgingly, I smiled and waved back at Abhilaksh, and so, we were back on talking terms. Or waving terms at least.

Sandy beckoned Abhilaksh, who took Mallika's permission and shifted five seats to come and sit with Sandy. He shook hands with me, ruffled Sandy's hair affectionately, and said, 'What is it, buddy?'

Sandy leaned toward him and whispered, 'Test drive her, man. She is game for you!' He muttered very softly but I overheard him. 'Go ahead, man. Prove Viraat wrong!'

Abhilaksh pinched Sandy's arm, fearing that I would overhear.

'Balls!' I mumbled and kept looking ahead.

The results were being announced. I had won the first prize, Karan was third, and jointly we had bagged the annual debating trophy. The crowd cheered as I walked up to the stage, with Karan following me. The crescendo reached a reassuring pitch as we raised the shield high up in the air. It was a shabbily made shield that had lost its sheen, yet, it felt as if we had conquered the moon. We walked back flashing the trophy at the cheering crowd. Mallika waved at us, smiling beautifully. God, she shone like a solitaire in that entire crop of average people. Proudly, we walked past the audience toward the exit.

'Congratulations!' Suddenly a sweet voice rose above the din and seized my attention. I turned around to see.

There stood a girl in a green skirt and a fawn top. She was thin and had large expressive eyes. Her hair was short and straight. She wore a light lipstick. Her hands were beautiful and her fingers were so long that they seemed to touch my chest when she opened her palm and extended her hand toward me. I greedily grabbed her hand and shook it with an uncalled-for gusto. The din around us had stilled. For that moment, holding her long, soft hand, and looking deep into those almond eyes, Mallika had been forgotten.

After an eternity, she demurely pulled her hand out of my grip, and smiled mischievously. Karan came forward and said with deliberate emphasis, 'Hi. I am his partner, Karan. I won the third prize. And jointly we won this trophy.'

I broke out of my trance. Sandy came rushing toward us. He had caught parts of the conversation and had seen the expression on my face. And from experience, he understood that I had fallen head over heels for this new girl. Even Sandy was salivating. He came and patted Karan's back and said, 'And this guy, Karan, normally gets the first prize. This year, for a change, he has settled for third.'

Karan turned around and scowled at Sandy. I stammered, 'And this is Sandy. We are a gang.'

'Hi. I am Komal Kapur.' Her voice was decidedly that of a prospective singing star. 'And I am in the English department, first year MA.'

'Great meeting you, Komal,' I stammered and looked sheepishly at her again, at her dreamy eyes, her luscious lips, her dangling earrings, and her brilliant forehead. She stood still. I waited for her to say bye and walk away, but she stayed on.

'Komal, we are going for lunch to StuCee. Want to come?' Karan jumped in before she could go.

'Well, you guys carry on. I don't want to intrude on the gang,' she said shyly, but her eyes told another story.

'Come on, Komal, our gang is not like the Parliament with limited seats! There is always room for more friends. We have a couple of other guys, Mallika and Abhilaksh,' Sandy insisted. He tried to look for them in the crowd, but they had disappeared.

'Yes, he is right. And since they became a couple, the place for singles is now vacant,' I chuckled.

Komal looked on, indecisively. Why is it that girls take so much time in minor things like befriending guys, but when it comes to major things like smooching buffoons like Abhilaksh, they just rush in without thinking? 'Fine! I can come along if you guys are okay with it,' Komal consented finally.

At StuCee, we had puri chhole and sweet lukewarm coffee. All along, I kept trying to steal glances at the new girl. I thought that given a choice, Komal would perhaps prefer me over the others, if it ever came to the process of selection. Which pretty girl would like a hairy grizzly chap like Karan? And Sandy was too old for any girl of

171

our age to fall for. Abhilaksh was already booked. I had conveniently overlooked the fact that the university campus brimmed with other good looking boys too.

From the next day onwards, we started hanging out almost every day. Mallika had drifted apart from us. Sandy claimed that he had given Abhilaksh the key to his uncle's apartment. I imagined Abhilaksh would take Mallika there every day in his yellow Zen, and then make out with her on that sodden mattress. Mallika didn't know that the flat belonged to Sandy's Ludhiana uncle; she was told that it belonged to Abhilaksh's uncle from Bhatinda. So, she too must have been comfortable rolling on the big, smelly mattress lying on the empty floor of the flat. Sandy told me that Abhilaksh loved her and so wouldn't go beyond fondling and kissing; that would keep Mallika happy and guilt free. *So he loved her from the core of his heart, not merely from the centre of his body*, I thought wryly.

Komal would hang out with us boys. Preeto and Vandana would occasionally join in. I stopped missing Mallika that much. Now, I was forcing myself to fall for Komal. Her teeth were better, whiter, I would mentally argue, comparing both the girls. And she didn't have a mole on her little nose.

'Campus recruitments are on for you guys, right?' Komal asked one afternoon, munching a chocolate.

'Yes, Komal,' I replied, 'I have got a couple of interview calls. I hope to get picked soon.' *And soon I would earn enough to support an English literature-educated girl as a girlfriend,* I thought.

'Komal, can you imagine, this chap got as many interview calls as I did,' Karan jumped in. The war between us boys over the sole girl never seemed to end. Why didn't God make an adequate numbers of pretty girls, I cursed.

'Tomorrow, the Amex people are coming. We have GDs and interviews the whole day,' I told Komal, 'they are the best pay masters.' *And once I am in that American bank, you'll be able to shop mindlessly on my credit cards. And if we last long enough to get married—then even for the house and our kids.* I was already imagining the offspring that I would have with Komal. Two of them—a boy and a girl. Surprisingly, in my head, the kids looked the same as the kids that I had imagined being born to me and Mallika, till some weeks ago. Irrespective of the mother, the kids looked the same in my thoughts.

'So, as it turns out, both of us have been shortlisted for Amex. But there are eight others, and only one of the ten will get the job,' Karan said.

'Both of you, competing for the same job!' Komal exclaimed. 'I don't know what to say. Well, best of luck to you both. May the best man win. But I am sure of one thing: the job will go to one of you two. The other eight have no chance,' she said sweetly and diplomatically.

Karan was beaming but I was disappointed. The kids in my head quickly melted away. For her, Karan and I had the same importance? How could girls be like that?

It was the D-day. A large, bearded man in a blue blazer and neatly ironed shirt entered the room filled with ten aspirants. The GD was the shortlisting process and both Karan and I made it with relative ease; being debaters helped us shout down the others and awe them with our reasoning prowess. The topic was 'Corporate Social Responsibility', and though we both thought it was a sham, we vehemently spoke in favour of the concept and the need for the same. Arguments seasoned and garnished with bits and pieces of morality and a few oft-quoted readymade anecdotes helped us glide through the process.

The five shortlisted students, which included some odd jokers, were meant to go through personal interviews. I went in first. The large, bearded man had taken off his jacket, and the necktie rested almost horizontally over his paunch, which heaved in and out as he spoke, 'Viraat Nijhawan? Twenty-three?' It was a voice as if arising from a deep and mysterious cave. I blinked. *What is twenty-three?* I wondered. This wasn't my roll number. It wasn't my house number or sector number, or number of times I had had wet dreams of both Komal and Mallika the entire week. So, then it must be my age, which was twenty-two years and eleven months. My mother would have slaughtered the fatso for saying that I was twenty-three years old. For her, I would be twenty-two till the day of my birthday. So when this bearded hippo of a man said twenty-three, it took me some time to register.

'Yes, sir. But I haven't turned twenty-three yet,' I stammered idiotically.

The large man looked up from a heap of papers and stared at me over the top of his glasses.

'Whatever, twenty-two or twenty-three. You are Viraat Nijhawan, right?' he asked for confirmation.

'Yes, sir. Surely. You can even match my real face with my snap there on the interview sheet.'

The man looked quite amused by now and broke into a smile. 'Of course. You look like this boy here.' He tapped the picture of me on the interview sheet. 'Unless you have an identical twin also studying here. Like in Hindi films.' He guffawed.

I smiled sheepishly.

The man was relaxed by now, smiling from ear to ear. He seemed too happy to evaluate me with any degree of seriousness. For a moment, I felt that the man was just humouring me to lift his own mood. I doubted if any serious selector would be smiling so much while interviewing someone whom he intended to evaluate and select.

'I am Kishore Kumar,' the man laughed. 'You can call me KK. I head the Personnel department at the Amex corporate office in Mumbai.' He was rotating a pencil between his fingers; it irritated me and diverted my attention for no reason.

'Nice meeting you, sir,' I stood up, grabbed KK's fat hand and shook it with gusto. His hand was limp and damp, as though he had just finished masturbating under his table. The pencil between his fingers dug deep into his fat skin and he looked a bit shocked.

'Young man, normally you don't shake hands with your interviewer,' KK blurted, smoothening the pencil mark on his fingers.

'Sir, but in America and in American companies, people are more informal,' I said and grinned shamelessly; confidence dripping off my face like sweat falling off the brow of a roadside labourer.

KK stopped smiling. 'But you can only enter an American company when I clear you, young man.' He cleared his throat.

Such benevolence! I exclaimed internally, and mumbled, 'Of course, sir. But I am sure that you will find me the most suitable candidate here.' Sandy had advised me to sprinkle extra drops of confidence in situations when knowledge was found wanting.

'It feels like you are not being your natural self,' KK stared at me hard. 'Are you into acting or something?'

How did he guess? I cursed. I quickly thought of an answer, 'Sir, aren't we all acting most of the time? We are always wearing a mask—at college, at work, at home. Except when we're asleep, anytime we're in the company of another human being, we start acting. Isn't it?'

KK laughed aloud. He looked very amused. I too smiled sheepishly. 'So, young man, do you think that I too am acting right now? You think that I too am floating around with a mask?' blurted KK, sipping a cappuccino and wiping the froth off his whiskers as he placed the cup back on the table between us.

'Of course, sir. If you were your natural self, why would you wear this uncomfortable necktie?' I pointed at that striped, long piece of clothing meant to be hanging vertically, which now rested horizontally over his heaving stomach.

KK stopped smirking, swallowed the lump in his throat, and went on to loosen the tie with slow relief. Then he loosened his belt and took a deep breath. I watched him with secret fear. What was the fat man going to do to look natural: take off his belt and lash me with several whooshing strokes? Or take off his trousers and sodomise me? Silly brainwaves! I felt entertained by my own thoughts and broke into a small giggle.

'Are you always this frank and creative....err....Viraat Nijhawan?' KK was so relaxed by now that he appeared too natural to be an interviewer.

'Not always. But, sir, you have this magical impact on me. I am totally at ease now.' I folded my left leg over my right knee. Was KK impressed or did he see me as an owl perched atop a banyan tree, relaxed and indifferent to his own blindness? I no longer cared.

'Good. We appreciate truthful, relaxed employees. That's the American philosophy.' KK's sunken eyes sparkled. Yes, he was impressed. My strategy seemed to be working well.

'I know, sir. The way America turned Osama bin Laden into a corpse,' I chuckled at my own joke. Then we both laughed aloud. The other four aspirants eavesdropping outside could perhaps hear our laughter. They might even presume that KK was some lost uncle of mine, I thought.

The interview continued for a good twenty minutes. The longest interview in the whole batch. In the end, he asked me the trick question to check my wits.

'What's the colour of the wall behind you?' he asked casually after listening to my banter about my career goals and life goals.

'Why, sir, it's white, of course,' I said without blinking. I knew such trick questions were supposed to catch us off-guard. That's why I did not stupidly turn around to check the colour of the walls behind me. They obviously would be the same colour as the walls in front of me. I had clearly impressed him.

At the end of the interview, I came out gleeful. Later, Karan's interview also went well. None of us were asked any academic questions. Karan had impressed the interviewer with his rhetorical manner of speaking as though he was at the podium. That was Karan's style in any case; he was forever eloquent.

The two of us got shortlisted and were called in together at the end of the long day. It was almost dinner time. KK looked tired by now and someone called Bhattacharya had joined him for the final round. Bhattacharya was a bald small man, who seemed higher in rank. I looked at KK's pointy shoes as he shook his foot, and wondered why large, fat men had such small feet. Perhaps such large fat men had small penises too! I had often glanced down neighbourhood urinals in toilets to compare the size of other people's genitals with my own, by instinct, and had invariably noticed that big men were smaller endowed. KK would fall in the same category since he had small feet, I guessed silently and smiled.

'Boys, this is my boss, Mr Bhattacharya. He is the DGM,' KK introduced the small bald man to us.

Karan and I acknowledged his exalted presence, nodding respectfully. We were never as respectful to our professors, or even our respective fathers.

'Congratulations, boys. You are both shortlisted. And now you will need to come down to Mumbai for an informal chat with our GM and for a medical test, before you join our great organization: The Amex.'

Medical test? Medical tests always freaked me out; the doctor holding my testicles and making me cough to detect hernia and then inserting something sharp in my anus to check for piles—that was the memory of the last medical test I had undergone after my class twelve exams when I had cleared the NDA exam. So, the mention of a medical test overwhelmed me again. 'Medical tests,' I mumbled and squirmed.

Bhattacharya droned on for some more time, enlightening us about the philosophy of the American corporate world. He was as skilled a rhetorician as Karan. I felt like breaking into applause at the end of that short speech.

'Thank you, sir. We shall prove worthy of your esteemed organization,' Karan matched Bhattacharya in eloquence.

'Tell me, where did you do your summer internship?' Bhattacharya asked. Karan seemed hesitant to say 'Smart Bra Company' so he said, 'Sir, it's a garment export company in Ludhiana, the Manchester of India. It's called SB Co Pvt Ltd.' In any case, Bhattacharya did not seem to care.

'And what about you, Viraat?' Bhattacharya asked perfunctorily.

'Sir, I did my internship at the prestigious Metal Bearing Company, Faridabad,' I said proudly.

KK sat up suddenly and his sunken eyes lit up, 'Really! That's great, Viraat.' Then he looked at Bhattacharya and continued, 'Boss, you remember, my brother Ashok Nigam? He is the GM of Metal Bearing Co.'

My heart skipped a beat. Oh God, this can't be happening! The GM of Metal Bearing Co., the guy who wanted his daughter to be wedded to me: Vasundhara, the mysterious girl who used to stealthily hang her undergarments on the drying line, the one whom I had craved to bed without having to wed, the girl who had called me a creep after which she and her father had chucked me out of their house! That Nigam was KK's brother? This KK, the fatso who would decide my future, was actually Kishore Kumar Nigam! My face went white and I must have looked like a bloodless zombie.

'Oh yes! I remember.' Bhattacharya grinned. He looked like a donkey in heat, as he excitedly spoke, 'KK, call your brother now and tell him that we are picking up one of his interns.'

The air in the room froze. A slithering lizard peeping out from behind a picture frame of a deformed Einstein on the wall behind Nigam seemed to mock me.

'Sir, Mr Nigam was the GM,' I gulped. 'He won't even remember me.' I could barely hear my own voice.

KK Nigam tilted sideways. I thought he was going to break wind, but he was actually trying to take out his mobile from the pocket of his trousers. 'Let me still tell him.' He smiled. 'He might be happy that one of his trainees is coming to work for his brother.'

KK Nigam punched numbers into his cell phone and after a few moments, shouted, 'Hello Bhaisahab. It's me. Kishore.' The voice from the other end resonated as the mobile had been put on speaker mode by Nigam to my utter dismay. Karan sat around, jealously listening to the conversation, trying to look interested. Bhattacharya was yawning up at the lizard on the wall.

'Yes, yes! Kishore. How are you?' The cold, low growl of the elder Nigam came to life and chilled me to my bones. The scum sounded as dangerous over the phone as in real life.

'I am in Chandigarh at the B School here, Bhaisahab. For campus recruitment,' KK said to AK.

'Ok. How is it there?' Ashok Nigam coughed out a small smoker's cough and growled. 'These days the chaps don't have much substance to them. All they want is fun. No seriousness. Far from the way we used to be! Remember?' The voice resonated distantly. I continued to stare at the ceiling where a tiny cockroach struggled to extricate itself from a cobweb. I felt like that cockroach.

'But there are a few good guys here, Bhaisahab. And they come much cheaper than the IIM graduates. And they are almost as good. That's why I go for small time B Schools with funny names, to hire chaps every year,' KK said, looking at his own pointy shoe that quivered along with his foot.

Karan looked at me, smirked and whispered, 'So, the corporate honchos think that ours is a vague B School, eh?'

I was not in a condition to respond.

'What else?' Ashok Nigam was curt even with his brother.

'Nothing much,' KK said respectfully. I was hoping the conversation would end but that was not to be. The feared thing happened, the way it always does, and KK said, 'Bhaisahab, we have selected one of your ex-interns. A very good, frank, and witty boy.'

'My intern? Who?' AK barked out of the speaker phone.

'You may not remember him. He was there just for two months last summer.'

I held my breath, clutched my armchair so hard that my knuckles went white. I still hoped that the dreaded conversation would finish—maybe the mobile battery would die or the network would act up, or even better, an earthquake would strike, dismantling the mobile tower itself. But there was no deliverance and KK went on to nail me with his words, 'He is a boy called Viraat Nijhawan.'

The line went silent for a few moments. I imagined the elder Nigam freeze.

'What did you say?'

'Viraat Nijhawan, Bhaisahab.'

There was a shriek at the other end. Vasundhara's distant shriek of horror, as if she had seen a ghost. They were on the speaker phone, these godammned Nigams. Can't people talk in private, I cursed.

'That rogue! How could you ever select a chap like him, Kishore?'

'Why? What happened?' KK looked embarrassed. He got his fingers to the pad of his phone and turned the speaker phone off.

The silence in the room was nauseating. For a long time, almost till eternity, KK kept listening. His paunch was quivering in a strange rhythm. Beads of sweat erupted on his brow. Bhattacharya looked startled. He looked at me and scowled with constricted eyebrows. KK stared hard at me even as he continued to listen. Karan widened his pupils at me and I could see my pale face reflected in his eyes. I looked down at my own shoes. Finally, when the call was over, I slowly rose from my seat and walked out of the room, feeling like a raped nun. No one stopped me. As I closed the door behind me, I heard KK say to Bhattacharya, 'This guy here was a pervert. We are saved.'

It was dark outside and the empty corridors of the campus appeared less dangerous and abhorrent to me than the room that I had just exited. I had lost the job that I had almost bagged a few moments ago. I had lost my dollar dream. Those bras hanging on the Faridabad terrace had taken their toll!

12

'WOW! THIS FEELS GREAT,' KARAN CARESSED THE PIECE of paper for the umpteenth time. It was his appointment letter from Amex. Three weeks since the disastrous turn of events, only one letter had arrived at the placement office and it was for Karan. He was treating us at StuCee with bread pakoras and sweet lukewarm coffee that had dancing froth competing with tads of grime from the waiter's nails.

Mallika, Abhilaksh, Sandy, Komal, and I sat on the grass. Across the lawn, four small pups and their mother sniffed the grass. I gazed at them, disenchanted. Soon those pups would be mating incestuously, by the time the next batch was ready to pass out. Karan's newly acquired job made me feel worse about my situation. I must be jinxed. During the past three weeks, I had fared badly in two more job interviews.

'Nice,' I said sullenly to Karan, as he showed off his offer letter.

'Nice?' Mallika nudged me, 'Come on, Viraat! It's great. The first one in the campus to land an American job is our dear chap here.' She patted Karan on his back. All this time, Mallika held Abhilaksh's arm with her other hand, as if she feared losing him.

I burned with jealousy and looked away. I had nothing. No job, no girlfriend. Nothingness seeped into me like ink into blotting paper.

'Come on, Viraat. Cheer up,' Komal stroked my hand. I felt a bit comforted by her touch; at least I had something to look forward to. Komal, it seemed, had grown fond of me. Last week, the two of us had gone to the cheapest discotheque in town, but I did not manage to hug her. Discos, I realized that night, were the most unromantic places—with loud music ripping one's ear drums, flashing neon lights alternating with interludes of dark and the necessity to dance, hop, step, and jump. We wasted all our energy on the dance floor rather than in bed. At the end of it, sweaty and tired, we went back home. We didn't kiss, we didn't hug, but we held hands for a brief moment, and for the rest of the time, tried to camouflage our own awkwardness. It was an uneventful date. Even the Amex interview had been more eventful than that night.

'What next?' I asked.

'I just want to clear the exams with minimum marks, so that I can get the hell out of this campus and join office in Delhi or Mumbai,' Karan proclaimed, scratching his beard. His life sounded idyllic.

'Great, man,' Sandy said.

'And what about you, Mallika?' Sandy asked her.

'Nothing. I will relax at home while I wait for someone to complete his studies and find a job,' she said, looking at Abhilaksh with affection. Abhilaksh stroked her hair. They looked blissful together.

'I'll go to the US,' Sandy declared. 'My dad's eldest brother lives there. He is a consultant with a big company. I will join it if all goes well. He knows them very well.' He then smiled sheepishly and stuttered, 'And I also have some experience in that field.'

'What company is that, Sandy?' Karan asked.

'Victoria's Secret,' Sandy whispered shyly. We burst out laughing.

'Man, you are so funny. From Smart Bra Company to Victoria's Secret!' I giggled, smiling after a long time and whispered into his ear, 'Seems like you were born to serve women. And support their breasts!'

Sandy punched my arm. For a moment, I forgot all about the hanging bras of Faridabad and my doomed fate.

'And what's your plan, Viraat?' Abhilaksh tried to break the ice. It was the first time in almost two months that we spoke.

I smiled at Abhilaksh, whose hand was still stroking Mallika's hair. 'Well, I can't do a job. Sucking up to some boss all my life isn't my cup of tea. I will do something else. Maybe start a business of my own and make a lot of money,' I said softly, watching a frog on the grass. That was the only option for someone who didn't find a job at the end of a B School course. Business could mean anything from running a tailoring shop to becoming a powerful land tycoon.

I looked at Komal, expecting her pat, but she looked rather disappointed. I wasn't sure how to respond. We finished our coffee and walked toward the main building.

Sandy and I trailed behind; walking past the stone wall, past the playful pups and Rambha. We entered the last patch of the shrub-lined passage. I had always loved the walk. There was silence in our steps. It was a silence that was strangely deafening. As we crossed the library door, I caught a glimpse of the Sardar librarian, seated like a statue, doing nothing. Suddenly, my face lit up. 'Hey, Sandy, are you still screwing his wife?' I spoke into Sandy's ears, trying not to let his ear-wax repulse me.

'Regularly, man,' Sandy winked at me mischievously, as we walked past the library. 'At my uncle's flat. Remember I told you? Harwinder and I do it there. She is too hot, man.'

'Wow, you lucky bugger.' I was jealous beyond belief. That I was jinxed was getting clearer to me by the day— job-wise, love-wise, sex-wise. I was a loser.

Sandy sensed my thoughts and chided me, 'Viraat, what's wrong with you, man? You have the looks. The physique. The intelligence. Yet you don't do anything worthwhile.'

'You are right, buddy.' I felt real remorse shear through me. 'Perhaps it's my destiny.'

'Nonsense,' Sandy said, placing his hand on my shoulder. 'Things will work out soon. Although I was much taller and bigger than Sandy, he held an invisible power over me. Sternly, he said, 'There is no such thing as destiny. It's all in your hands.'

'What do you mean?'

'I mean you need to have sex once in a while! And I can help you manage that.'

'How?' I felt excited at the possibility. Mallika was now off the radar, and the possibility of bedding Komal also seemed remote. Then who?

'Leave that to me,' Sandy whispered as we entered the classroom to join the others. The lecture had already started and Prof. Dubey was beginning to parrot out some management theory. 'Meet me after class,' he said and winked at me.

At seven in the evening, Sandy took charge of me and we both slipped away from the others, stealthily riding off on his Vespa. My heart was beating in an unusual fashion. Sandy was right, I needed release. I gulped the fresh air and steadied myself to face what was coming my way.

Sandy's uncle's flat was small, dark, and designed for debauchery. It was a one-bedroom flat, with a mattress and a folding chair. There was a tiny kitchen that had a few cheap cups without saucers and a few stainless steel plates, and the rhythmic sound of water dripping from the kitchen tap.

I turned to inspect the tiny toilet: it was adorned with a lidless commode that had pale urine marks over its rim, a patchy mirror, and a low wash basin that was perhaps designed to facilitate the washing of genitals after copulation. 'Now what?' I whispered nervously to Sandy. Beads of sweat glistened on my brow.

'Relax. We need to wait for some time. The girls are on their way,' Sandy winked.

'Girls? Or girl? Are there two of them?' I felt uneasy.

'Yes, two.'

'Hey, but we can't make out here together. It's a small room,' I caught hold of his arm and said. 'Man. I hope you are not planning an orgy.' I glanced around to see if there was a hidden camera somewhere. I didn't wish to become a South Indian porn star.

'Let's see,' Sandy said mysteriously.

'What the hell do you mean, Sandy? Look, I can't do that sort of stuff.' I was quite perturbed. I could not strip naked in front of another man and still manage a performance. That was impossible. And if I couldn't manage that, I would be shamed beyond words in front of the whore. That would be terrible.

'Fine. Don't worry, man,' Sandy consoled me. 'You take

the main room and we shall play on the kitchen platform.'

'Can't we take turns? You wait outside with your lady and then I do the same.'

'No way! We can't be seen standing out, silly.'

The bell rang. My heart started thumping against my temples. Sandy opened the door, and I froze when I saw who was standing outside. It was Harwinder, the fair, bubbly wife of the Sardar librarian. Oh god!

She walked in and smiled. Sandy closed the door and walked behind her, grinning at me. He seemed to be enjoying my distress. 'This is Harwinder. You know her, right?' Sandy said. I shivered and nodded. She held out a soft and damp hand and I shook it nervously.

I swallowed the lump in my throat, continuing to hold her hand and stammered, 'But Harwinder, why would you want to do it with me? Aren't you Sandy's muse?' I felt so jittery I could barely feel her touch; making out with her was going to be impossible.

Harwinder winked at Sandy, pulled her hand back, and smiled. 'Listen, Viraat, I think I need to tell you the whole scene,' she looked back and forth between me and Sandy, paused a bit, and then went on. 'You see, both my sister and I are married to these two brothers. Jasvinder, my sister, is older to me by two years and is married to my husband's elder brother, Tarjit Singh.'

'Your sister? Where is she?'

'Jasvinder is downstairs, in the auto rickshaw. She will

come in once we have talked this out and if it's okay with you,' Sandy whispered. 'Go on, Harwinder.' He cajoled her lovingly.

She continued, 'So, to cut the long story short, my brother-in-law, Tarjit is also like my husband. He is a scientist at CSIR, and stays in the lab for sixteen hours a day. And both of us feel royally ignored in the process.' Harwinder sounded sad. 'Actually, I got out of my loneliness very early in my marriage. Thanks to Sandy.' Harwinder patted Sandy's back affectionately.

'Then why did you marry the man if you didn't love him? And if you knew what was already happening to your elder sister?' I asked, my voice sounding distant and strange. Oh god! I thought. Why did I have to preach? Why not just enjoy the fruit that was about to come my way? But I had already spoken, and so I needed to take my argument to its logical conclusion. 'Why did you marry the man who you knew was just like your brother-in law? Someone who was going to ignore your needs for the rest of your life?' I must have sounded like Karan debating at the podium.

Harwinder's eyes became moist, but only for a split second. She evaded the question and wiping the corners of her eyes, she said, 'So that I can have my cake and eat it too.' She pinched Sandy's fair forearm, 'And this, your friend here, is my cake.' She playfully bit him on the cheek.

'And you can become the cake for Jasvinder. And she can be yours. If you can promise to keep this a secret,' Sandy hissed.

My eyes glistened; between the two of us, we would be fornicating with the entire clan, I thought. I felt wicked, but was too excited to let the chance slip. So, I just nodded.

Sandy went down and in a few minutes walked in with Jasvinder trailing him. She was coy. Compared to her younger sister, she was plumper and darker. What bad luck, I thought: the younger, fairer, and prettier of the two had already gone to the older, shorter, and feminine looking Sandy. But beggars can't be choosers.

It had gotten very dark, and the deed had been done. In the distance, a dog howled and I sat up on the mattress. I shivered as I had no clothes on. Jasvinder turned around and squatted to gather her clothes from the chair. Sandy and Harwinder were slurping tea in the kitchen. They had finished quite some time ago, familiarity having shortened the duration of their coitus.

'Can we come in?' Sandy said from the kitchen, knocking softly on the door.

Jasvinder stroked my bare back and got up from the mattress. I noticed that her bum was quite flabby and that it wobbled when she tiptoed into the toilet. I hurriedly put on my jeans and T shirt and pulled open the kitchen door. Sandy and Harwinder walked in, lovingly, arm in arm. Jasvinder came out of the toilet rather quickly. Minutes later, the ladies were gone.

The whole thing seemed unreal. I was dazed and my stomach churned, making me feel sick. Frustration can make men copulate with any kind of woman, but it is the aftertaste that speaks the truth, I realized. I felt disgust descend on me.

'Let's go, buddy. What are you waiting for?' Sandy nudged.

Sandy stepped forward and patted my back, a wicked smile playing on his chubby, smooth cheeks. At that moment, he seemed like a pimp. 'So my mattress here has been quite useful, eh!' he said.

I said nothing and stood there like a zombie. My head was reeling. Sandy punched me gently and continued, 'This mattress here has been the battleground for many victories. Our ex-craze Mallika lost it to Abhilaksh on this very humble bed.'

Suddenly, I rushed into the kitchen, bent over the sink, and puked. Then I buried my head into the sink and turned on the large tap over my head. I kept the tap on for a long time. Silently, I wept under the flow of water, my tears mixing with the water. Sandy stood at the kitchen door, watching silently. For once, he didn't make fun. Perhaps he understood my pain. My virginity had been wasted away and spent on an older, married woman I didn't know. I had been deflowered cruelly.

'Failure can do strange things to men,' Sandy whispered softly to me, hugging me in sheer sympathy. 'Yet they call women the weaker sex!'

13

THE FINAL EXAMS WERE OVER WITHOUT MUCH PAIN. HALF of the exams didn't even necessitate much studying. A course like MBA, true to what Karan always said, was more like an exercise in creative writing; except, of course, a few technical subjects like Business Statistics and Industrial Economics, which one could hope to pass by studying two full nights. Most other papers on subjects such as Organizational Behaviour, Business Environment, Marketing, Industrial Psychology, and Industrial Relations, were abstract. Good language skills, nice handwriting, and some story-telling capabilities helped Karan and me breeze through the exams.

In the Business Ethics paper, Sandy even wrote about a cooked-up, story of a romance between a General Manager and his secretary, and the impact of that on the organizational behaviour of eager peons outside his door! In the paper on Social Responsibility of Business, I wrote an essay on the process of photosynthesis by plants grown around polluting factories; something I had learnt in class eight in Life Sciences. It was with such creativity that everyone sailed through the exams.

'Perhaps Prof. Dubey and his colleagues love reading fiction,' Mallika said and laughed.

'Come on, Mallika! We are plain intelligent,' Karan boasted.

I smiled kindly, having learnt to be civil to Mallika.

'I know how intelligent you guys are!' Vandana came from behind and lightly slapped Karan on his backside.

The others soon joined us and we headed toward StuCee.

'When is the farewell party?' I asked everyone in general.

'I suppose that would be happening this Saturday,' Karan said.

'Hope you aren't going to give a speech, Karan, because there is no debating contest!' Preeto laughed. Karan laughed and looked the other way.

Abhilaksh, who was walking hand in hand with Mallika, said, 'No way. I hope not. Karan, please refuse, even if the Dean insists. We hear you debate all the time. Can't bear it on the last day, that too at a party.' Laughter surrounded Karan, who turned around and ran after Abhilaksh, caught hold of him, threw him on the grass, and punched him playfully. Everyone cheered and laughed aloud. Mallika disengaged them and lovingly brushed the grass off Abhilaksh's back. I looked at them with jealousy. Lucky bastard!

'The farewell party will be fun. We will go and talk to Prof. Dubey and request him that we don't want any serious stuff. We need to chill out on our last day on campus. Some dancing, some dumb charades, karaoke and stuff like that,' said Preeto.

It was the last Saturday of April. The weather was getting warmer and the bougainvilleas that hugged the campus walls were in full bloom. As the sun set, students gathered on the lawns behind the campus. They wore their best casual clothes. The boys tried to look cool and the girls tried to look hot.

There was jarring music playing from an old and scratched CD placed in an older, redundant CD player. Damn, the university was so impoverished that it couldn't even afford a decent music system!

'Some day, when I am rich, I will gift the university a nice Bose system, and then come and dance with the students, but only if they invite me as the chief guest,' I murmured to no one; for if I had ever spoken out those thoughts, my batch mates would have laughed at me. How could a guy like me—who had no job in sight, no girl, and who had lost his virginity to a married nymphomaniac—aspire so high? How on earth could such a useless, worthless, narcissistic guy ever aspire to be a chief guest at a 'prestigious' B School farewell party some day? People would have booed me out; ripping whatever little remained of my self-respect to pieces.

Meanwhile, Preeto had seized the mike and was making everyone play silly girlish games that made no sense to me. Sandy and Karan sneered at her and slipped away to smoke a joint. At such times, I felt very left out; I always craved to be taken along with them.

At the party for our B School batch, other students from the university had also come as guests. Most of these other students were girls, however, and I supposed that we MBA boys were hot catches since we were bound to manage some sort of employment and were good prospects for the future. Komal had dropped by too, along with some of her girl friends.

Dancing soon commenced. A square wooden platform had been erected in the middle of the lawn and a few cheap neon lights had been strung on a big mango tree near the stage. That was our makeshift discotheque.

I saw Komal looking at me, her eyes shining like pearls. She was standing at the other end of the lawn. Sandy and Karan had still not returned. Being their last day on campus and having found jobs and having given up their desire for Mallika, they were free souls who did whatever they wanted to do. I shrugged, and whispered, 'To each his own.' My lips curled and cursed in silence. From the other end, Komal was still looking at me intently. She seemed to be mouthing something at me, but I couldn't tell what she was saying. I walked up to her. 'Shall we dance?' I said into her ear. She extended her hand and we walked to the dance floor.

At that moment, as if on cue, the loud song changed to a softer one. I didn't know the song, not like I particularly cared for English songs anyway, but the song that was playing sounded lovely. I held her gently and we swirled around the dance floor. It must have been a long song because we didn't realize that most of the people had already made a beeline for the food counter. Even when the music picked up its tempo once again, we continued to dance in soft, romantic steps. It had grown late and the music soon stopped. We finally broke away from each other and stepped off the makeshift dance floor.

'Wasn't that beautiful, Komal?' I exclaimed. She smiled. I let go of her soft hand and stood there awkwardly.

'Yes, Viraat. It was nice,' Komal said softly. 'And my god, you're sweating!'

'Yeah. It's getting warm, and I sweat more than usual,' I said and laughed. 'Dancing with you...wow. I mean, it was exciting.'

'It was nice, though I wouldn't call it exciting,' Komal said, looking around for her friends. Abhilaksh and Mallika too had slipped away quietly; perhaps to go and make out in Sandy's uncle's flat. I brushed the thought away. It was time to concentrate on Komal. 'Live in the present,' I had often heard the saying on spiritual channels on TV. And so, I focussed on Komal, who was still standing there, as if waiting for me to do or say something.

'It's warm h-here,' I stammered, wiping sweat off my forehead. 'Let's get some fresh air.'

'Yes, sure. But just a short stroll,' she said. 'Just a stroll and fresh air, not you getting fresh with me.'

I nodded, not sure whether those words were a warning or an invitation.

We walked out of the venue through the rear exit. A lonely walkway with grass on both sides, a howling dog in the distance, and a full moon in the sky made the evening seem other-worldly. I was surprised at the upswing in my own mood. It was over six months since I had seen Abhilaksh and Mallika kissing in Kashmir. Since the time of that incident this was the first time I was feeling truly happy. We walked in long strides leaving the noise of the party behind us. There was no one around. I was hoping not to bump into Karan and Sandy. Or get called back by Vandana or Preeto to help them pack their karaoke set. Or that Komal's friends from the English department didn't come looking for her. But no one bothered us. We stopped walking and I said, my voice trembling ever so slightly, 'Komal, I want to ask you something...'

Komal looked down at her shoes, digging a hole with her left heel, and said, 'Yes, Viraat. Tell me.'

'May I kiss you, Komal?' My own voice seemed distant to me. I stood there frozen, ready for a slap. The least I expected was that Komal would turn back and walk away. I even expected Karan and Sandy to appear from behind the trees and mock me. But nothing happened. Instead, Komal came forward, held me by the neck, pulled down my face toward hers, and kissed me. I was stunned.

We kissed for a long time. Then, slowly, Komal stepped back, giggled and said breathlessly, 'You are a good kisser, Viraat.'

Had she kissed other random people to be able to compare? But such thoughts didn't matter anymore. 'Live in the present,' the words echoed in my mind. I stepped forward to kiss her again but she suddenly clutched me by the arm and started walking. There was silence. It surprised me how, in the silence of the night, the sounds of small creatures like crickets and frogs seemed so loud.

'So, Viraat. What's happening with you?' Komal asked gently.

'Nothing, everything seems to be down at the moment. No job, and no idea of how to find one. And until a few minutes ago, no girl!'

'Really!' Komal laughed.

'But, of course, now I have you,' I put my arm around her waist as we strolled back to the party.

Komal punched me playfully in the stomach and ran ahead of me toward the party. I ran after her. By now, most of the people had eaten. The waiters, watchmen, helpers, and the caterers had queued up to polish off the leftovers. People were saying their goodbyes to each other.

Some people hugged, some cried, others joked about the fun times, and some shook hands stoically.

Just then, I spotted Sandy and Karan coming toward me. They looked stoned out of their wits and were staggering. Komal had already grabbed a plate and was fishing for leftovers of chicken in the curry-smeared bowl. Karan walked up to me, a cloud of marijuana smell engulfing him, and said, 'Well done, buddy!' He was his usual loud self, and his words made the caterers turn back and take notice.

Komal choked on her food.

'Why? What happened? Has Viraat received a job offer?' Preeto came forward and asked. The words cut through me like a knife. I was filled with embarrassment, more at the thought that Karan had seen us kiss. Komal too, stuttered near the smeared dal makhani bowl and froze. She stilled herself to listen, even though she looked the other way.

'What do you mean, bastard? What "well done"?' I growled.

Sandy came forward, hugged me, and squeaked in my ear, 'It's okay, buddy. Karan is just kidding.'

'Then why did he say "well done, buddy" to me?'

'Oh, nothing man,' Sandy slurred through his words, 'we were behind StuCee and we saw you running behind some girl.'

I heaved a sigh of relief. They hadn't seen us kissing. And they hadn't seen Komal.

'So, now tell us. Who were you chasing, buddy?' Karan tried to tickle me.

'No one, man. You must have been hallucinating after smoking so much,' I disengaged myself and walked toward the food counter.

All of us sat down to eat. Strangely, Mallika and Abhilaksh had also returned by then, glowing and satiated. Perhaps it was destined for the entire gang to be together on our last evening on campus.

'Guys, I have an announcement to make,' Karan stood on a chair and shouted. The chair almost tipped over, but Abhilaksh held it just in time.

'Go on!' Vandana cheered him.

Everyone giggled, but Preeto silenced them, 'Listen up, guys, our dear Karan has an important announcement to make!'

'We shall all meet at the StuCee, on this day, the 20th of April, every year, come what may!' Karan shouted and clapped aloud, alone.

'Aye, aye,' Abhilaksh egged him on.

'What aye aye, you silly guy?' said Sandy. 'You are going to be here next year anyway. But I am going to the US of A. I have already got my visa call to the US Consulate.' He breathed in deeply, to fill his chest with air and pride.

'I can't come here every year. I am getting married to a guy in the Merchant Navy, and I will be sailing around the globe with him,' Vandana announced.

We turned around to look at her, 'Really, Vandana? You are getting married?'

'Yes, this December. We finalized it this morning,' she said giggling.

There was a brief silence.

Finally, Preeto said, 'That's why you did the MBA, Vandana? To spend two years waiting to get married? So that you could carpet-bomb the matrimonial columns! I mean, how can you marry a stranger and trail him everywhere? What about your career?' Preeto was livid.

'So what, Preeto?' Mallika stepped forward to speak in Vandana's defence. 'I am also waiting to get married and be a homemaker. What's wrong with that?' She stroked Abhilaksh's arm. Abhilaksh appeared a bit troubled, but said nothing.

Vandana didn't say anything.

'Listen guys, stop quarrelling. It's our last day,' Karan said, as he tried to climb on to the chair once again.

'Why don't you talk from down here?' I tried to pull him down. 'Here, take this serving spoon in your hand and imagine it to be the mike, you ace debater. Then you won't get the urge to climb onto the podium.'

Everyone laughed aloud. But nothing could stop him. Karan clutched the large serving spoon in his right hand and climbed the shaky chair. He announced, 'Friends, Indians, and countrymen, lend me your ears.'

Komal giggled, 'He should have been in English MA. What is he doing here?'

Everyone guffawed and hooted.

Sandy whistled and said, 'Listen to him, guys. When on dope, he speaks the truth!'

A semblance of order descended around us momentarily. 'Go on, Karan,' Sandy exhorted him.

'I want to take a pledge, that come what may, on this day, the 20th of April, each year, wherever I might be on this globe, I shall return to meet all of you, my dearest, closest, loveliest, funniest, wittiest, and coolest pals. I shall be here. At StuCee. University campus, Chandigarh. For the rest of the years of my life.'

Sandy cheered him and pulled him down from the chair, and stood on it. 'I, Sandy, too pledge that each year I shall be back from the US of A, on this day, to be with our gang.' He paused and looked around. People stood surrounding the chair, looking at him with gaping mouths. There were amused by the melodrama of it all. And then, Mallika clapped. And then, Abhilaksh. And everyone else followed.

'Abhilaksh and I are also going to be here, this day, each year,' Mallika said and clutched Abhilaksh's hand and raised their hands in the air. 'And the party is going to be on us each year.'

'Why on you?' Preeto shouted.

'Because we are going to be the richest,' Mallika

shouted, upping her collars. 'Abhilaksh is going to be a businessman. I want him to be rich. So that he can spoil me!' She giggled.

'And the bill is going to be in my name, guys,' Preeto said aloud. 'Because I am going to be settled here. I am going to do my PhD and teach here, at this very campus. And StuCee gives thirty percent discount to the faculty. So, even if Mallika and Abhilaksh are going to pay, I will get the bill in my name and get them the discount.'

'But what's the point, man?' Sandy squeaked, 'They don't supply marijuana at StuCee. Who will pay for that?'

Everyone laughed. There was such euphoria as though the world had squeezed in to fill that little lawn with pure bliss just for us. At that moment, no other place on earth was filled with such joy.

14

WHEN WE LEFT THE CAMPUS, ALL IN DIFFERENT DIRECTIONS, toward different aims, goals and destinations, none of us realized that we would no longer be inseparable parts of each others' lives, the way we had been for the past two years, day in and day out. Fate and time tore us apart like the pulling of a cork from a wine bottle; our lives would never fit back into the same place. We got unscrambled like letters in a crossword puzzle, creating new meanings for our individual selves, rendering the original chaos dead. Henceforth, we were individuals in pursuit of our own dreams; our collective reality had been smudged, perhaps forever.

The day Sandy left for New Jersey, at midnight in May, no one from the gang was there to bid him adieu at the Delhi International Airport. Strangely, he had expected no one to be there. En route to the US, he later wrote to me in a hilarious e-mail, he dreamt he was watching a pole dancer. He woke up with a start just when the girl in his dream landed on his lap and was about to perform the American lap dance around his crotch. He jumped in fear that she might fleece him of all his dollars. As he woke up, he found himself hiding an erection from the air hostess who had been nudging him for some time, beckoning him to fill in the immigration form. I had laughed as I read the e-mail, but I was seething inside that my friend would be earning in dollars while I was not even earning.

Karan also took a flight—to Mumbai. He was alone at the Chandigarh airport, happy and excited at the impending fulfilment of his corporate dream. He resolved to give up marijuana, as it might nibble away at his intellect and reasoning, weakening his ability to assess market risks. Single malt whiskeys, a weekly game of golf, and stifling his raging libido was his formula to propel him up the banking ladder. He sent us pictures of his small cubicle in the Amex office at Worli, making sure he included the sexy receptionist too.

Mallika had nowhere to go. After university, when she joined cooking classes, no one from the gang was there to taste her recipes and tease her about her inadequate culinary skills. Her game plan was to watch TV serials in the afternoons, visit the gym in the evenings, and party hard each night on the crutches of the ample money that Abhilaksh would plough into the household furnace, month after month. She was completely satiated by her dream and did not miss the gang even a wee bit.

As for Abhilaksh, when he left for his summer internship at Metal Bearing Co., Faridabad, this time as an MBA intern, nobody from the gang was there to wish him luck. There, at the plant office reception, even the busty Rosy had almost forgotten him. I gues Abhilaksh missed me for a few hours in our old cubicle, for old time's sake; after all he was still a student and had not yet been bound by anxieties of dreams of a future. However, he wasn't too fond of me anyway and he was happy to have no competition in the ogling of Rosy. Moreover, there was nobody to share his oblong cubicle, in which, on a few lazy summer afternoons, he could even masturbate peacefully below his desk, straight-faced, looking at Rosy through the glass partition, with an expression of stoicism on his face. And thus, all the while, even Abhilaksh didn't think of the gang, except when he was periodically trailed and subbed by his would-be wife, Mallika.

Vandana got married in court one fine day, and there was no time for celebrations. Her husband Captain Anil Jain, the odd looking sailor with a toothbrush moustache and contrived smile, never got to meet the gang. He and Vandana had to catch his next vessel from Vizag, from where they were to sail to China. It was a vessel filled with iron ore, smelling of fuel and sweat, and was a far cry from the romantic *Titanic*. It disillusioned Vandana's dreams and yet unlike the *Titanic*, kept her afloat and alive. Her entire honeymoon, and perhaps most of her youth, would be marked and characterized by coitus at sea: copulating in sync with the big ship's movements. For the present, as she packed her bags and got her marriage certificate securely laminated at the uncle's shop next to StuCee, she had no time to think of the gang.

Preeto joined the PhD programme at university, acquired her maiden pair of reading glasses, and was already frowning upon the freshers and their pranks. She had turned into half-faculty, at least in her thoughts, mannerism, and dreams. Thin vertical scowl lines had gotten etched on her forehead. Another couple of lines and she would be a Reader; add a few strands of grey hairs at the temples and an inadequate nitwit as a husband, and she would be fit to be promoted to Professor. A few bespectacled, constipated kids buried beneath fat books later, she would be ready to be elevated to Dean of the B School. But for now, she was just doing her PhD and she never ever thought about the gang.

The gang had evaporated, except in my mind, the only one who was not yet wedded to a secure path. I was as confused and angry as ever. Often, I would go to StuCee and hang around, sipping sweet coffee and watch the stray dogs trying to outdo one another in entangling the sole bitch. On some weekends, I would take a bus to Delhi, go to Connaught Place, sit at the barricade across the huge Allahabad Bank Building, and just think. I thought about the gang: wondering what each one of them would be doing. My thoughts were just like me—aimless and random. I had no job, no plans, and no girl. I had no work, no aspiration, no killer instinct, and no peaks to conquer. So I was full of the gang and I was painfully lonely.

'But you must have some ambition in life,' Dad said to me one evening at the dining table.

I had no friends to hang out with, so whenever I wasn't at StuCee or loitering about engulfed in loneliness, I would be at home.

Mom had made rajmah, my favourite, and I relished her food after a long while.

'Let him eat in peace,' she whispered to Dad. She feared that I might get up and leave the table, the way I had done a couple of times during the past month.

'He needs to stop being at peace all the time, Sudha. I am worried,' Dad scowled at her and she went into the kitchen to fetch warm dal.

'Son, tell me. Is there a girl?' he asked. He was unusually soft.

I didn't have the energy to deny it. 'Yes, Dad. There was. And there is,' I replied.

'How long have you known her?' Dad persisted softly, like an interrogating cop .

'I mean to say, there was one girl. And now there is someone else.'

'So, you must forget the one who was. She's the past. And grab the one who is your present. Live in the present,' he said. 'Why don't you tell me about the present girl, son?'

'She is studying English. I want to marry her. Not now,

maybe later on,' I took a sip of water, and continued. 'She is a very good girl, Dad. '

'Then why not do so, son?'

Mom came in with hot dal. I kept quiet; I was shy and hesitant before my mother. Dad sent her back to the kitchen, asking her to re-heat the egg bhurji.

I continued, 'Dad, she is too good for me. I mean, I am not yet worthy of her.'

'I don't know what you mean by that but if you feel that you need to become worthy of acquiring her, you must work toward that goal. And while you do that, tell her to wait for you.'

What Dad said made some sense. Suddenly, I felt a rush of energy. The aim seemed clearer. I could never have Mallika and this time I did not want to lose Komal.

'But how do I do that, Dad? I have no job.'

'Son! Girls want a secure future and a well-stocked kitchen and wardrobe. Once these things are assured, they want lots of love and attention from the husband, respect from the kids, and freedom from their in-laws,' said Dad. He was being very wise today, wiser than Gabriel, the Archangel. I gaped at him wide-eyed, feeling the sparkle.

Mom came back with the egg bhurji, a bit too quickly, I thought. Microwaves, I cursed. She was pleased to see the transformation in my demeanour, and patted my back. 'Earn money, son,' she said. 'Lots of it. It will keep you busy.'

After dinner, I shut myself up in my room and thought

hard about my life. I thought about the rage that was building up inside me about my joblessness. I thought about the helpless feeling that overcame me when I saw everyone around me doing something with their lives. I hated the pseudo-sympathetic looks others gave me when they heard I had no job. I did not want to be the object of anyone's pity or jibes. In that moment, I was gripped by a steely resolve. Who needed a job in the first place, I thought to myself. It was only money that mattered. And I wanted lots of it. Dad was right—as long as I brought enough money home, I would be able to find a girl. And the world did not care if you were a saint or a crook, as long as you had a fat bank balance. So I resolved to get rich. I didn't need a job for that. I would start a business of my own, and would do whatever it took, to make it succeed.

'I will start a business, Dad,' I declacred to him the next day.

Dad smiled and nodded. 'What business do you have in mind?'

What I had in mind was a touchy subject for Dad, so I broached it carefully. 'Dad, I had seen a James Bond movie in which the villain creates land from an ocean bed. And he keeps saying that land is something that isn't manufactured; in fact, it is the rarest of the supplies, getting rarer every day.'

'Yes. That's right. So?' Dad raised an eyebrow, unsure of where I was heading.

'Dad, we have family land, thirty kilometres beyond Mohali. How big is it?'

'It's about ten acres. Our ancestral land,' he answered. 'And we have given it out for cultivation to the local farmers. They give us half of the crop, *bhag batai* you see.' The pride in Dad's voice didn't escape me.

'Yes, Viraat,' Mom added, 'your grandfather wanted to cultivate it but he died before he could retire from the school where he used to teach. We are city-bred people and don't know how to cultivate ourselves, so we gave it for *bhag batai*.'

'Your mother is right. We, urbanized, educated people, can't farm. How will *you*?'

'I am not talking of cultivating the land, Dad. What I'm saying is that a lot of city people want to own a piece of the countryside. They all crave for a second home, away from the madness of the city,' I was trembling with excitement as I spoke. I felt as though I was debating on the stage of the Youth Festival, with Karan on the other side of the spectrum, striving to outdo the ace debater. My arguments came out clear and emphatic.

'So? What are you trying to say?' Dad stopped eating.

'Dad,' I spoke slowly, 'I will parcel out our land into plots, make walkways, small roads, one common green area, and sell the plots.' I was excited, but still wasn't sure of my parents' reaction.

'Shut up, you idiot!' Dad shouted. 'In our family, we don't sell land. It's our tradition to keep and own land.'

He was furious and quivering. He looked at Mom and said, 'Your son wants to render us landless!'

Mom was bewildered. She said, 'Viraat, what are you saying? That is our only asset left.' She stood behind my chair and stroked my back, 'Son, don't you know that all the remaining land was taken away by the government under the land ceiling law and by your uncles, and some parts by encroachers? This one is the only property we're left with.'

'And this will also go away like that. Come on, Mom! What's the point of retaining an asset that's low paying but has so much latent value?' I looked at Dad, and continued softly, 'Dad, I will sell this as smaller plots, and with the money you can buy a much larger field to till and cultivate by the time you retire.'

He got up with a jerk, pushing back the chair he was sitting on, which fell with a crash. He was livid. Mom tried to stop him but he left the room in a huff. I had tears in my eyes. I sat there for a very long time, till my mother patted my head and said, 'Don't worry, I will convince him. By morning he will give in. I know him too well. He can't say no to his only son.' Then she held my chin and pulled my face up so that I was looking into her eyes. 'But, Viraat, this is our only asset. We were saving it as security for when we are old. It will ensure we are cremated well.'

'Mom, please don't be dramatic. Don't worry, I will cremate you well when the time comes.' I sounded silly even to myself. She scowled at first, and then broke into a laugh.

The next morning, Dad had agreed. The ten-acre farmland, not too far from Chandigarh, had huge potential, if the local farmer family who had been tilling it for the past two decades vacated it. Suddenly, I was filled with a sense of purpose.

Quickly, I set out to woo the farmer, bribe the patwari, and oil the revenue machinery. The ten-acre land saw de-greening after twenty long years. The peasant and his family were out in a week; the wheat had been harvested, and paddy was yet to come in, so it was the best time to weed out other useless things such as the green shrubs, vegetable plants, a noisy kerosene-operated tubewell motor, a band of stray dogs, three pigs, two cots, and an earthen pot. The land was finally in my hands. I promised a plot each to the patwari and the tehsildar, and got the land ready for sale. By mid-June I had struck a deal with a land broker to ensure quick sales.

My MBA had taught me the carrot and stick approach. It actually worked. People worked for my project, as I worked upon people, without any money to offer. I simply offered them dreams. I succeeded faster than I had ever succeeded with girls. Each of my twenty plots got sold. I called the project 'Green Paradise'. There was no greenery left though, and the paradise lay hidden in the dreams and fantasies that I sold. I made my first five million rupees in three months, more than what any of my MBA classmates would make in an entire year of slogging in their air-conditioned offices.

Land excited me far more than I had ever imagined even as I set out to wriggle my way through the stubborn, conniving and exasperating bureaucracy at the lower levels. My success depended on keeping them happy, and I figured it was futile to take the high moral ground when all around me, life thrived on favours and favouritism. It was the way of the world and I was determined to make the most of it and earn my happiness rather than get weighed down by morals. I had seeped through the system like ink in blotting paper.

Sooner than I realized, I had ceased to be the idealistic young university graduate. I had given up my jeans like a snake shedding it skin. Unknowingly, I had embarked upon an image makeover so that the farmers, the patwaris, the tehsildars and other thugs who infested the government offices, felt comfortable enough to be bribed. I gave up cappuccino, slang-ridden English, T-shirts perfumed kerchiefs and fake branded sunglasses. I had transformed almost overnight: embracing loose pants with short crumpled kurtas. The kurta had deep pockets for carrying things like small bribes, the keys of my newly acquired old Maruti 800, and a comb to keep my now oily hair down. I wore dusty sandals.

The change was so sudden that my mother, the gardener, the milkman were all astonished. The lust for money had transformed me into a totally different human being. I was a different man altogether: I became Nijhawan-ji to the farmers and patwaris. My surname obliterating my first name was perhaps a sign of success; something that I thought happened to many as they grew up from students to working men. And with the suffix 'ji' added to my surname, I knew I mattered. Finally.

Occasionally, I met Komal, just to ensure that her mind and heart had bits and pieces of me to remember. When I met her, I got into my old, youthful avatar—washed the oil off my hair, wore jeans and replaced the crumpled, earth-smeared kurta with a T-shirt.

It was Monday evening. Komal looked lissom, fresh and well rested. I was tired, and thoughts of an impending land permission kept nudging me the whole time I was with her. We sat on the steps going down to Sukhna Lake. That was our usual meeting spot: secluded for me, yet safe for Komal. She silently stared at the ripples of water, as I tossed little pebbles into them.

'So, Komal, what's happening in life?' I whispered, playing with her hair.

'Everything except you is happening with my life.' She turned toward me and looked into my eyes. There was a tinge of sadness there.

'I mean, how are your studies going?' I was unsure of what I really wanted to say, and so I blabbered.

'Studies! Well, it's cool. I happen to be studying

218

English Literature, not Business Management. So it's nothing great,' she shrugged.

'All fields are equally important, Komal.'

'Come on, Viraat, you know that's bullshit. Many girls like me are admitted into courses like these so that they remain busy till their parents find a suitable boy for them. You know that.'

I kept silent and looked back into the lake. The monsoon had set in and the air was sultry.

'Suitable boy! So, your parents are already thinking of marrying you off?'

'Why not? What else will I do with a degree in English Literature?'

'You could do journalism or write content to earn. Maybe become an author too.'

'Journalists in print have to turn into blackmailers to survive and support their families. And authors and writers in India can't make a career out of writing unless they create huge controversies or win big awards.' She sighed. 'I can't do either. So perhaps I will get married in a year or two. And join cooking classes till then.'

There was silence. Perhaps she expected me to say something. But I was too young. I still wanted to make a lot of money, buy a Mercedes and buy my parents a big house in Sector 5 after my dad's retirement. I liked her a lot but I was still unsure whether I was ready to commit to her. But I did not want to lose her either. So the silence hung heavily between us. I looked at Komal sitting by my side. She was beautiful, in a different way from Mallika. Mallika was fairer, Komal was taller; Mallika giggled much more, had fuller lips and amazing energy; Komal was more intense and brooding. Thoughts of Mallika had finally loosened their grip over me. I did not know if Komal was the one for me, but that did not matter. I was free and I was successful too.

'Komal, you know I am going to be rich soon,' I tried to divert her thoughts away from marriage.

She looked at me, broke into a smile, and patted my back. 'How soon?' she asked.

I liked her but I didn't want to ruin her marriage prospects by asking her to wait for me. I simply said, 'Pretty soon.'

We got up and climbed the stairs to the promenade around the water. I wanted to hold her hand and she seemed willing, but the thought of matrimony cautioned me. Slowly we walked toward the entrance façade. There was nothing pleasant around, except Komal. I wanted to kiss her but held myself back. We kept strolling toward the gate. Occasional joggers—sweaty, burly men in shorts—huffed past us. Looking at those joggers, I became concerned about my own fitness levels and physique, and hoped Komal found me attractive. I glanced at her, but she was looking at the darkening waters of the lake. The last dark patch, a hundred yards before the big entrance façade, was my only chance to kiss her. Softly, I touched her palm. She slowed down her pace, perhaps giving me this last chance for the possibility of our second kiss. I held her hand firmly and she stood still. She looked up and came closer. The sounds of distant dogs and splashing waters added to the symphony of my heartbeats; the three sounds working like an orchestra. I felt a bit jittery; the thought of marriage scared me a bit, but soon enough my libido spurred me and I held her in an awkward embrace, tight and hurting.

She looked up and whispered softly, 'Kiss me, Viraat.' I bent and placed my trembling lips over hers. It wasn't too long I was sure, when, all of a sudden, someone grabbed me by the neck, pulling me back violently. He twisted my arm and another turbaned man punched my face. I cried out in pain. Warm liquid flowed down my nose and into my mouth. I realized that I was bleeding. Komal shrieked in horror and scampered away toward the main gate. She ran as fast as she could and didn't even turn back to see my fate.

'You sister-fucker,' a familiar voice bellowed. 'Sleeping with other people's wives!' The two Sardars rained blows on me for a long time. I had curled up like a foetus. It was the librarian Sardar, and perhaps his brother. I was writhing in pain and yet the blows did not stop. I was happy that Komal had run away and had not heard when the beaters yelled again and again, 'You fucker! Bastard! Spoiling our women!'

'Enough, bhaisahab,' one of them said after what

seemed like an eternity. 'Let's go now.' And they left.

After a very long time, I got up with a lot of effort and limped toward the gate. No one paid me any attention. Torn shirt, bleeding nose, ruffled hair, dusty clothes—I walked to the parking lot and sat in my car. Slowly, I twisted the key and as the car cranked to life, I smiled and muttered, 'My debt to the librarian's brother has been paid off.'

The dusty car swerved toward Madhya Marg, gurgling and speeding all the way back home. Being beaten up was nothing unusual in the land business, so I didn't have much difficulty explaining my predicament to my mother. I was just glad that both my mom and Komal didn't know the truth.

15

DIWALI AND DHANTERAS SPURRED PEOPLE'S SHOPPING sprees. I was already launching my third project, grander than the first two. I had registered my firm and opened an office on an encroached piece of land next to Omi Dhaba. I had dutifully paid off the slimy small-time functionaries to turn a blind eye. I had also paid Omi for letting me put up a prominent red and yellow hoarding that read 'Fast Track Real Estate'; the name intrigued everyone.

I knew I had just six months more to prove myself before the gang congregated at StuCee, exactly a year after graduating. I wanted to buy my own Toyota before that, so that I could take everyone out for a ride, with Mallika seated in the front with me. For the reason of speed, it had to be the 'Fast Track Real Estate Pvt Ltd'.

Business boomed. I offered a 20 percent discount to the university teachers and staff, after escalating the price by 30 percent. More than a third of my plots got sold in the 'happy hours', mostly to the university staff, simply because of the visibility of the hoarding.

The office had two brick and mortar rooms without the plaster, though there was an AC that vibrated noisily and continuously like the televised proceedings of the Legislature. There was a wooden table draped in a green tablecloth that looked like a curtain from an ophthalmic ward of a government hospital. There was a rugged revolving chair on which I sat, staring at my prey—the small plot buyers filled with anticipation—who sat opposite me on a couple of uncomfortable chairs that got the full blast of the icy AC, which was meant to ensure the numbing of their brains. In the adjoining room sat two thugs whom I had employed; they were school dropouts, sons of the local police head constable, and were best suited for recovering outstanding dues from customers and passing part of it to the police and the patwaris. Wads of soiled money lay scattered in my drawer along with the 'kutcha register' or a ledger for noting the account of black money received and disbursed. The account was scribbled in pencil, and could be erased, smudged, fudged, forged or destroyed, depending on the situation. There goes the lesson on double entry computerized entry system taught by Prof. Gupta, I mused each time I scribbled numbers into that ledger. My MBA degree was just a waste, I often felt, as I counted the wads of money; it was something that had to be effectively unlearned, in order to be able to make filthy money in real life.

In the three months that followed, I had finished selling the plots and had also acquired more land from farmers from the surrounding villages. These farmers may have been illiterate but they drove a hard bargain. I learned it was wiser to pay them generously, perhaps even more than the market rates, so that I could get possession of their land swiftly and without trouble. Almost seventy percent of the entire transaction was in hard, unaccounted cash. I could feel the pulse of the parallel economy of black money that I had studied about in my MBA.

I set up a cycle of buying agricultural land, converting it to non-agricultural usage by paying bribes liberally, advertising aggressively, putting nicely designed hoardings on the sites, arranging site visits in AC vans each Sunday, giving hefty discounts to middlemen and other brokers, and offloading the plots at five times the price of acquisition. Just parcelling out land into smaller units unfolded a value that wasn't possible in another business. I never imagined so much hunger existed in society for land.

One Monday afternoon, Preeto came to see me, after her classes. She had heard from the Dean about the brilliant land business that I had set up right opposite the university. The Dean had heard of my success in the realty business and wanted her to invite me to give a lecture on 'Business Ethics' since the question of ethics was so practically played out in my field.

'Business Ethics!' Preeto laughed her head off, as she

225

sat facing me, glancing at every inch of 'unethicalness' that suffused the little unauthorized office space of Fast Track Real Estate Pvt. Ltd. I joined her with my uproarious laughter.

The burly thug stuck his head in to see if everything was okay. Assured that the lady seated in the boss's room was too academic, pimpled, freckled and speckled to be a threat, he resumed digging his ear wax.

'But why? I can surely lecture them on Business Ethics and the futility of it—on how to keep ethics at bay,' I said as I took a sip from the tiny glass of sweetened tea, the surface of which was layered with brown cream.

Preeto giggled. She looked around: uneven bricks gaped from behind chipped whitewash on the wall behind my chair. A cobweb swayed above my head where the low ceiling met the uneven brick wall. There, one fat, blue-eyed fly trapped inside a cobweb danced the dance of death. Preeto looked at me—oily hair, a big dangling wristwatch, and a white kurta with sleeves folded till the biceps. 'Viraat,' she muttered softly, 'You certainly look different.'

'Of course,' I smiled. Even my smile had turned vile. 'I have to don the clothes required by my profession. It's our uniform. Like cops, army men and firemen have uniforms, like pilots and even the whores of Amsterdam have uniforms, so do us property dealers.'

Preeto squirmed and looked at the ceiling. I had changed so much in the six months that she didn't know how to relate to me. Just to change the topic, she chuckled, 'And you look a bit healthier too.' I had decidedly gained weight. I didn't say anything to that one.

A sleepy land official was escorted in by one of the thugs. I stared at him with big eyes, opened my drawer, took out a wad of cash and tossed it on the table, Gandhi-side up. 'Here, Ram Chandji. Take! It's ten thousand.'

'But you had said twenty!' the sleepy patwari protested. The thug behind him patted his back and said, 'Take whatever sahib is giving. He knows the Collector. And the SP, CBI also.' Acquaintance with high-ranking officials amounted to savings, and so the unhappy patwari reluctantly left the room.

'Sorry, Preeto. So where were we?' I cleared my throat like a village elder. 'Yes, the lecture to students. Sure, whenever you say.'

Preeto nodded.

'How are the others?'

'Well, they keep in touch sometimes. They write or call at times,' she said, putting down the empty tea cup on the table.

'And where is everyone?' In my rush to make it big in my business, I had not kept up with my friends, either on the Internet or their mobiles. At first, I had deliberately distanced myself from them because they all had jobs and I didn't. When my own business started to take off, I found it awkward to find my way back into their lives. My life had changed so much from the B School days.

I was not the cool, reserved youngster anymore. I had transformed into a cunning, kurta-clad wheeling-and-dealing businessman.

'Mallika is home, having done a course in cookery, make-up, and home science. Evening courses. During the day, she prepares term papers and notes for Abhilaksh, who, of course, is enjoying himself thoroughly. Sandy is in America, as you know, I think doing a job somewhere and struggling daily to survive. On weekends he mows his small lawn and sweeps his car bonnet and shops for the week,' she said.

'And what about Karan?'

'He is enjoying Mumbai, commuting between Goregaon and Nariman Point in the morning and returning the same route each evening, cursing Mumbai traffic, and missing the serene roads of Chandigarh. In between the two commutes, he remains harassed in the corporate rigmarole. He told me how much he missed our debating trips to various colleges, winning trophies, and winking at girls' backs while walking the Sukhna Lake promenade.'

'Oh! So no one seems happy!' I felt a bit sad. 'When we were students, we could hardly wait for the damn course to end and get to be masters of our own destinies. And now! Look at everyone.'

'I swear!' Preeto sighed, 'But you seem happy, Viraat. Making money, sitting so close to the university, having your own office and flexible working hours.'

I wasn't sure. Money always took away all flexibility. I asked, 'And what about Vandana? She must be sailing the globe.'

'Oh, she is fine. She once called me from Sicily or some place. She seemed excited.' Preeto leaned forward to whisper, 'Though she confided in me that her sailor husband was a big boozer and drank so much all the time that he could hardly make her happy. You know what I mean,' she said and winked.

I guffawed, suddenly feeling proud of my own virility.

'And you seem really happy, Preeto?' I asked her softly, trying not to sound too intrusive.

'I am happy, Viraat. I always wanted to teach, and that's what I am doing. So it's fine. And I wanted to thank you guys, you and Sandy.'

'For what?' I didn't get what she was saying.

'You guys enticed that Sardar librarian's wife. He left her. They have filed for a divorce. And the chap has proposed to me. Librarian getting married to the Reader in the same department!'

'Oh really! Wow, that's great. Congratulations, Preeto!' I didn't know whether to feel happy for Preeto or sorry for Harwinder. The blows from the two Sardar brothers still stung.

'I think they were a wrong match. She was a nice girl but wasn't cut out for him. He needed someone more academically inclined. Someone who is as passionate about the library as he is. Someone who can grow old talking about books and acquiring reading glasses along the way!' Preeto smiled.

'And tell me one thing, Preeto,' I asked her softly. 'You didn't mind a divorcé? I mean you never had someone else in mind?'

She paused for a moment, trying to find the right words, and then spoke, 'Viraat, I believe I wanted someone who is gentle, mature and understanding; someone who isn't necessarily ambitious, who is around me, even though silent and unresponsive, or even unromantic,' Preeto made a lot of sense and I nodded. 'He understands me. And we work at the same place. He also has a university quarter allotted, has a permanent job, pension, gratuity, and provident fund. He has no plans of leaving Chandigarh. And so when my parents grow old, I can still be around for them. I can continue to enjoy the lake and the wide roads, the hills in the backdrop, and the serenity of this place while the world elsewhere is spinning mad. I have always been forced to be independent, with my father getting posted all over the country. I think I want some stability in my marriage.'

Another way to look at things! It surprised me and made my acidic ambition seem alien to me for a moment. What was I running after, compensating for the loss of Mallika by trying to win the world? I wasn't sure.

'I am so happy for you, Preeto.'

'Thank you. And can we fix up your lecture some day?'

'Preeto, come on, I am not the kind of person who'd be an ideal to follow. I don't deserve to pollute the minds of students.'

Preeto patted my shoulder. She seemed to understand. I was not the same Viraat who had studied with her six months back. Now I was a devious property dealer, loaded with money but devoid of morality. Yet I was her friend, and classmates would always remain attached to one's sweetest memories.

'Bye, Viraat,' she said. 'And use some of that money to clear those spider webs!'

I smiled and nodded. Preeto left. She was nicer than I ever thought, much nicer than Mallika.

The rest of the day, I was a bit pensive. I left early. I decided to go for a jog around the lake. I parked my car and tried jogging around the grassy promenade. I missed the old days and even the pain associated with them. I tried jogging fast but after a bit, I felt breathless and sat on the wall that abutted the rim of the lake. I wasn't as fit as I was six months ago. I couldn't imagine that it would take only six months for me to descend so deeply into weary worldliness.

I dragged myself back to the car. Diwali was approaching and the chill in the air had become perceptible like new money is on middle class people. It was just catching on, nip turning to chill, and yet, I had beads of cold sweat dancing on my brow.

I sat in the car and watched the hawkers being fleeced by municipal staff. A mad beggar woman with grimy, knotted, lice-infested hair passed by and laughed aloud. I snapped out of my reverie and rolled up the glass. I started the car and switched on the stereo. An old Mukesh song filled the air with more sadness, and I quickly turned it off. 'Damn! Why were old films full of sad songs,' I cursed.

Meeting Preeto again didn't really help, even though she had been nice to me. 'Live in the present,' I said to myself. Suddenly, I felt like a drink. A lot of it. I turned on the car engine and drove to the Lake Club.

I parked the car and entered the pub 'The Drinking Zone' at the Lake Club. The boisterousness of the place filled me with relief and squeezed all thoughts and reflections out of my brain. I made my way through the noisy drinking men and went straight to the bar counter. 'Pour me a Solan Number 1 whiskey, double, with soda and lots of ice,' I said to the bartender. The bartender was disinterested and impersonal, he smiled at no one in particular. 'Bartenders always poured 5 ml less and made one drink for themselves out of six drinks served,' Sandy had once told me, advising me to always get my drink poured in front of my eyes.

I drank fast, as I didn't really know how to drink alcohol. The swivelling bar stool kept me busy. There were big, fat, noisy and loud people all around. It was a cheap bar and attracted noisy customers. However, I liked the noise; it helped me drown my thoughts. And that evening, I drank faster than ever. Things and people around me grew more agreeable in a while. The bartender seemed to be smiling more; the smile quotient seemed to increase with every peg I ordered. The white kurta and blue jeans would have been a very uncool thing to wear in the university campus but I realized that a lot of men around me at the bar wore such desi couture. It seemed the done thing in a bar like this which brimmed with the new rich.

The swivelling stool gave me the advantage of being able to survey the entire room. There were sunken sofas and lazy waiters, there were sooty ashtrays and thin columns of cigarette smoke rising from almost each congregation. There were peanuts, wafers, and popcorn strewn on most tables, like sea shells lying scattered on a coast post the ebbing of a high tide. Dangling from the roof, dim light bulbs collectively managed to produce a joke of an illumination.

'One last drink, please,' I pushed my glass toward the bartender. Then I asked, just for the sake of sobriety, 'This would be the fifth large. Right?'

The bartender smiled from ear to ear and nodded, 'Sir, why count? You are in perfect shape. Drink till you can.'

I felt proud. Bartenders really knew how to make a virtue out of the art of boozing. 'But I have to drive back.' Somehow I felt I had the ability to clear off the vapour of drunkenness from my mind by a mere mental command. 'One should develop the ability to look and feel sober in bouts and jerks, in between the continuum of drunkenness,' Sandy's words of wisdom echoed in my mind, 'Whenever you start drinking, practice the art of returning to soberness, intermittently.'

'How does one do that?' I had quizzed.

'Man, didn't you read in the book I gave you, on sex education, how you can be a more satisfying lover?'

'What?' I had looked up, rubbing my eyes.

'There is a technique which all men must practice if they want to be good lovers. When you piss, don't do it in one go, but instead, hold your bladder half way through, and then piss again. In a "go-stop-go-stop-go" way. That's the way you must urinate. It's an exercise that helps a man gain better self-control in bed.'

'Ya, I do that all the time. That's why my commode is full of urine spots!' Karan had joined in, guffawing aloud.

'Shut up, Karan. I don't want to hear you preach,' I had shouted. 'But, Sandy, what's the relation between drinking and the urine stopping exercise?'

'Self-control man, self-control,' Sandy had said. 'That's what makes a man a real man. When you drink, never get carried away. Be conscious, count your pegs, and keep telling yourself that you are okay. You must be able to count people, walk straight.'

That was what I was trying at the moment, and it seemed to work. I rose up to go to the toilet, and as I walked past people, I consciously tried to be observant and perceptive. People, chairs, tables, peanuts, chicken drumsticks, cocktail samosas, sodden tissue napkins, and the corridor toward the toilet—everything was clear. I wasn't drunk at all and could perhaps have another drink, I told myself confidently.

As I was about to turn toward the corridor that led to the restroom, I suddenly heard a familiar feminine voice. There, in a dark corner, I noticed a couple seated around a small round table for two, which was in an alcove in the wall that gave them privacy. A dim bulb hung above the table, and from where I was standing I couldn't make out their faces. The lady was laughing drunkenly.

I stood still, ignoring the pressure in my groin. I listened intently. The feminine voice rose above the rest. My eyes bulged as I expanded my pupils to look into the dark. The man had a fat neck and seemed to be smoking a pipe. The woman was laughing and giggling. The man smoked his pipe and turned his face sideways to release smoke away from where the woman sat. Twice, the man leaned over, held his pipe away, and kissed the woman on her lips, and then turned to smoke the pipe again. It was an alternating action: turning the pipe away, kissing the woman, then taking a puff—as though the pipe smoke was a mouth freshener that stifled his bad breath.

I moved closer to them and stood silently. 'Oh darling,' the woman was saying, 'we must travel more often like this. It's so much fun. In the office, I can't even smile at you.'

'Yes, darling,' the man said, his voice was heavy and deep. 'We do travel, sweetiepie. This is our fourth trip in a year.' The man was balding and had a thick neck and fat shoulders. The woman had short hair and seemed much younger. Her shoulders were smooth and sexy in the sleeveless top she had on. I moved a little closer to see who she was and then froze. I was so close that perhaps the man sensed the presence of another human being behind him and swiftly turned back, rose up with a start, and looked completely startled when he saw me. The man was speechless, as he tugged at the woman, pulling her up by the arm. The woman looked up, gave out a small scream and stood up. 'Viraat, is that you?' she stammered.

'Yes, Rosy, it's me,' I said coldly. 'And nice to see you here, sir. In this mood,' I said sarcastically. The man was Ashok Kumar Nigam, the GM!

The alcohol inside me had been metabolized and its liquid residues were swirling inside me so much that I wanted to rush to the restroom and empty out my bladder. But the moment was too significant to be skipped. I laughed aloud and said, 'So Mr Nigam. Do you recognize me? This is me, Viraat Nijhawan, your ex-intern. I live here in Chandigarh.'

The man and the woman stood still. His face was flushed and Rosy was trembling.

'I am the same Viraat who had almost got a good job through the campus interview. The one who was almost picked up by a nice, fat gentleman called KK Nigam, who happened to call you to break the news to you, and unfortunately for me and perhaps for him, he happens to be your brother! And you screwed up my career!' I shouted so loud that two stewards rushed to the table.

'What's the matter, sir?' asked the head steward. They were too stunned to say anything, because by then I had climbed on their table and was shouting, 'Ladies and gentlemen, lend me your ears.' I almost felt like Karan at the podium. People around turned to look at the ruckus.

'Please, Viraat, for my sake, stop it,' Rosy pleaded.

'For your sake! This man screwed my happiness. And here he is, flirting with you!' I screamed, looked at the trembling couple, and suddenly broke into loud laughter.

Some people had stood up and were watching with interest. I did not stop. I wanted to settle scores with the man who had done me so much damage.

'Here, gentlemen, is Mr Ashok Kumar Nigam from Faridabad—the top-notch General Manager of the top-notch Metal Bearing Co. And this fine lady here is Rosy, fifteen years younger to him—his office receptionist.' People encircled the table on which I stood. 'This man is a symbol of morality. He seldom smiles. Doesn't allow his young daughter to have boyfriends and enjoy herself. This is pure corporate sexual dominance and exploitation.' I took a swig from Nigam's glass that lay on the table. Nigam's glass had better whiskey, perhaps a single malt, and so I gulped down the whole thing. At least a thousand rupees loss to Nigam, I thought, by then feeling quite drunk.

My bladder was bursting but I continued. 'And this villain, this Mogambo of my life, totally screwed up my career. Because of him, I couldn't get a job. And today, here I am, a wretched property dealer.' I shouted. 'Rich enough, but still a wretched property dealer.' I teetered on the edge of the table, lost my balance and managed to jump down. I punched him in the stomach and screamed, 'THIS MAN HERE! NIGAM. THIS RASCAL IS SCREWING HIS RECEPTIONIST!'

There was complete silence. A press photographer clicked a few photos of the ruckus, as Rosy and Nigam hid their faces. I left them there and tottered toward the toilet.

I opened my fly on the way as I entered the restroom and relieved myself in the right place. I washed my hands, splashed water on my face, smiled into the mirror, and shouted, 'JUSTICE!'

Life was good; it afforded me a chance to settle my scores.

16

'HOW ARE YOU DOING, SLEEPY HEAD?' KARAN'S VOICE echoed in my ear, rather early on that winter morning.

I rubbed my eyes and spoke into the phone, 'Hey Karan! It's early. And so cold.' I looked out of the window to see a thick pall of fog. It was the first day of the New Year and last night's party at a local MLA's farmhouse had lasted till the wee hours of the morning. My head was throbbing with the amount of alcohol I had consumed. 'You corporate guys don't celebrate the New Year or what?'

'No, man; today's a working day. And in the corporate world we have to be on time, every single day.' Karan had pride in his voice, and it surprised me.

'Corporate slaves,' I muttered softly so that Karan would not hear, before adding audibly, 'Good for you, you corporate honcho.'

'What about you, Viraat?' Karan asked. Over the phone,

he sounded like an All India Radio newsreader from the 1950s.

'Well, I went to a wild party last night, which was attended by some of the most powerful people around.' I could hear the cynicism in my own voice. I wasn't proud of partying with rustic politicians and semi-literate land mafia, drinking large swigs of Peter Scot with full soda, watching a Ukrainian belly dancer especially flown in from Mumbai gyrate for the crowd, tandoori chicken drumsticks and cigarette butts strewn all around the venue. The entire scene would have been unimaginable to any member of the gang. What a contrast to last year's party at StuCee, with coffee and poori channa. *How had I changed so much over the past year?* I wondered.

'So, what else? How are you doing?' I asked.

'I am doing fine, earning a decent living.' Karan spoke, and then lowering his voice, he whispered, 'But listen. Have you met Mallika of late?'

'No, I met Preeto around Diwali. But for the past two months, I've been out of touch. Too busy with my projects.' This time I felt proud. 'You see, we are launching this golf course plot scheme next month after Uttarayan.'

'Listen,' Karan didn't seem interested in my work, and that irked me a bit. 'Mallika has not been herself of late.' There was concern in his voice.

I sat up on my bed and asked, 'Why? What happened to her?'

'She had a nervous breakdown.' It was incredible how

Karan's voice seemed to drawl and linger over the phone.

'What!' I jumped out of bed. The cold marble under my feet wasn't as cold as the words that came in from the other side. 'What are you saying, Karan? A nervous breakdown? And Mallika? This isn't possible. You must be joking.'

'No, Viraat,' Karan was serious. 'This is why I've called you. You should go and meet her. Find out what happened and then call me back.' We quickly said our goodbyes and hung up.

In the next half an hour, I was heading for Mallika's house in Sector 15. The city was sleepy, and the hangover from last night's party seemed to suffuse the air everywhere. Past the closed shops, past the faulty traffic signal, past the roadside shoe cobblers and the empty auto rickshaw stand, the familiar route took me to house number 376.

While ringing the doorbell, I felt a chill engulf my heart. I was beginning to get scared when Mr Mattoo opened the door. He was sleepy and less cheerful than his normal self.

'Hello, Viraat,' he said, extending a limp hand. 'Seeing you after a long time. How have you been?'

I folded my hands and said Namaste to him. 'I heard Mallika is a bit unwell, uncle?' I whispered. There was an air of grimness and morbidity to my voice that I was trying my best to hide. *She is still alive, damn it,* I reprimanded myself. *Don't sound so glum!*

'Go and ask her yourself, if you can elicit a reply,' Mr

Mattoo heaved a sigh. 'I have been more unwell than her, actually. She is just confused and sad. Something to do with Abhilaksh, I believe.' He showed me to the stairs.

On the first floor, I knocked at her door thrice, each time with increasing firmness. When there was no reply, I pushed the door open and peeped in. The curtains had been drawn and the room was wrapped in deliberate darkness. The bed looked dishevelled and despite the wintery air outside, the room felt stuffy as I peered inside. The left corner of the room had a bay window and a cushioned seat where I could see Mallika sitting now, reclined against a big cushion, her hair ruffled, and face peering out of the window. There was an air of purposelessness about her.

'Hey, Mallika,' I said softly, as I let myself in, closing the door behind me. Mallika turned toward me slowly and merely nodded an acknowledgement of my presence. She did not smile. From a distance, I could see the bags under her eyes. She looked so different and so morose. I walked up to her and drew the curtain aside. A stream of sunlight flowed in, illuminating the floating dust particles along the length of the rays. 'What happened, Mallika?' I spoke so gently that my own voice seemed alien to myself.

'How are you, Viraat?' She was listless.

'I am fine, Mallika. But what happened to you?' I stood close and stroked her hair. I was amazed at myself for this spontaneous show of affection.

'Just upset. And sad,' she whispered. 'You had no

time to check up on me, Viraat?' She dug her nails into my forearm and pulled me closer. She took my hand and buried her face in my palm, wetting it with her tears.

'I am so sorry, Mallika. I thought you were happy with Abhilaksh and I busied myself with work.' I continued stroking her hair, 'Had I known you were not well, I would have come running.'

She got up, pulled the pink plastic chair from the computer table and asked me to sit down, 'What will you have?' she asked and then hastily said, 'I'm sorry I can't offer you anything, as dad is alone at home. And he hasn't been keeping well.'

'Don't worry about me. I don't want anything. But tell me, what happened? I am really concerned,' I had never been so worked up about anything as I was about this woman now.

She remained silent for a long time, gazing aimlessly at the ceiling, where there as nothing to look at, not even an insect-gobbling lizard. I waited for her to break the silence. Her effervescence, her charm, her enthusiasm, the zing in her voice, the sassiness in her laugh had all disappeared.She seemed like a completely different person. I was saddened by what had happened to her, yet I remained still and silent.

'Abhilaksh isn't what I thought he was!' she finally said. 'He cheated on me!' There was a long silence, and I felt a strange pleasure run through my spine at her words. My own reaction surprised me, but I was no longer sad. In fact

I was pleased that Abhilkash was the cause of her sadness.

'Really?' There was excitement in my voice, 'What did he do?'

'I would rather you ask me about all the things I did for him!' she sobbed. 'I kicked a great job offer in Mumbai to be with him in Chandigarh. I wrote all his term papers and assignments. I took all those stupid cooking classes just to equip myself, unlearning my MBA skills and learning the skills of a housewife, just so that I could marry him once he finished his studies and got a job. He never wanted his wife to work, so I sacrificed all my dreams for him, all my ambitions. I ignored my parents' wishes to marry a Kashmiri boy and forced them to agree to the idea of me marrying a Punjabi. I cut off contact with all my friends and focused all my attention on him and only him. And after all this, he cheated on me.' By now she was crying uncontrollably. I held her for some time and then poured a glass of water for her from a mug that was lying on the ironing table.

'Silly boy, this water's from the bathroom,' she suddenly giggled. 'I had filled it to iron my dupatta.' I laughed aloud and she joined me. It was a strange and sudden shift from crying to giggling. 'You are as clumsy as ever, you lazy oaf.' She thwacked my back. 'Go and get me drinking water from the fridge.'

When I was back I asked, 'So tell me what that bugger did?'

'We were having a big fight over his plan of settling

abroad, in Canada,' Mallika spoke slowly, sipping the water from the bottle. 'I wanted him to stay in Chandigarh, so that I could look after dad. You can see he is growing old faster than I thought.'

'Ya, I just met him. He seemed pale and unwell.'

'Yes, I wanted Abhilaksh to settle in Chandigarh or Delhi. He wants to go to Canada. We had a long argument on the issue. Then, I finally gave in and told him we would go to Canada together.'

'Then?'

'Then he said that he wanted to go alone first in order to settle in properly. He wants to start a taxi business in Toronto and own a fleet of taxis. And then eventually open a restaurant. He told me that he wants to establish himself professionally and then come back and decide when to marry me.'

'That is ridiculous. It could take several years.'

'Yes! And I am older to him by a year. By the time he is settled, I will be in my thirties. And then he'll come and "decide" when to marry me!' Mallika was livid.

'So, what happened finally?'

'He applied for a work visa but his visa application got rejected. And now he wants to legally marry a Canadian Sikh girl, his family friend's daughter, get Canadian citizenship, and then he says he will divorce her and marry me. Can you believe that!'

'What a wretch,' I shouted. I felt a sense of wicked joy, a feeling of 'I- told-you-so' seeped through me. 'Don't worry,

Mallika, I will take care of you!' I wanted to say, 'I will marry you, maintain your expensive shopping sprees and your spa visits. Just dump that bastard!' I wanted to say all that, but did not. Pure tact prevented me from venting out my excitement. Instead, I said nothing.

I went back to visit her again in the evening, and then the next day and the next. In about five visits, I could open her up to the idea of going out for coffee to StuCee. In about a fortnight, we were close again. Mallika seemed to have obliterated the painful experience with Abhilaksh from her psyche, although some of the effects still lingered. I had started jogging to lose weight; I replaced my crumpled white kurtas with trendy T-shirts. On the work front, the thugs at my office had become worried—the golf course plotting project clearances were not being pursued and the scheme was getting delayed. The customer payments and the bribe payouts were all getting delayed and jumbled up. The Omi Dhaba guy had refused to extend time for our hoarding due to non-payment of dues, so the village headman and the farmers would wait at the office endlessly and leave cursing. Yet even amid all this I was happy. I did not care for anything other than Mallika and our time together.

Komal tried to call me a couple of times and left a few messages. She even came home once on a Monday, an off day for the real estate business. But I escaped from the back door, jumping over the back hedge, taking my servant's Luna to escape in time to meet Mallika at StuCee. I was wrapped up in Mallika all over again, and nothing else seemed to matter. I was in a state of pure bliss. Business, parents, drinking, money, power, ambition, drive, dreams, and aspirations—none of it seemed important. I was brimming with happiness and joy. Yes, I was in love.

But was she in love too? I wondered at times, as we walked each evening along the lakeside promenade, or as I listened to her chatter endlessly, seated in StuCee. But the answer wasn't important. What was important was my own sense of contentment while she was around. In a month's time, I had succeeded in restoring Mallika back to her old self. She blossomed back to her exuberant self.

'You know what, Viraat? Abhilaksh is quitting his MBA, just three months before the end of the final term!' Mallika said softly, looking down at her own pretty feet, twitching her big toe. Her unpainted big toe was more beautiful than the Koh-I-Noor diamond, I thought; my gaze following her as always. I loved that when she was around, nothing else mattered.

'Really!' I muttered, absent-mindedly, gazing at her feet. It did not matter if Abhilaksh was quitting, but in that instant I realized that perhaps it should matter. It could be better for me if he left earlier. Three months was good enough for Abhilaksh to vanish from the scene.

'Yes. Saleena, the Canadian girl, is here next week. She has come to pick him up. As in, marry him and fly him off to Canada.'

'Oh,' I didn't know what to say that might suppress my own excitement at the prospect of Abhilaksh's early departure.

'She gave him an ultimatum. For the next one year, she has no leave available from the bank she works in.' Mallika was smiling now, 'And the funny thing is that her parents had booked everything in advance: the caterer, the reception hall at the Taj in sector 17, even the granthi at the Gurudwara to solemnize the marriage. All sitting in Canada; over the phone. And so, she and her parents are flying in on Friday and the next Sunday they are getting married. On Wednesday, Abhilaksh will apply for citizenship and wait.'

'But why does he have to quit his MBA just three months before the finals?' I mumbled. My tone belied the concern I was trying to feign.

'I also asked him the same thing but he says he doesn't find the MBA degree useful anymore. Besides, Saleena wants him to spend a few months in Delhi sitting at his would-be-uncle's taxi stand on Janpath, learning the tricks of the trade here in Delhi. Saleena told him that's the best school, the taxi stand on Janpath. She told him that the Toronto drivers were no different. Seems like taxi drivers all over the world have their crudity in common.' Mallika suddenly broke out into violent laughter. 'And, Viraat, the funniest thing is that her parents had shortlisted three guys, and told all three—marry now or get lost. A first-come-first-serve kind of ultimatum. Abhilaksh was the first one to jump at the offer.' She paused, had a sip of coffee and exclaimed, 'Even the wedding card design had been decided by them. The boy's name, they left blank. Her father scanned and mailed the card to all the three boys. And Abhilaksh was the first one to e-mail his consent back to them.' She was hysterical. It was rare to find her laugh so loud.

I was indeed amused. I always thought Abhilaksh was a bit of an opportunist and a social climber, but that he could go to such an extent was astonishing. Abhilaksh had come all the way from Delhi to Chandigarh, joining an MBA course just to get closer to Mallika. He skipped an IIM entrance offer. He betrayed my friendship. And now that his Canadian dream was ahead of him, he sacrificed not only his MBA degree just when he was three months away from completing it, but he was also dumping Mallika. And to top it all, he had the audacity to tell Mallika that once he got the Canadian visa, he would divorce Saleena and marry Mallika and call her to Canada, cutting her off from her roots, her city, and her family! And all this while he had been using her for getting his reports, term papers and dissertations done—making her sacrifice her dreams and join a cooking course instead. A nauseating feeling filled my guts and I grimaced, clenched my fists and cursed, 'What a ruthless fucker!'

Mallika had stopped laughing and started weeping instead. Small teardrops gathered at the corners of her eyelids. Being betrayed in love often does this to people, making them alternate between laughter and tears within minutes.

I held her hand. For a very long time, we didn't say a word. January is a cold month in Chandigarh, yet my palms were moist with sweat. I looked into her eyes and it was painful to watch them well up.

Weeks passed by. I bought my Toyota Corolla by the end of March and Mallika was the first person to ride in it with me. She was almost back to her peppy self although traces of her sadness stayed, appearing occasionally. By that time, Abhilaksh had left. Mallika told me that Abhilaksh had suddenly stopped coming to class, leaving everyone guessing.

'He is selfish and secretive as always,' I muttered, and Mallika nodded in silence.

'He must be manning some taxi stand on Janpath, bossing over rowdy drivers.' The sarcasm in her tone consoled me. I loved her even more when she said such things about Abhilaksh.

'Forget him, Mallika. You deserve better,' I whispered, as we ate our vanilla ice cream cones, sitting in my Corolla. How could girls be so blind, I cursed silently, thinking of Mallika and me; they search the world for the right person, when that person is sitting right next to them.

'You are right. I must get over him,' she wiped her pink lips with a tissue and threw it out of the window. If only she would discard Abhilaksh from her life in the same way, I thought to myself.

'What are your plans, Mallika?' I asked gently, as I drove her back toward her house.

'Haven't really thought of anything yet,' she was pensive. 'I have been so consumed with the idea of a life with Abhilaksh till now...' she sighed and continued after a moment, 'and now that he has left, I am lost and confused. Although I'm not depressed anymore. Thanks to you, buddy!'

'Why don't you take up a job?' I pulled the car into the driveway of her sprawling bungalow.

'I can't leave Chandigarh. Dad is not keeping too well. He is asthmatic and has become diabetic as well.' There was sadness in her voice, 'He is growing old.'

I looked at her profile. I figured only a girl could think like that; how many times had I thought of my own parents? Boys are so self-centred, so ambition-driven, so ruthless! I realized suddenly, as I saw concern for her father dripping from her words. I walked her to the door, as she fished out the spare set of keys from her large handbag. From amid all those objects, she pulled out the house keys, tried six of them, one by one, and then finally managed to open the lock.

At the door, she turned back and looked at me, 'Won't

you come in, Viraat?' Her eyes however seemed to want the opposite, so I stuttered and said, 'No, Mallika. I will see you tomorrow. Same time, then?'

'Hmmm. Just call me tomorrow morning, please,' she said and smiled, adding in a whisper a second later, 'Why do you spend so much time with me, Viraat?'

I stood there, quivering in my boots. My feet were cold, yet I could feel my soles sweating. 'Mallika,' I said, 'I could spend a whole lifetime with you.'

Mallika stood still at first, a little stupefied, but when she recovered, she raised her eyebrows and laughed aloud, 'You really know how to play a prank, Viraat. And with such deadpan seriousness.'

'I am serious, Mallika.' I was surprised at my own courage. If only I had said those words two years back, or even a year-and-a-half back, Abhilaksh would not have happened. Mallika said nothing, turned around slowly and walked away.

'See you, Viraat,' she sounded tired; tired of relationships.

I closed the door behind me and walked to the car. Suddenly I felt weak, as if I had given away something vital. I felt as if my guts had been wrenched out and I was left powerless.

17

ABOUT THREE WEEKS BEFORE THE ANNIVERSARY OF OUR
graduation ceremony, I called Preeto. 'Hi Preeto! Hope you
remember we had decided to meet on the first anniversary
of our graduation day last year.'

'Of course I remember, Viraat. But only you, me and
Mallika are here. All the rest are away. Sandy is in the
US, Karan in Mumbai, and Vandana on some vessel! You
think they'll come?'

'They will,' I said firmly and confidently, 'and it is our
duty to remind everyone.'

'I will definitely do that,' Preeto asserted, 'I will write
them a nice e-mail—nostalgic and sentimental. And I
will also mail everyone's phone numbers to you; you can
do the calling up bit.' She added quickly, 'I can't afford
making international calls.'

'Don't worry. I will call everyone. Repeatedly,' I

assured her. 'Just mail their contact details to me. You will have the latest numbers in the alumni records.'

The first one to be called was Karan. It was April 1, and so Karan wasn't sure, 'Trying to make a fool out of me, buddy?' Karan asked cautiously.

'No, Karan. I am serious.' I shouted, 'If you want, I can call you back tomorrow. On April 2.'

'Yes, that's a good idea,' Karan surprised me, and saying, 'do that,' he hung up.

'Damn! What a crazy man,' I cursed into the phone.

The next day, I called again, trying to sound breezy, 'Hey, Karan! Here I am, calling you again. You have to reach StuCee on the 20th of April.'

'Bro, I can only try.' In between, he was chatting with someone else, and I could imagine him seated in a conference room, full of corporate slaves.

'What do you mean "try"?' I asked indignantly. 'It was the gang's promise. You haven't forgotten that, have you?'

'It's busy in the corporate world, man,' Karan tried to argue.

I interrupted him curtly, 'I don't care what you corporate slaves do. For me, you are a pal, a member of the gang.' Then I demanded, 'How can you forget the promise we made, the great times we had, our moments of togetherness? Don't you want to re-live those times; even if it is for a day?' Before Karan could argue any further, I barked into the phone, 'And buddy, I have planned everything—lunch at StuCee, dinner at the Yankee Doodle

Bar, followed by fun all night long at the disc.' I was as excited as a kid. 'I have everything lined up. Just come for a day, Karan.' I pleaded. 'Just for a day. You can return on the 21st.' I paused.

There was silence at the other end for a few moments, and then Karan said, 'Okay, buddy. I will take two days off and come over.'

'Yippee,' I yelled, and cut off the connection.

Next was Sandy who told me that he had booked his tickets six months ago, since pre-booking was cheaper. He was a true-blood NRI, converting dollars into rupees. Planning things so much in advance that it sounded ridiculous sometimes.

'Man, we Americans believe in perfect prior planning.'

'Like the Iraq invasion!' I guffawed.

'Shut up,' Sandy whispered sternly, 'the FBI could be snooping in.'

'But you booked your ticket six months in advance, just to save a few dollars?'

'Yes! What's wrong with that?' Sandy's soft, feminine voice came from the other end, 'People here plan their funerals and even choose their coffins in advance: teak coffins with mahogany inlay; a decent funeral costs a fortune, and one can pre-book and pre-pay one's own funeral.'

'You can't be serious, Sandy!'

'I am telling you the truth, buddy,' Sandy laughed at the other end, 'people pawn away their homes in what they call "reverse mortgage system". Till they live, they enjoy the house. After they die, the bank takes over the house and pays for the funeral on pre-decided terms.' He was laughing loudly. 'The children won't bury you well otherwise.'

'What a cruel, insensitive society,' I growled, 'that's why they don't wail at funerals. And then, they drink wine after the burial!'

There was silence, and then Sandy asked, 'How is your love life, man? Komal?'

'We will talk about it when we meet. But you are coming for sure, right?'

'Of course, pal,' Sandy said warmly.

The last but not the least, was Vandana. Since she was sailing eternally, the best thing was to send her an e-mail. By April 7, she had replied saying that she was pregnant and so, as per cargo ship rules, she could no longer sail with her husband. He was sailing in a chemical vessel whose fumes could be dangerous for the unborn kid. So she was returning to Chandigarh to stay with her mother for at least six months.

Abhilaksh was not to be invited. But Preeto argued that he was definitely a part of the gang; and even though I (and now Mallika too) disliked the idea of him being present, there was no alternative but to invite him. We could only hope that he would not turn up and save everyone the embarrassment. As for Komal, she had been invited by me, more out of confusion about the definition of the 'gang' than anything else. Even if they were fringe members of the gang, they were members nevertheless.

Mallika, Preeto, and I gathered at the venue two days in advance to plan out the event. The menu had to be poori chhole and coffee at StuCee. After that we had planned to go for a film, triple-riding the bikes, followed by dinner and drinks at Yankee Doodle Bar, and then finally to the disco at the Piccadily. Everything had been planned out. We had even decided to host the outsiders, with me, as the wealthiest of the lot, agreeing to foot the bill. At moments like these, I felt a sense of pride in my money. After all, what good was my money if it could not be seen by people who mattered?

'Mallika, we are all set for the reunion tomorrow,' I whispered softly, as I drove her back home. Summer was in the air. In a few weeks I would be back to my real estate money making racket. Where would Mallika be? That was the question lingering in my mind. So I asked, 'Mallika, what are your plans?'

She said nothing. Meanwhile, I had to swerve the car to save a cyclist. Once the barrage of expletives that followed subsided, I spoke again, 'Why don't you join me, Mallika?'

'Join you, as in?' She was curious.

'I mean, join my real estate business. You have great taste. You can be my interior designer. And I'm not saying this to do you a favour. I am being selfish, trying to procure a talented person for my upcoming apartment scheme at Panchkula for next month.'

'Interior decorator!' Mallika broke into laughter. 'You can't be serious!'

'I am always serious when it comes to you.' I pulled the vehicle into her driveway and stopped the car.

'But I am not qualified for it, Viraat,' she said. 'You need to study for this. And there are many qualified interior decorators you could hire.'

'But for me, it's your taste that's important. You can do a better job than any of the so called qualified chaps.'

'My taste!' A sudden sadness engulfed her voice like a cloud covering the moon out of nowhere. 'My taste was Abhilaksh. And you know how he turned out to be!'

I looked into her eyes. They were sad. We sat in the car silently. For a long time, we just looked into each other's eyes, trying to discover ourselves. I gently lifted my hand and touched the side of her face, softly caressing her hair and the nape of her neck. It happened spontaneously; she said nothing and continued to glance at me. I wasn't sure how I smelled after a sweaty day; perhaps she also thought of similar things, but it didn't seem to matter. After what seemed like an eternity, I pulled her face, softly, toward my own. She didn't blink, she didn't turn away, she didn't push me, and she didn't break into a giggle. And then, softly, I kissed her. Her lips felt warm and moist, and for a very brief moment, I felt her kiss me back. And I felt the moistness of her tears roll on to my cheeks. Only girls could kiss and cry at the same time!

'Hey, Mallika, don't cry please,' I had never known how to speak so softly.

'I am just upset with Abhilaksh!' *Abhilaksh? Again?* I cursed silently. *Then why the hell did she kiss me?*

'Goodnight, Mallika,' I said curtly. She still loved the man who had dumped her royally. Women!

'Goodnight, Viraat.' She got out of the car, bent down to the window, and whispered, 'Hope you understand my feelings!'

'No, I can't,' I wanted to say, but instead, I just nodded and shifted the gear to reverse the car.

A kind of perplexed mindlessness engulfed me. The girl still loves the rascal who ditched her! I turned my car to the Lake Club and hit the bar. Whenever I was upset, I would either jog at the lake, or drink with vengeance. Anything to numb the brains would do, and since drinking required less effort than jogging, I drank.

'Do you have some cocktail called "Fucking Loser" on the menu?' I asked the bartender.

The wily chap smiled and said, 'Not on the menu, sir, but you'll find them here all the time seated on these stools. My menu has only winners, not losers.' And then he got busy shining up the glasses with a red velvet cloth.

I drank for some time, but soon grew bored. My head was filled with thoughts of Mallika. Much more than Abhilaksh would ever be in Mallika's head. I got up, signed the cheque, and tottered toward the exit. In the dark parking area, I looked around and spotted a brand new black Mercedes parked in a dark corner. Drunk, I walked to the Mercedes, opened my fly and urinated on its tyre. 'Bloody life,' I stood leaning against the car, and broke into hysterical crying. I wept till I felt the alcohol evaporating through my tears. Finally, staggering back to my car, I sat with my head on the steering wheel for some time. When I felt I was sober enough to drive, I started the car engine, and slowly drove back home.

'I can do it,' I shouted aloud, my voice reverberating inside the car.

18

'VIRAAT, ARE YOU STILL ASLEEP?' PREETO WAS SHOUTING over the phone. 'Today's the reunion! Wake up, silly!'

I rubbed my eyes and sat up. I felt a bit hungover, which had more to do with an emotional overdose rather than the whiskey.

'Yes, I know Preeto,' I yawned into the phone, 'but I may not come.'

'You can't be serious, Viraat. We are the hosts. Even Sandy has come all the way from the US early this morning!' she shrieked. I said nothing. 'Are you listening?' Preeto shouted again.

'Let me call you back in some time.' I pressed the red button on my cell and got out of bed. I went into the toilet, splashed water on my face, and peed in one go (without the usual self-control). I still felt disoriented. My phone rang again. This time, it was Sandy.

'Hello, my buddy!' Sandy seemed excited and fresh, despite his eighteen-hour flight from the US.

'Hi, Sandy,' I muttered, sounding like a damp squib.

'What's wrong with you, man? You sound a bit in the dumps.'

'No, no. It's nice to hear your voice, man,' I wanted to say nice things but my tone gave me away.

'Shut up and tell me what happened,' Sandy was curt, something that was a rare occurrence. Men could be curt when trying to find out what was wrong; coming straight to the point, like pimps negotiating prices.

Over the next five minutes, I narrated the whole story to him. Sandy was like my feminine agony uncle. In between, Preeto's incoming call flashed on my cell, and so I added her into the conference.

'Hi Sandy, Viraat,' Preeto piped in. 'Hey, Sandy, what's wrong with Viraat? He says he is not coming for the reunion.'

'He is an emotional fool, Preeto. As always!' Sandy blurted. 'He can't get over Mallika. And Mallika can't get over Abhilaksh, who is already married!'

'Yes, I know that,' she said.

'You knew about it all along and you didn't do anything about it?'

'What could I have done, Sandy?'

'Shut up, Preeto. You could have done what friends do,' Sandy chided her. Being the eldest of the gang gave him some privileges.

'Now that you are here, Sandy, we will talk to Mallika.' There were some more arguments, and then the two of them decided to head to Mallika's house before the reunion.

'But you better be there at StuCee at noon,' Sandy warned me and put the phone down.

Mallika was thrilled to see Sandy. And she seemed less sad and confused than Sandy had imagined. Women could be so unpredictable: crying when one should laugh, and normal when one would expect them to be emotional.

'Hi, Mallika,' Sandy hugged her. 'Great to see you!'

Her father was standing there, but as always, he left the room when her friends were around. Exactly what boys would expect from fathers of pretty girls. They sat around her bed.

Sandy said to her after they had exchanged pleasantries, 'Mallika, you must forget Abhilaksh. He is not worthy of you. He is going to migrate to Canada. It's closer to me in the US and I know life in the American continent. It's very different from here, very mechanical. A bit ruthless, too. You don't belong there.'

'Mallika, try to understand,' Sandy sounded exasperated, 'Abhilaksh can be handled only by the Canadian girl, Masculina.' He was sarcastic and angry.

'Saleena, not Masculina,' Mallika doubled up on the bed, laughing wildly. 'Hey that's a nice name for that bitch.'

Sandy didn't smile. He looked at Mallika and said,

'Whatever her name is, it doesn't matter to me. What matters to me is your happiness, Mallika. And your happiness isn't with Abhilaksh. It isn't in Canada.' Sandy looked at Mallika, and then at Preeto, 'Why don't you say something, Preeto?' Sandy said sternly. The squeakiness in his voice could assume a harshness sometimes.

'Yes, Mallika, Sandy is right,' Preeto joined in, and then fell silent again.

There was a prolonged silence, and then Sandy spoke, 'Mallika, you should opt for Viraat instead.' His voice was soft, full of concern.

'Viraat?' Mallika looked bemused.

'Yes, Viraat. You know that he has been in love with you much before you even met Abhilaksh.' Sandy had gotten up and paced the length of the room as he spoke, 'Viraat is more your type, Mallika. He is going to settle down in Chandigarh. He is nice looking. What more would a girl want?' Sandy exclaimed. Mallika kept sitting on the bed, her eyes fixated on the barren floor.

'And now he is rich too,' Preeto nudged her.

'Yes,' Sandy supported her. 'That's also important. Indeed, very important. In fact, he is the richest in the gang right now and growing richer by the day. You know that, don't you? You have driven around in his brand new Corolla.' Sandy winked. Mallika grimaced and looked to the other side where Preeto sat.

'And, Mallika, for any woman, it is wiser to marry

someone who loves her, rather than marrying someone whom she loves,' Preeto proclaimed. 'Makes more sense. Such a man will pamper you all his life.'

'But Abhilaksh said he will divorce Saleena once he gets his Canadian citizenship,' she sounded like a fool, even to herself.

'That might take years, Mallika. Don't be an idiot,' Sandy shouted. He was feeling helpless trying to convince a girl in love. For someone as pragmatic as Sandy, this love triangle was unnerving and he was getting steadily exasperated. 'In any case it's your call,' Sandy heaved a sigh and stopped pacing up and down. He turned toward the door to leave. 'Come on, Preeto, let's push off,' he snapped, 'no point in trying to make her see reason.' They rushed down the stairs. Mallika followed to see them off. At the gate, Sandy turned around and said, 'And listen, Mallika, you better be at StuCee at noon.' He winked at her and said, 'Your Abhilaksh will also be there.'

Then they drove straight to StuCee. There were familiar faces, the same men in the shops, the same waiters, the same sweepers and gardeners, the same dogs and bitches, even the same sparrows and squirrels.

'Strange thing, Preeto,' Sandy said, pointing at a furry squirrel that stood balanced on her two hind legs and begged for food, almost smiling, 'Even the squirrels here aren't scared of humans.' As an afterthought he added, 'You know, in America, even the squirrels are big, fat and suspicious. Just like the Americans.' He laughed at his own joke, and his squeaky laughter alarmed the squirrel, who scampered away.

In a few moments, Mallika rode in on her scooty, looking pretty and cute even in her helmet. Her eyes sparkled from a distance and her lips broke into a smile when she saw the gang. Sandy and Preeto waved at her as she parked her scooty. She got off and took a phone call. The call made her lose her brilliance. She stood near her scooty, under the shade of a big tree, and spoke into the phone. Then she sat down on the scooty seat, as she continued to talk, argumentatively it seemed from a distance. The conversation seemed long and Sandy clapped loudly to draw her attention. When that didn't get her attention, he whistled like a loafer.

'What's happening? Hope her dad isn't unwell or something,' Sandy asked Preeto.

'No, it's something more serious,' she said. 'It is definetly Abhilaksh calling.'

Mallika finished her conversation and put her cell phone away. She looked pale. She gestured to both of them, started her scooty, and whizzed away.

'She will be back', Preeto whispered to Sandy, glancing at the little bubble of dust behind her scooty. 'And Abhilaksh will be with her when she returns.'

Preeto was right, because the next moment they saw her take a turn toward the road leading to the boys' hostel. Although Abhilaksh had stopped attending classes and had gone to Delhi to work at the taxi stand, he had retained his hostel room till the end of the term, and he stayed there whenever he came back to Chandigarh over weekends.

Karan entered the cafe running and hugged each one of us one by one.

'Hey man, good to see you all!' he said.

We settled down on the stone platform outside StuCee. The fountains were dancing in the distance. Nothing had changed.

'Where are the others?' I asked casually.

'Others?' Preeto looked at me sympathetically, 'Well, others might be coming in. *Together.*'

Meanwhile, Vandana came in a cab. She looked amply pregnant. She seemed quite odd, but the boys didn't make fun of her. They had matured in the one year of leaving university, learning the ways of the world. *Young people are quick learners*, I realized as I watched Sandy hold her hand, helping her climb the small slope.

'You look so cute, Vandana,' Karan was saying to her. I smiled seeing that the boys had become so gentlemanly.

'Where are the others?' she asked.

And then Komal came. From a distance, we all looked at the tall, lanky girl, striding toward us across the lawn. Komal looked lean, in control, and quite pretty, when I didn't compare her with Mallika. Damn! Why couldn't I ever love Komal the way I loved Mallika?

'Hi, guys!' Komal said, waving at no one in particular. Her eyes avoided mine. Everyone greeted her with gusto, and she settled down on the stone platform. 'Sitting here?' she quizzed, 'I thought we are going to be seated inside, at that corner table. It's getting hot nowadays.'

'Yes, Komal, we are just waiting for Mallika,' I said.

'And Abhilaksh,' Karan hissed. Komal smirked and this time looked at me. Her eyes spoke.

'Komal is right! We should go in,' I was determined.

As we got up to walk up the ramp leading to the restaurant, we saw Mallika with Abhilaksh pillion-riding her scooty. The rogue was using her to give him a lift, I cursed. What a wretch of a man! Everyone shook hands with Abhilaksh but nobody hugged him.

We all went up together and settled into the pre-booked corner round table that was away from the rest. I ordered cold coffee for myself.

'Hey, Viraat, you have put on some weight!' Vandana commented.

'You too, Vandana,' there was an unnecessary meanness in my voice. Abhilaksh and Mallika sat together. I was sure they were holding hands under the table.

'Hey, and Abhilaksh, how is the Janpath taxi stand treating you?' Preeto asked.

'It's interesting. Much more interesting than academics.'

'Don't be mean to Preeto, man,' Sandy snubbed him, 'She finds teaching more interesting than emptying out your brains upon the belligerent and uncouth taxi drivers of Delhi.' Abhilaksh looked a bit cheesed off but said nothing.

'And congrats on your wedding to Saleena,' Karan said, addressing Abhilaksh. There was sarcasm in his voice. Abhilaksh didn't say anything and looked at Mallika. In a sly voice, unsure of what she said, she announced, 'Abhilaksh has married her just for the citizenship, guys. They didn't even celebrate their first night.'

For the first time that afternoon, Komal looked at me with a meaningful look.

Mallika continued, 'And guys, you know what! He is going to divorce her and then we shall be married and I shall move to Canada.' She sounded foolish. Silence hung heavy in the room. Abhilaksh said nothing; his attention was buried in a bowl of channa into which he was delving, perhaps to fathom a few grains of truth for himself, I thought, glancing at him with disgust. But there was nothing I could do about it.

Nobody spoke much, except Komal, who patted Mallika's hand across the round table and whispered softly, 'Good idea, Mallika.' I scowled at her with disdain; obviously she wanted Mallika out of her way so that she could continue to fool around with me, and perhaps run away in case of trouble, leaving me to fend for myself.

We ate our oily purees quietly. I could not get my mind off what was happening right in front of me. Abhilaksh was caressing Mallika's shapely calves. There was an overall lack of cheer in the gang. The exuberance and wildness of youth were missing. Our love triangle had impacted the gang's mood in the same way Botox stifles facial expressions. Whatever little *joie de vivre* was floating around in spurts and dribbles, felt cosmetic.

'Guys, why are you all so silent, so formal?' Sandy chided. It spurred some artificial fizz in the environment, but it wasn't like the old times.

'No reunion can relive the reality of the past,' Karan muttered. No one noticed him; people were looking at their food, and the girls were talking softly among themselves on subjects like pregnancy and the best brands of lipsticks. It appeared like a party of grownups.

In two hours, we finished several rounds of cold coffee and a few rounds of poori chhole. Since Sandy was jet lagged and Karan had a few calls to make, they decided to skip the matinee film show and left, promising to meet up in the evening at the Yankee Doodle Bar.

The evening was better. We could decipher less of one another due to the absence of daylight; the girls could conceal their emotions beneath thicker layers of make-up, and the boys could drink and play with the clink-clank sounds of ice cubes floating in their glasses. I had resolved not to drink whiskey since Mallika and Abhilaksh's presence could make me blabber beyond control. Emotions and whiskey always made a heady mix and impacted me enormously. So I drank beer, which would fill my stomach with more barley and less alcohol. Two hours of drinking later, we spent sometime at the disco, where Mallika and Abhilaksh thankfully did not dance intimately. The gang now seemed happy to me.

Vandana was too pregnant to drink or dance; yet she was around, drinking sodas and lemonades.

'Storing up milk for the baby so that I can be Mother Dairy,' was the excuse she gave when Mallika came by to sit down and take a breather from the dance floor. 'Have a sip of water, Mallika,' she advised. 'Too much dancing can dehydrate you. And you are sweating,' she said, pointing at the damp patches around her armpits.

Mallika smiled and took a swig out of the bottle. The music was blaring. She looked at the dance floor where Karan and Sandy were doing some weird bhangra moves. Komal was dancing quite energetically, all by herself; she didn't appear to be bothered about me as I swayed lightly at a distance, gloomily looking in Mallika's direction. Most people danced with abandon—throwing their arms up randomly, shaking their hips, throwing their hair back, and looking up into the lights on the ceiling. Some had glasses balanced precariously in their hands.

'It's amazing, this disc thing,' Mallika said to Vandana. 'Most people won't understand a word of the numbers being played, nor do they know the nuances of Western dance. Still they dance.'

'Ya! It's like technology,' Vandana philosophized, 'the less brains you need to use the gadget, the more you use it. Look at cell phones; even my dhobi has one.'

'I guess that's why the Indian dances, classical music, and stuff like that is no longer popular. No one understands it,' Mallika said getting up to go, but Vandana held her

271

hand, 'Mallika, wait a minute. Sit down.' She pulled her and made her sit down. Mallika looked enquiringly at Vandana. 'Mallika, what's going on in your life?' Mallika's face abruptly lost the smile and she turned sombre.

She said nothing. Vandana spoke softly, 'For god's sake, Mallika, don't screw up your life. I just want to tell you that you should use your brain, not your heart.' She patted her hand. 'The heart is just a pump. The brain is what controls everything. Take control of your life.' Mallika looked at her, her pupils dilated and she nodded lightly. 'Take control of your life, Mallika,' she repeated. 'The youth, the student life, the college saga of love and all the good times we have had in the campus are all great but they are still a very small part of life, when you think about it a few years later,' she said insistently, trying to shout above the music, in an effort to be heard. 'These memories stay with you, but the impact fades away. This is not life.'

'What about chasing your dreams?' Mallika asked.

'Provided those dreams are sensible, and have been filtered by the brain. Mallika, listen, all this hype about following your dreams, whether in a career or in love, is fine. But as youngsters, we dream of many things—sex, drugs, parties, confused career choices—but if we start following all those dreams, we will only end up running in circles. The dream has to be thought through. You have to see yourself ten years down the line, living that dream. If you are happy seeing yourself like that, then go for it, and don't look back. But confused fantasies aren't dreams; *they are just confused fantasies.*'

Mallika looked at her long and deep, and asked, 'Vandana, how come you grew so wise, so soon?'

Vandana smiled, 'There is a child growing inside me now. I married a man, Mallika, not a boy. And I am not unhappy. At times, it's enough not to be unhappy. My love for him has grown after marriage. It's okay; rather, it's good. And I am sure it's less draining emotionally. All arranged marriages aren't bad. All choices suggested by your elders can't be bad, just as all dreams can't be logical and good.' She pressed Mallika's hand affectionately. 'Make the best choice and live your life.'

Mallika put her hand on Vandana's and got up; she was smiling. She danced again, but didn't drink anymore. At 1 a.m., we split up. There were hugs and exchanging of addresses, and the gang seemed quite enthused. The evening had been perhaps the closest to reliving the old times. Old wine in new bottles.

I drove back silently with Mallika seated by my side, and Komal at the back. Nobody spoke a word. The sounds of heavy breathing and uncomfortable shifting filled the air inside the car. I dropped Mallika and then drove Komal to her hostel. We were both quiet on the way back, even after Mallika had left the car and Komal had come up in front. Once outside Komal's hostel, I asked her, 'Are you sure you won't have a problem entering your hostel at this hour?'

'We have curfew hours but I had taken medical leave for the day,' she said and winked, flashing a yellow piece of paper. 'Here is my slip. I told my warden that I wanted to go to Ambala to see my family doctor and would come back in the wee hours,' she giggled.

I smiled, 'Smart move.'

'I can do that anytime, Viraat.' She sounded emphatic. Sex seemed to be on her mind. 'Anytime for you, Viraat,' she whispered softly.

I said nothing, and she didn't try to kiss me goodnight; something stopped her.

'Bye, Viraat,' she regained the aloofness in her voice. 'Thanks for *dropping* me.'

I didn't say anything. I followed her with my gaze. She had a nice posterior, was hot, but something was amiss. I was confused. Well after she had entered her hostel building, I drove back home.

Abhilaksh, Sandy and Karan had hired a cab to drop Vandana safely to her parents' home in the cantonment. 'Hey Abhilaksh,' Sandy smirked as the cab sped off on empty roads after dropping Vandana, 'are you really gonna split up with your Canadian girl? What's her name? Saleena?'

'Yes, Saleena.' Abhilaksh nodded.

'And you are not even gonna fornicate with her!' Karan guffawed and Sandy joined him. He had known that was coming. Abhilaksh scowled at both of them and looked out of the window.

'Lucky man!' Karan spoke, clinically dissecting each word, 'He has got one wife and one girlfriend who is going to be his wife.' He poked Abhilaksh's rib, 'And then, later, the trend will continue? Eh?'

'Shut up, Karan!' Abhilaksh sounded tired. He was unable to fight back or even show his anger with some degree of authenticity.

Sandy quietened Karan with a scowl. A sleepy cop at a police checkpost waved at the cab to stop it. Sandy threw out a hundred rupee note. The cop smiled at the note and didn't bother to look who was inside the car.

'Wish the American police was also as practical,' Sandy said and laughed. 'I have been working my ass off to get a driving licence and they keep failing me. We should have some of them sent here for training on how to make the most of the cop job.' The taxi driver smiled from ear to ear like a buffoon.

En route, Abhilaksh was the first to be dropped off. Karan and Sandy indulged in customary backbiting and bitching before Karan got off. Sandy's American accent had incited the cab driver to fleece him more, since he was the last one to get off. He paid the cab driver without arguing, who in turn happily scratched his crotch and left.

'Scratching of balls is perhaps the taxi drivers' way of saying goodbye,' Sandy commented. 'I must tell Abhilaksh about it tomorrow, since he specializes in taxi drivers.'

The night was happy for most of the gang members, except perhaps for the three corners of the triangle.

The next day, I was up by nine. There were some remnants of last night's emotions buzzing inside my head like the last few bees trapped inside a smoked-out honeycomb. By the time I showered, I felt much better and the bees had disappeared. I was ready for my 'Fast Track Real Estate'. The thugs at the office were happy to see me in my kurta and jeans after such a long absence.

'We must speed up the land acquisition at Panchkula!' I shouted at one of the goons, who nodded happily.

'Yes, boss. All important decisions have been pending, lots of bribes and all,' he said.

I was quite sombre. I took out stick-on slips, pink for SDM, yellow for tehsildar, red for patwari, and scribbled amounts with a pencil, and gave them to my accountant. 'Off you go!' I was determined to get things sorted out today.

'What about the farmers, boss?' the grinning thug asked, folding up his kurta sleeves, showing his biceps.

'Handle them with care, Raghu. Farmers are the trickiest part of the drama.' The chap nodded and left with a few bundles of notes tucked in the depths of his kurta pockets.

Throughout the day, the place buzzed with all types of

people. Customers came with their dreams, patwaris came with their greed, and the rest of the rogues came just to feel relevant. I was in my element—driven, authoritative, and determined. After a very long time, the disempowering feeling of love didn't seem to bother me.

Sandy had left to visit his relatives in Ludhiana and impress them with the usual NRI talk; weaving a web of mystique around the foreign land. 'Folks back in towns and villages feel everyone in America is a millionaire,' he had told me over the phone on his way to Ludhiana. 'And they feel that the moment you land in America, you get to fuck at the drop of a hat.'

Karan had left for Mumbai. He had to be back in office on time. On his way, he dropped by my shack and sneered at the uncouth office and at the kind of people who converged there. I had smiled it off and told him, 'Fuck off, man. I earn ten times more than you. And I have no boss.' Another empowering moment, when men were men, and there was no talk of women, who, I realized, could weaken even the mightiest.

It was late evening, almost time to close the office. The accountant was counting the cash and stacking the suitcase. Each day, I would take cash home, and would stuff it under my bed, inside the lockable bed-box. And each morning, twenty percent of my income that came in the form of white money would be deposited in the bank by the accountant. Payments to farmers were substantially in cash, and the bribes were paid fully in cash. My next target was to acquire a Mercedes and a gun licence. The land business necessitated both.

If left to my dreams, I would have given up everything in return for spending the rest of my life with Mallika, but now it was all about land and guns. The thin line between dream and nightmare had blurred.

But the lesson on dreams was not complete yet.

19

AS ALWAYS, I WAS THE LAST ONE TO LEAVE OFFICE. Like every other day, I refreshed the mailbox on my computer screen and deleted all the spam mail, went through the remaining unread mails cursorily, and just before logging out, I refreshed a second time, out of habit. My eyes became riveted to the top of the mailbox. I had one new e-mail. It was from Mallika. My heart skipped a beat. The same debilitating feeling engulfed me. I swallowed hard, realizing that even her mail could make me dizzy. I took a swig from my water bottle and clicked on it. I took in each word, one by one.

Hi, Viraat,
Wuts up. First of all, I want to thank you for organizing the reunion. It was wonderful. It gave me so much to think about. And thank you for helping

me pull myself out of the silly depression I had gone into during the past few months.

Before you start calling me a fool again, which I know I have given you all reason to, I want to tell you that I have been thinking a lot. Especially in the last few hours. And thankfully, I am much clearer now on the way ahead.

You know, I always thought that my ultimate dream was to get married to Abhilaksh. Somehow, I had seen him as the most perfect panacea for all my problems. That's why I decided to wait for him even when he married someone else. I believed him when he promised he would divorce her for me. Probably, that's why my faith in him stayed despite him even making me do all his assignments and term papers, while he himself floated around like a free bird. But all the time, he was crafting me and moulding me into a housewife. He was shaping me, certainly not for myself, but for himself. Just himself.

I have thought a lot last night and almost the whole day today. I could sleep barely a wink after the night at the disco. Vandana's words jolted me out of my reverie. And over the long, late night conversation with Abhilaksh after reaching home, I realized the full meaning of what she was saying. He refuses to see my point, my need to be able to settle down in Chandigarh, so that I can perhaps look after my ageing father. And then I thought, even

if he had agreed to be back here, what's the point?
He is married, and I don't want to be the cause of
his preplanned divorce. Why should I let him use
me, even for his divorce?

My heart was thudding so loud, that if my goons were
around, they would have thought that their boss was
having a heart attack. Thankfully, no one was there. I
took another sip of water and scrolled down to read the
rest of it. My fingers were trembling. I couldn't wait to
read what was coming. Eagerly, with quivering fingers,
I scrolled down.

I have understood with great difficulty that it is
not about Abhilaksh. Or you, for that matter. It's
about me. I have to live for myself first, and I have
to see where my decisions take me ten years down
the line. Today's issues are trivial, I agree. But if I
take impulsive steps today, I will be responsible for
ruining my own future. We all dream, sometimes
passionately, at times in a silly way. Everyone keeps
saying 'follow your dreams'. But I would rather say,
first be sure if that's a dream worth following. In fact,
whether it's a dream at all or just a fantasy. Is it a
dream that has the steam, the passion, the force,
and a bit of logic behind it? And my dream can't
just be to be with another person. Abhilaksh alone
can't be my goal. If it means giving up everything,

going far away, getting uprooted, giving up a career, leaving my father and just being with Abhilaksh, despite him being a selfish, scheming, divorced man—it just can't be my dream.

So, Viraat, I have decided not to pursue Abhilaksh. He is my past now. Then what's my future?'

My mouth went dry and my hands were trembling more than ever before. My heart was banging in my ribcage like a chimpanzee thumping against his cage in a zoo. I desperately wanted to know what Mallika's future vision was.

Viraat, my future is about me. I know you are very fond of me. In fact, you perhaps love me very dearly. But again, as I said, you must realize that people, just people, can't be someone's dreams. They can perhaps form a part of your dream to some extent or even to a substantial degree. But any person, however much you may love him or her, can't be your dream in its entirety. Viraat, please see the light and don't make the mistake that I made—of making someone your dream.

Tears welled up in my eyes. I rubbed my eyes and read further.

I like you too. You have been a true friend. You have brought me out of a phase that could have killed me. And since you love me so much, you will be the best boss I can ever have.

I smiled remembering my offer to her.

Can I join you, Viraat? I will be a good employee. And a good friend, too. And I promise to work hard with you and make the company grow. I am good at design, and as you had said to me once, I can contribute as an interior designer. If nothing else, doing Abhilaksh's assignments has at least helped me increase my knowledge on accountancy, business economics, and organizational behaviour. I will be an asset to your venture. And we will soon have a proper, well managed, transparent, large company, with a good office. One day, we could give the biggest and the best in the business a run for their money, who knows?

I shall await your reply eagerly. Am ready to join tomorrow.

Love always,
Mallika

I stopped and then read further, one last line, aloud.

P.S.: And along the way, if our dreams match, we

could perhaps get together at a personal level. Till then, let's keep it that way—at 'perhaps'.

Slowly, I rose from the chair. I clicked on the reply icon. With firm fingers this time, I typed out the reply, standing.

Mallika,

You are most welcome to join me. As a partner in business. And going by your knowledge bank, if you work well, I will offer you twenty-five percent sweat equity. Let's grow the company together. And Mallika, be assured, that I shall be working toward the latter possibility. We will create new dreams, together. And chase them to glory.

My regards to uncle.

And to you,

Love,

More than always,

Viraat

I sent her the reply, logged off, switched off the lights, and closed the shutters. There was no one outside except the Omi Dhaba staff at a distance. I took a fresh breath of air. I felt rejuvenated.

Almost mechanically, I punched Preeto's number and texted her, 'Hi Preeto, I am now ready to lecture the fresh batch next session. And the topic will be 'How to Recreate Your Dreams.'

ACKNOWLEDGEMENTS

This book was born out of the inherent ability of the human mind to remember vividly even the smallest experiences of early youth—its follies, its fun, its frolic, its merriment, its romances, its flings, its dreams, and its deviances. I hope this book will strike a personal chord with readers from all across.

It took me close to three years to pen down this book. For helping me on this wonderful and enjoyable journey, I would like to thank Stuti Sharma and Radhika Shah for their constant guidance and support.

I would also like to thank my colleagues—Anita Karwal and Bidyut Swain—for their invaluable inputs. My publisher Milee Ashwarya of Random House India for believing in me.

And above all, my wife, Gitanjali, for allowing the laptop to be seated on my lap for long nocturnal hours!

A NOTE ON THE AUTHOR

VIPUL MITTRA (not the hare, but the other being in the picture), lives in Ahmedabad with his family. His first book, *Pyramid of Virgin Dreams*, was a best-seller. He happens to be a member of the Indian Administrative Service (IAS). His satirical and unabashedly witty style of writing is rooted in everyday life and holds universal appeal. To know more about the author, visit www. vipulmittra.com. To write, interact, or share your views on the book, visit www.thedreamchasersbook.com

TheDreamChasersBook

@vipul_mittra